THE BITER BIT
& OTHER STORIES

WILKIE COLLINS

THE BITER BIT
and Other Stories

ALAN SUTTON

First published in this edition in the United Kingdom in 1983 by
ALAN SUTTON PUBLISHING LIMITED
PHOENIX MILL · FAR THRUPP · STROUD · GLOUCESTERSHIRE

Reprinted 1986, 1990

British Library Cataloguing in Publication Data

Collins
  The biter bit and other stories.
  I. Title
  823'.8[F]   PR4494.B/

  ISBN 0-86299-070-X

Cover picture: detail from The Moonlight Walk
by Honoré Daumier.
National Museum of Wales.

Typesetting and origination by
Alan Sutton Publishing Limited.
Photoset Bembo 9/10.
Printed in Great Britain by
The Guernsey Press Company Limited,
Guernsey, Channel Islands.

CONTENTS

BIOGRAPHICAL NOTE

William Wilkie Collins was born on 8 January 1824, in New Cavendish Street, London, the elder son of William Collins, a fashionable and successful painter of the early nineteenth century, who counted among his friends Wordsworth and Coleridge. William Collins was a religious man, and in his strict observances may have been a repressive influence on his son, who appears to have inherited his mother Harriet Geddes' attractive and friendly personality. Wilkie was named after his godfather, Sir David Wilkie, RA, a bachelor and close friend of the family.

Little is known of Wilkie's early life. His brother, Charles, was born in 1828, and the family lived comfortably, first in Hampstead, then in Bayswater, where Wilkie attended Maida Hill Academy. The following year the whole family left for Italy, where they spent two years, visiting the major art collections and learning Italian. On their return, Wilkie attended a private boarding school in Highbury, where his story-telling talent was recognized and exploited by a senior prefect who demanded, with the threat of physical violence, to be entertained. 'Thus,' wrote Collins, 'I learnt to be amusing on a short notice and have derived benefit from those early lessons.'

When he left school in 1840, he showed no inclination to enter the Church, as his father wished, and chose, without enthusiasm, the world of commerce, accepting a post with Antrobus & Co., tea importers. He was totally unsuited to the regularity of business life, preferring to escape to the vibrant atmosphere of Paris. He started to write articles and short stories, which were accepted for publication, albeit anonymously, and in 1846 his father agreed to that he should leave commerce and take up law, which would, in theory, provide him with a regular income. He studied at Lincoln's Inn Fields, and was finally called to the bar, but his legal knowledge was to be applied creatively in his novels, rather than practically in the law courts.

In his early twenties Collins painted as well as writing. He had many friends who were artists, and he supported the new Pre-Raphaelite movement. In 1848 he had a picture exhibited in the Royal Academy. In the same year his first book was published: the memoirs of his father, who had died the previous year. These were diligently researched and provided a training ground for the emerging writer, developing his thorough methodical approach to compilation and exercising his descriptive ability. His first novel, *Antonia* was published by Bentley's two years later. Although of no great literary merit, it was written in the then popular mode of historical romance, and so enjoyed instant success. The following year Bentley's published *Rambles beyond Railways*, an account of a holiday in Cornwall, which reflected Collins' life-long love of wild and remote places.

It was in the same year, 1851, that Wilkie Collins first met Charles Dickens, an introduction effected by their mutual friend, the artist, Augustus Egg. The meeting was significant for both, leading to a close friendship and working partnership from which both benefited. Dickens had found a friend of more stable temperament than himself, affable and tolerant, responsive to his restless demanding nature. From Collins he acquired the skill of economic and taut plotting, as evidenced in *A Tale of Two Cities* (which may be interestingly compared with Collins' story of the French Revolution, *Sister Rose*, 1855), and in his later novels. Collins was welcomed by the Dickens family, and spent many holidays with them in England and France. He was encouraged and guided in his writing by Dickens, and he must have been stimulated by the latter's enthusiasm and vitality. The two authors worked together on Dickens' magazines, *Household Words*, and *All the Year Round*. Collins was employed as an editor, and many of his works appeared first in these publications, while both writers collaborated on several short stories.

A Terribly Strange Bed – Collins' first work in the macabre genre – was the first of his short stories to appear in *Household Words*, in 1852. The following year the magazine saw the publication of *Gabriel's Marriage*, a story of a Breton fishing community. In the interim, Dickens had turned down *Mad Monkton*, a study of inherited insanity, as unsuitable subject matter, and this was later published by *Fraser's Magazine* in 1855. These two, along with *Sister Rose, The Yellow Mask*, and *A Stolen Letter*, were originally published in *Household Words*, and reprinted in *After Dark*, 1855, for which anthology Collins wrote the successfully economic and melodramatic *Lady of Glenwith Grange* (an inspiration for Miss Haversham?). *A Rogue's Life*, Collins' venture into the picaresque, was serialized in 1856. This was followed in 1857 by *The Dead Secret*, a full length novel, which in its complexity suggests the author's technical potential. *The Biter Bit*, which was published in 1858 and is commonly held to be the first humorous detective story, shows Collins' development of the epistolary form. Both of his two greatest novels, *A Woman in White* and *The Moonstone*, appeared first as serializations in *All the Year Round* – as did the less well known *No Name*. This unconventional study of illegitimacy was published in its full form in 1862, two years after the masterpiece of suspense and drama *A Woman in White* and six years before his original detective story, *The Moonstone*, appeared as complete books.

Another interest shared by Collins and Dickens was a love of the theatre. *The Frozen Deep*, 1857, written by Collins and starring Dickens, was inspired by an interest in the Arctic exploration of the time. It was followed by a series of minor productions, the stage version of *No Thoroughfare* (with combined authorship), enjoying a record run of two hundred nights in 1867.

Anyone meeting Collins in those days would have seen:

> A neat figure of a cheerful plumpness, very small feet and hands, a full brown beard, a high and rounded forehead, a small nose not naturally intended to support a pair of large spectacles behind which his eyes shone with humour and friendship.

R.C. Lehmann, *Memories of Half a Century*

But how many would have glimpsed, as did the young artist, Rudolf Lehmann, the strange far-off look in his eyes, which gave the impression of investing 'almost everything with an air of mystery and romance'? It was suggestive of a depth of personality not accessible to many, but demonstrated by the author's expressed unconventional views of the class and social *mores* of the day; which were further borne out by what is known of his personal life. During the 1860s, Collins met and fell in love with Caroline Graves, who had a daughter by a previous marriage. He never married her, but lived with mother and daughter for most of the remainder of his life. In 1868, Caroline mysteriously married another, and Collins entered into a relationship with Martha Judd, by whom he had three children. However, by the early 1870s, he was once more living with Caroline, who was still known as Mrs Graves. It has been suggested that Martha Judd may have been employed originally by Collins as an amanuensis. Over the years Collins' health had been deteriorating. He was a victim of gout, which attacked his whole body, including his eyes. He suffered a particularly severe attack in 1868, when his mother died, and he was working on *The Moonstone*. A dedicated woman, capable of disregarding his suffering and attending only to his words was employed, to whom Collins dictated the rest of the work, but she has never been named.

In 1870 Charles Dickens died. During the previous ten years Collins had produced his best work: the three novels serialized in *All the Year Round*; *Armadale*, 1866, in the *Cornhill Magazine*, and *Man and Wife*, 1870, in *Cassell's Magazine*. But with Dickens' death, something in Collins seemed to die too, although his popularity remained undiminished. His novels, produced regularly until his death, were widely read, and his was some of the first fiction to appear in cheap editions. In the 1870s he enjoyed some success with the stage versions of his novels, which were produced both in London and the provinces. Not only was Collins' work popular in England; his novels and plays were translated and produced in most European countries, including Russia, and were widely available in America. In 1873 Collins was invited to give readings in the eastern United States and Canada. Although his reading lacked the vitality of Dickens, the Americans were charmed by him.

Of course, it was not only Dickens' death which adversely

affected Collins' work. His gout was becoming persistent, and he relied increasingly on laudenum to relieve the pain. However, he never lost his mental clarity, taking care to be properly informed about medicine, drugs and chemistry, as is clearly shown in *Heart and Science,* 1883 and the detailed notes he left for his last novel, *Blind Love,* 1890 – completed, posthumously, at his request, by Walter Besant. During his later years, his social life was restricted by poor health, but he did not become a recluse as has been suggested. He maintained close friendships with Charles Reade, Holman Hunt, the Beard and the Lehmann families, and theatrical people, including Ada Cavendish and Mary Anderson. In 1889, after being involved in a cab accident, Collins' health rapidly declined, and he died while suffering from bronchitis on 23 September. He was buried at Kensal Green Cemetery.

SHEILA MICHELL

THE BITER BIT

THE BITER BIT

[Extracted from the Correspondence of the
London Police]

*From Chief Inspector Theakstone, of the Detective Police,
to Sergeant Bulmer of the same force*

London, 4th July, 18—.
Sergeant Bulmer, – This is to inform you that you are wanted
to assist in looking up a case of importance, which will require
all the attention of an experienced member of the force. The
matter of the robbery on which you are now engaged, you
will please to shift over to the young man who brings you this
letter. You will tell him all the circumstances of the case, just
as they stand; you will put him up to the progress you have
made (if any) towards detecting the person or persons by
whom the money has been stolen; and you will leave him to
make the best he can of the matter now in your hands. He is to
have the whole responsibility of the case, and the whole credit
of his success, if he brings it to a proper issue.

So much for the orders that I am desired to communicate to
you.

A word in your ear, next, about this new man who is to
take your place. His name is Matthew Sharpin; and he is to
have the chance given him of dashing into our office at a jump
– supposing he turns out strong enough to take it. You will
naturally ask me how he comes by this privilege. I can only
tell you that he has some uncommonly strong interest to back
him in certain high quarters which you and I had better not
mention except under our breaths. He has been a lawyer's
clerk; and he is wonderfully conceited in his opinion of
himself, as well as mean and underhand to look at. According
to his own account, he leaves his old trade, and joins ours, of
his own free will and preference. You will no more believe

that than I do. My notion is, that he has managed to ferret out some private information in connection with the affairs of one of his master's clients, which makes him rather an awkward customer to keep in the office for the future, and which, at the same time, gives him hold enough over his employer to make it dangerous to drive him into a corner by turning him away. I think the giving him this unheard-of chance among us, is, in plain words, pretty much like giving him hush-money to keep him quiet. However that may be, Mr. Matthew Sharpin is to have the case now in your hands; and if he succeeds with it, he pokes his ugly nose into our office, as sure as fate. I put you up to this, Sergeant, so that you may not stand in your own light by giving the new man any cause to complain of you at headquarters, and remain yours,

Francis Theakstone.

From Mr. Matthew Sharpin to Chief Inspector Theakstone

London, July 5th, 18—.

Dear Sir, – Having now been favoured with the necessary instructions from Sergeant Bulmer, I beg to remind you of certain directions which I have received, relating to the report of my future proceedings which I am to prepare for examination at headquarters.

The object of my writing, and of your examining what I have written, before you send it in to the higher authorities, is, I am informed, to give me, as an untried hand, the benefit of your advice, in case I want it (which I venture to think I shall not) at any stage of my proceedings. As the extraordinary circumstances of the case on which I am now engaged, make it impossible for me to absent myself from the place where the robbery was committed, until I have made some progress towards discovering the thief, I am necessarily precluded from consulting you personally. Hence the necessity of writing down the various details, which might, perhaps, be better communicated by word of mouth. This, if I am not mistaken, is the position in which we are now placed. I state my own impressions on the subject, in writing, in order that we may clearly understand each other at the outset; and have the honour to remain, your obedient servant,

Matthew Sharpin.

From Chief Inspector Theakstone to Mr. Matthew Sharpin

London, 5th July, 18—.

Sir, – You have begun by wasting time, ink, and paper. We both of us perfectly well knew the position we stood in towards each other, when I sent you with my letter to Sergeant Bulmer. There was not the least need to repeat it in writing. Be so good as to employ your pen, in future, on the business actually in hand.

You have now three separate matters on which to write to me. First, You have to draw up a statement of your instructions received from Sergeant Bulmer, in order to show us that nothing has escaped your memory, and that you are thoroughly acquainted with all the circumstances of the case which has been entrusted to you. Secondly, You are to inform me what it is you propose to do. Thirdly, You are to report every inch of your progress (if you make any) from day to day, and, if need be, from hour to hour as well. This is *your* duty. As to what *my* duty may be, when I want you to remind me of it, I will write and tell you so. In the meantime, I remain, yours,

Francis Theakstone.

From Mr. Matthew Sharpin to Chief Inspector Theakstone

London, 6th July, 18—.

Sir, – You are rather an elderly person, and, as such, naturally inclined to be a little jealous of men like me, who are in the prime of their lives and their faculties. Under these circumstances, it is my duty to be considerate towards you, and not to bear too hardly on your small failings. I decline, therefore, altogether, to take offence at the tone of your letter; I give you the full benefit of the natural generosity of my nature; I sponge the very existence of your surly communication out of my memory – in short, Chief Inspector Theakstone, I forgive you, and proceed to business.

My first duty is to draw up a full statement of the instructions I have received from Sergeant Bulmer. Here they are at your service, according to my version of them.

At number 13, Rutherford Street, Soho, there is a stationer's shop. It is kept by one Mr. Yatman. He is a married man, but has no family. Besides Mr. and Mrs. Yatman, the other inmates in the house are a young single man named Jay, who lodges in the front room on the second floor – a shopman, who sleeps in one of the attics, – and a servant-of-all-work, whose bed is in the back-kitchen. Once a week a charwoman comes for a few hours in the morning only, to help this servant. These are all the persons who, on ordinary occasions, have means of access to the interior of the house, placed, as a matter of course, at their disposal.

Mr. Yatman has been in business for many years, carrying on his affairs prosperously enough to realise a handsome independence for a person in his position. Unfortunately for himself, he endeavoured to increase the amount of his property by speculating. He ventured boldly in his investments, luck went against him and rather less than two years ago he found himself a poor man again. All that was saved out of the wreck of his property was the sum of two hundred pounds.

Although Mr. Yatman did his best to meet his altered circumstances, by giving up many of the luxuries and comforts to which he and his wife had been accustomed, he found it impossible to retrench so far as to allow of putting by any money from the income produced by his shop. The business has been declining of late years – the cheap advertising stationers having done it injury with the public. Consequently, up to the last week the only surplus property possessed by Mr. Yatman consisted of the two hundred pounds which had been recovered from the wreck of his fortune. This sum was placed as a deposit in a joint-stock bank of the highest possible character.

Eight days ago, Mr. Yatman and his lodger, Mr. Jay, held a conversation on the subject of the commercial difficulties which are hampering trade in all directions at the present time.

Mr. Jay (who lives by supplying the newspapers with short paragraphs relating to accidents, offences, and brief records of remarkable occurrences in general – who is, in short, what they call a penny-a-liner) told his landlord that he had been in the city that day, and had heard unfavourable rumours on the subject of the joint-stock banks. The rumours to which he alluded had already reached the ears of Mr. Yatman from other quarters; and the confirmation of them by his lodger had such an effect on his mind – predisposed as it was to alarm by the experience of his former losses – that he resolved to go at once to the bank and withdraw his deposit.

It was then getting on towards the end of the afternoon; and he arrived just in time to receive his money before the bank closed.

He received the deposit in banknotes of the following amounts; – one fifty-pound note, three twenty-pound notes, six ten-pound notes, and six five-pound notes. His object in drawing the money in this form was to have it ready to lay out immediately in trifling loans, on good security, among the small tradespeople of his district, some of whom are sorely pressed for the very means of existence at the present time. Investments of this kind seemed to Mr. Yatman to be the most safe and the most profitable on which he could now venture.

He brought the money back in an envelope placed in his breast pocket; and asked his shopman, on getting home, to look for a small flat tin cash-box, which had not been used for years, and which, as Mr. Yatman remembered it, was exactly of the right size to hold the banknotes. For some time the cash-box was searched for in vain. Mr. Yatman called to his wife to know if she had any idea where it was. The question was overheard by the servant-of-all-work, who was taking up the tea-tray at the time, and by Mr. Jay, who was coming down stairs on his way out to the theatre. Ultimately the cash-box was found by the shopman. Mr. Yatman placed the banknotes in it, secured them by a padlock, and put the box in his coat pocket. It stuck out of the coat pocket a very little, but enough to be seen. Mr. Yatman remained at home, up stairs, all the evening. No visitors called. At eleven o'clock he went to bed, and put the cash-box along with his clothes, on a chair by the bedside.

When he and his wife woke the next morning, the box was gone. Payment of the notes was immediately stopped at the bank of England; but no news of the money has been heard of since that time.

So far, the circumstances of the case are perfectly clear. They point unmistakably to the conclusion that.the robbery must have been committed by some person living in the house. Suspicion falls, therefore, upon the servant-of-all-work, upon the shopman, and upon Mr. Jay. The two first knew that the cash-box was being inquired for by their master, but did not know what it was he wanted to put into it. They would assume, of course that it was money. They both had opportunities (the servant, when she took away the tea – and the shopman, when he came, after shutting up, to give the keys of the till to his master) of seeing the cash-box in Mr. Yatman's pocket, and of inferring naturally, from its position there, that he intended to take it into his bedroom with him at night.

Mr. Jay, on the other hand, had been told, during the afternoon's conversation on the subject of joint-stock banks, that his landlord had a deposit of two hundred pounds in one of them. He also knew that Mr. Yatman left him with the intention of drawing that money out; and he heard the inquiry for the cash-box afterwards, when he was coming down stairs. He must, therefore, have inferred that the money was in the house, and that the cash-box was the receptacle intended to contain it. That he could have had any idea, however, of the place in which Mr. Yatman intended to keep it for the night, is impossible, seeing that he went out before the box was found, and did not return till his landlord was in bed. Consequently, if he committed the robbery, he must have gone into the bedroom purely on speculation.

Speaking of the bedroom reminds me of the necessity of noticing the situation of it in the house, and the means that exist of gaining easy access to it at any hour of the night.

The room in question is the back room on the first floor. In consequence of Mrs. Yatman's constitutional nervousness on the subject of fire (which makes her apprehend being burnt alive in her room, in case of accident, by the hampering of the lock if the key is turned in it) her husband has never been accustomed to lock the bedroom door. Both he and his wife are, by their own admission, heavy sleepers. Consequently the risk to be run by any evil-disposed persons wishing to plunder the bedroom, was of the most trifling kind. They could enter the room by merely turning the handle of the door; and if they moved with ordinary caution, there was no fear of their waking the sleepers inside. This fact is of importance. It strengthens our conviction that the money must have been taken by one of the inmates of the house, because it tends to show that the robbery, in this case, might have been committed by persons not possessed of the superior vigilance and cunning of the experienced thief.

Such are the circumstances, as they were related to Sergeant Bulmer, when he was first called in to discover the guilty parties, and, if possible, to recover the lost banknotes. The strictest inquiry which he could institute, failed of producing the smallest fragment of evidence against any of the persons on whom suspicion naturally fell. Their language and behaviour, on being informed of the robbery, was perfectly consistent with the language and behaviour of innocent people, Sergeant Bulmer felt from the first that this was a case for private inquiry and secret observation. He began by recommending Mr. and Mrs. Yatman to affect a feeling of perfect confidence in the innocence of the persons living under their roof; and he then opened the campaign by employing himself in following the goings and comings and in discovering the friends, the habits, and the secrets of the maid-of-all-work.

Three days and nights of exertion on his own part, and on that of others who were competent to assist his investigations, were enough to satisfy him that there was no sound cause for suspicion against the girl.

He next practised the same precaution in relation to the shopman. There was more difficulty and uncertainty in privately clearing up this person's character without his knowledge, but the obstacles were at last smoothed away with tolerable success; and though there is not the same amount of certainty, in this case, which there was in that of the girl, there is still fair reason for supposing that the shopman has had nothing to do with the robbery of the cash-box.

As a necessary consequence of these proceedings, the range of suspicion now becomes limited to the lodger, Mr. Jay.

When I presented your letter of introduction to Sergeant Bulmer, he had already made some inquiries on the subject of this young man. The result, so far, has not been at all favourable. Mr. Jay's habits are irregular; he frequents public houses, and seems to be familiarly acquainted with a great many dissolute characters; he is in debt to most of the tradespeople whom he employs; he has not paid his rent to Mr. Yatman for the last month; yesterday evening he came home excited by liquor, and last week he was seen talking to a prize fighter. In short, though Mr. Jay does call himself a journalist, in virtue of his penny-a-line contributions to the newspapers, he is a young man of low tastes, vulgar manners, and bad habits. Nothing has yet been discovered in relation to him, which redounds to his credit in the smallest degree.

I have now reported, down to the very last details, all the particulars communicated to me by Sergeant Bulmer. I believe you will not find an omission anywhere; and I think you will admit, though you are prejudiced against me, that a clearer statement of facts was never laid before you than the statement I have now made. My next duty is to tell you what I propose to do, now that the case is confided to my hands.

In the first place, it is clearly my business to take up the case at the point where Sergeant Bulmer has left it. On his authority, I am justified in assuming that I have no need to trouble myself about the maid-of-all-work and the shopman. Their characters are now to be considered as cleared up. What remains to be privately investigated is the question of the guilt or innocence of Mr. Jay. Before we give up the notes for lost, we must make sure, if we can, that he knows nothing about them.

This is the plan that I have adopted, with the full approval of Mr. and Mrs. Yatman, for discovering whether Mr. Jay is or is not the person who has stolen the cash-box:

I propose, today, to present myself at the house in the character of a young man who is looking for lodgings. The back room on the second floor will be shown to me as the room to let; and I shall establish myself there tonight, as a person from the country who has come to London to look for a situation in a respectable shop or office.

By this means I shall be living next to the room occupied by Mr. Jay. The partition between us is mere lath and plaster. I shall make a small hole in it, near the cornice, through which I can see what Mr. Jay does in his room, and hear every word that is said when any friend happens to call on him. Whenever he is at home, I shall be at my post of observation. Whenever he goes out, I shall be after him. By employing these means of watching him, I believe I may look forward to the discovery of his secret – if he knows anything about the lost banknotes – as to a dead certainty.

What you may think of my plan of observation I cannot undertake to say. It appears to me to unite the invaluable merits of boldness and simplicity. Fortified by this conviction, I close the present communication with feelings of the most sanguine description in regard to the future, and remain your obedient servant,

Matthew Sharpin.

From the same to the same

7th July.

Sir, – As you have not honoured me with any answer to my last communication, I assume that, in spite of your prejudices against me, it has produced the favourable impression on your mind which I ventured to anticipate. Gratified beyond measure by the token of approval which your eloquent silence conveys to me, I proceed to report the progress that has been made in the course of the last twenty-four hours.

I am now comfortably established next door to Mr. Jay; and I am delighted to say that I have two holes in the partition, instead of one. My natural sense of humour has led me into the pardonable extravagance of giving them appropriate names. One I call my peep-hole, and the other my pipe-hole. The name of the first explains itself; the name of the second refers to a small tin pipe, or tube, inserted in the hole, and twisted so that the mouth of it comes close to my ear, while I am standing at my post of observation. Thus, while I am looking at Mr. Jay through my peep-hole, I can hear every word that may be spoken in his room through my pipe-hole.

Perfect candour – a virtue which I have possessed from my childhood – compels me to acknowledge, before I go any further, that the ingenious notion of adding a pipe-hole to my proposed peep-hole originated with Mrs. Yatman. This lady – a most intelligent and accomplished person, simple, and yet distinguished, in her manners – has entered into all my little plans with an enthusiasm and intelligence which I cannot too highly praise. Mr. Yatman is so cast down by his loss, that he is quite incapable of affording me any assistance. Mrs. Yatman, who is evidently most tenderly attached to him, feels her husband's sad condition of mind even more acutely than she feels the loss of the money; and is mainly stimulated to exertion by her desire to assist in raising him from the miserable state of prostration into which he has now fallen.

'The money, Mr. Sharpin,' she said to me yesterday evening, with tears in her eyes, 'the money may be regained by rigid economy and strict attention to business. It is my husband's wretched state of mind that makes me so anxious for the discovery of the thief. I may be wrong, but I felt hopeful of success as soon as you entered the house; and I believe, if the wretch who has robbed us is to be found, you are the man to discover him.' I accept this gratifying compliment in the spirit in which it was offered – firmly believing that I shall be found, sooner or later, to have thoroughly deserved it.

Let me now return to business; that is to say, to my peep-hole and my pipe-hole.

I have enjoyed some hours of calm observation of Mr. Jay. Though rarely at home, as I understand from Mrs. Yatman, on ordinary occasions, he has been indoors the whole of this day. That is suspicious, to begin with. I have to report, further that he rose at a late hour this morning (always a bad sign in a young man), and that he lost a great deal of time, after he was up, in yawning and complaining to himself of headache. Like other debauched characters, he ate little or nothing for break-fast. His next proceeding was to smoke a pipe – a dirty clay pipe, which a gentleman would have been ashamed to put between his lips. When he had done smoking, he took out pen, ink, and paper, and sat down to write with a groan – whether of remorse for having taken the banknotes, or of disgust at the task before him, I am unable to say. After writing a few lines (too far away from my peep-hole to give me a chance of reading over his shoulder), he leaned back in his chair, and amused himself by humming the tunes of certain popular songs. Whether these do, or do not, represent secret signals by which he communicates with his accomplices remains to be seen. After he had amused himself for some time by humming, he got up and began to walk about the room, occasionally stopping to add a sentence to the paper on his desk. Before long, he went to a locked cupboard and opened it. I strained my eyes eagerly, in expectation of making a discovery. I saw him take something carefully out of the cupboard – he turned round – and it was only a pint bottle of brandy! Having drunk some of the liquor, this extremely indolent reprobate lay down on his bed again, and in five minutes was fast asleep.

After hearing him snoring for at least two hours, I was recalled to my peep-hole by a knock at his door. He jumped up and opened it with suspicious activity.

A very small boy, with a very dirty face, walked in, said, 'please, sir, they're waiting for you,' sat down on a chair, with his legs a long way from the ground, and instantly fell asleep! Mr. Jay swore an oath, tied a wet towel round his head, and going back to his paper, began to cover it with writing as fast as his fingers could move the pen. Occasionally getting up to dip the towel in water and tie it on again, he continued at this employment for nearly three hours; then folded up the leaves of writing, woke the boy, and gave them to him, with this remarkable expression: – 'Now, then, young sleepyhead, quick – march! If you see the governor, tell him to have the money ready when I call for it.' The boy grinned, and disappeared. I was sorely tempted to follow 'sleepyhead,' but, on reflection, considered it safest still to keep my eye on the proceedings of Mr. Jay.

In half an hour's time, he put on his hat and walked out. Of course, I put on my hat and walked out also. As I went down stairs, I passed Mrs. Yatman going up. The lady has been kind enough to undertake, by previous arrangement between us, to search Mr. Jay's room, while he is out of the way, and while I am necessarily engaged in the pleasing duty of following him wherever he goes. On the occasion to which I now refer, he walked straight to the nearest tavern, and ordered a couple of mutton chops for his dinner. I placed myself in the next box to him, and ordered a couple of mutton chops for my dinner. Before I had been in the room a minute, a young man of highly suspicious manners and appearance, sitting at a table opposite, took his glass of porter in his hand and joined Mr. Jay. I pretended to be reading the newspaper, and listened, as in duty bound, with all my might.

'Jack has been here inquiring after you,' says the young man.

'Did he leave any message?' asks Mr. Jay.

'Yes,' says the other. He told me, if I met with you, to say that he wished very particularly to see you tonight; and that he would give you a look in, at Rutherford Street, at seven o'clock.'

'All right,' says Mr. Jay. 'I'll get back in time to see him.'

Upon this, the suspicious-looking young man finished his porter, and saying that he was rather in a hurry, took leave of his friend (perhaps I should not be wrong if I said his accomplice) and left the room.

At twenty-five minutes and a half past six – in these serious cases it is important to be particular about time – Mr. Jay finished his chops and paid his bill. At twenty-six minutes and three-quarters I finished my chops and paid mine. In ten minutes more I was inside the house in Rutherford Street, and was received by Mrs. Yatman in the passage. That charming woman's face exhibited an expression of melancholy and disappointment which it quite grieved me to see.

'I am afraid, Ma'am,' says I, 'that you have not hit on any little criminating discovery in the lodger's room?'

She shook her head and sighed. It was a soft, languid, fluttering sigh; – and, upon my life, it quite upset me. For the moment I forgot business, and burned with envy of Mr. Yatman.

'Don't despair, Ma'am,' I said, with an insinuating mildness which seemed to touch her. 'I have heard a mysterious conversation – I know of a guilty appointment – and I expect great things from my Peep-hole and my Pipe-hole tonight. Pray, don't be alarmed, but I think we are on the brink of a discovery.'

Here my enthusiastic devotion to business got the better of my tender feelings. I looked – winked – nodded – left her.

When I got back to my observatory, I found Mr. Jay digesting his mutton chops in an armchair, with his pipe in his mouth. On his table were two tumblers, a jug of water, and the pint bottle of brandy. It was then close upon seven o'clock. As the hour struck, the person described as 'Jack' walked in.

He looked agitated – I am happy to say he looked violently agitated. The cheerful glow of anticipated success diffused itself (to use a strong expression) all over me, from head to foot. With breathless interest I looked through my Peep-hole, and saw the visitor – the 'Jack' of this delightful case – sit down, facing me, at the opposite side of the table to Mr. Jay. Making allowance for the difference in expression which their countenances just now happened to exhibit, these two abandoned villains were so much alike in other respects as to lead at once to the conclusion that they were brothers. Jack was the cleaner man and the better dressed of the two. I admit that, at the outset. It is, perhaps one of my failings to push justice and impartiality to their utmost limits. I am no Pharisee; and where Vice has its redeeming point, I say, let Vice have its due – yes, yes, by all manner of means, let Vice have its due.

'What's the matter now, Jack?' says Mr. Jay.

'Can't you see it in my face?' says Jack. 'My dear fellow, delays are dangerous. Let us have done with suspense, and risk it the day after tomorrow.'

'So soon as that?' cried Mr. Jay, looking very much astonished. 'Well, I'm ready, if you are. But, I say, Jack, is Somebody Else ready too? Are you quite sure of that?'

He smiled as he spoke – a frightful smile – and laid a very strong emphasis on those two words, 'Somebody Else.' There is evidently a third ruffian, a nameless desperado, concerned in the business.

'Meet us tomorrow,' says Jack, 'and judge for yourself. Be in the Regent's Park at eleven in the morning, and look out for us at the turning that leads to the Avenue Road.

'I'll be there,' says Mr. Jay. 'Have a drop of brandy and water? What are you getting up for? You're not going already?'

'Yes, I am,' says Jack. 'The fact is, I'm so excited and agitated that I can't sit still anywhere for five minutes together. Ridiculous as it may appear to you, I'm in a perpetual state of nervous flutter. I can't, for the life of me, help fearing that we shall be found out. I fancy that every man who looks twice at me in the street is a spy – '

At those words, I thought my legs would have given way under me. Nothing but strength of mind kept me at my Peep-hole – nothing else, I give you my word of honour.

'Stuff and nonsense!' cried Mr. Jay, with all the effrontery of a veteran in crime. 'We have kept the secret up to this time, and we will manage cleverly to the end. Have a drop of brandy and water, and you will feel as certain about it as I do.'

Jack steadily refused the brandy and water, and steadily persisted in taking his leave.

'I must try if I can't walk it off,' he said. 'Remember tomorrow morning – eleven o'clock, Avenue Road side of the Regent's Park.'

With those words he went out. His hardened relative laughed desperately, and resumed the dirty clay pipe.

I sat down on the side of my bed, actually quivering with excitement.

It is clear to me that no attempt has yet been made to change the stolen banknotes; and I may add that Sergeant Bulmer was of that opinion also, when he left the case in my hands. What is the natural conclusion to draw from the conversation which I have just set down? Evidently, that the confederates meet tomorrow to take their respective shares in the stolen money, and to decide on the safest means of getting the notes changed the day after. Mr. Jay, is beyond a doubt, the leading criminal in this business, and he will probably run the chief risk – that of changing the fifty-pound note. I shall, therefore, still make it my business to follow him – attending at the Regent's Park tomorrow, and doing my best to hear what is said there. If another appointment is made for the day after, I shall, of course, go to it. In the meantime, I shall want the immediate assistance of two competent persons (supposing the rascals separate after their meeting) to follow the two minor criminals. It is only fair to add, that, if the rogues all retire together, I shall probably keep my subordinates in reserve. Being naturally ambitious, I

I desire, if possible, to have the whole credit of discovering this robbery to myself.

8th July.

I have to acknowledge, with thanks, the speedy arrival of my two subordinates – men of very average abilities, I am afraid; but, fortunately, I shall always be on the spot to direct them.

My first business this morning was, necessarily, to prevent mistakes by accounting to Mr. and Mrs. Yatman for the presence of two strangers on the scene. Mr. Yatman (between ourselves, a poor feeble man) only shook his head and groaned. Mrs. Yatman (that superior woman) favoured me with a charming look of intelligence.

'Oh, Mr Sharpin!' she said, 'I am so sorry to see those two men! Your sending for their assistance looks as if you were beginning to be doubtful of success.'

I privately winked at her (she is very good in allowing me to do so without taking offence), and told her, in my facetious way, that she laboured under a slight mistake.

'It is because I am sure of success, Ma'am, that I send for them. I am determined to recover the money, not for my own sake only, but for Mr. Yatman's sake – and for yours.'

I laid a considerable amount of stress on those last three words. She said, 'Oh, Mr. Sharpin!' again – and blushed of a heavenly red – and looked down at her work. I could go to the world's end with that woman, if Mr. Yatman would only die.

I sent off the two subordinates to wait, until I wanted them, at the Avenue Road gate of the Regent's Park. Half an hour afterwards I was following in the same direction myself, at the heels of Mr. Jay.

The two confederates were punctual to the appointed time, I blush to record it, but it is nevertheless necessary to state, that the third rogue – the nameless desperado of my report, or if you prefer it, the mysterious 'Somebody Else' of the conversation between the two brothers – is a woman! and, what is worse, a young woman! and what is more lamentable still, a nice-looking woman! I have long resisted a growing conviction, that, wherever there is mischief in this world, an individual of the fair sex is inevitably certain to be mixed up in it. After the experience of this morning, I can struggle against that sad conclusion no longer. – I give up the sex – excepting Mrs. Yatman, I give up the sex.

The man named 'Jack' offered the woman his arm. Mr. Jay placed himself on the other side of her. The three then walked away slowly among the trees. I followed them at a respectful distance. My two subordinates, at a respectful distance also, followed me.

It was, I deeply regret to say, impossible to get near enough to them to overhear their conversation, without running too great a risk of being discovered. I could only infer from their gestures and actions that they were all three talking with extraordinary earnestness on some subject which deeply interested them. After having been engaged in this way a full quarter of an hour, they suddenly turned round to retrace their steps. My presence of mind did not forsake me in this emergency. I signed to the two subordinates to walk on carelessly and pass them, while I myself slipped dexterously behind a tree. As they came by me, I heard 'Jack' address these words to Mr. Jay:–

'Let us say half-past ten tomorrow morning. And mind you come in a cab. We had better not risk taking one in this neighbourhood.'

Mr. Jay made some brief reply, which I could not overhear. They walked back to the place at which they had met, shaking hands there with an audacious cordiality which it quite sickened me to see. They then separated. I followed Mr. Jay. My subordinates paid the same delicate attention to the other two.

Instead of taking me back to Rutherford Street, Mr. Jay led me to the Strand. He stopped at a dingy, disreputable-looking house, which, according to the inscription over the door, was a newspaper office, but which, in my judgment, had all the external appearance of a place devoted to the reception of stolen goods.

After remaining inside for a few minutes, he came out, whistling with his finger and thumb in his waistcoat pocket. A less discreet man than myself would have arrested him on the spot. I remembered the necessity of catching the two confederates, and the importance of not interfering with the appointment that had been made for the next morning. Such coolness as this, under trying circumstances, is rarely to be found, I should imagine, in a young beginner, whose reputation as a detective policeman is still to make.

From the house of suspicious appearance, Mr. Jay betook himself to a cigar-divan, and read the magazines over a cheroot. I sat at a table near him, and read the magazines likewise over a cheroot. From the divan he strolled to the tavern and had his chops. I strolled to the tavern and had my chops. When he had done, he went back to his lodging. When I had done, I went back to mine. He was overcome with drowsiness early in the evening and went to bed. As soon as I heard him snoring, I was overcome with drowsiness, and went to bed also.

Early in the morning my two subordinates came to make their report.

They had seen the man named 'Jack' leave the woman near the gate of an apparently respectable villa-residence, not far from the Regent's Park. Left to himself, he took a turning to the right, which led to a sort of suburban street, principally inhabited by shopkeepers. He stopped at the private door of one of the houses, and let himself in with his own key – looking about him as he opened the door, and staring suspiciously at my men as they lounged along on the opposite side of the way. These were all the particulars which the subordinates had to communicate. I kept them in my room to attend on me, if needful, and mounted to my Peep-hole to have a look at Mr. Jay.

He was occupied in dressing himself, and was taking extraordinary pains to destroy all traces of the natural slovenliness of his appearance. This was precisely what I expected. A vagabond like Mr. Jay knows the importance of giving himself a respectable look when he is going to run the risk of changing a stolen banknote. At five minutes past ten o'clock, he had given the last brush to his shabby hat and the last scouring with breadcrumb to his dirty gloves. At ten minutes past ten he was in the street, on his way to the nearest cab-stand, and I and my subordinates were close on his heels.

He took a cab, and we took a cab. I had not overheard them appoint a place of meeting, when following them in the Park on the previous day; but I soon found that we were proceeding in the old direction of the Avenue Road gate.

The cab in which Mr. Jay was riding turned into the Park slowly. We stopped outside, to avoid exciting suspicion. I got out to follow the cab on foot. Just as I did so, I saw it stop, and detected the two confederates approaching it from among the trees. They got in, and the cab was turned about directly. I ran back to my own cab, and told the driver to let them pass him, and then follow as before.

The man obeyed my directions, but so clumsily as to excite their suspicions. We had been driving after them about three minutes (returning along the road by which we had advanced) when I looked out of the window to see how far they might be ahead of us. As I did this, I saw two hats popped out of windows of their cab, and two faces looking back at me. I sank into my place in a cold sweat; – the expression is coarse, but no other form of words can describe my condition at that trying moment.

'We are found out!' I said faintly to my two subordinates. They stared at me in astonishment. My feelings changed instantly from the depth of despair to the height of indignation.

'It is the cabman's fault. Get out, one of you,' I said, with dignity – 'get out and punch his head.'

Instead of following my directions (I should wish this act of disobedience to be reported at headquarters) they both looked out of the window. Before I could pull them back, they both sat down again. Before I could express my just indignation, they both grinned, and said to me, 'Please to look out, sir!'

I did look out. The thieves' cab had stopped.

Where?

At a church door!!!

What effect this discovery might have had upon the ordinary run of men, I don't know. Being of a strong religious turn myself, it filled me with horror. I have often read of the unprincipled cunning of criminal persons; but I never before heard of three thieves attempting to double on their pursuers by entering a church! The sacrilegious audacity of that proceeding is, I should think, unparalleled in the annals of crime.

I checked my grinning subordinates by a frown. It was easy to see what was passing in their superficial minds. If I had not been able to look below the surface, I might, on observing two nicely-dressed men and one nicely-dressed woman enter a church before eleven in the morning on a week day, have come to the same hasty conclusion at which my inferiors had evidently arrived. As it was, appearances had no power to impose on *me*. I got out, and, followed by one of my men, entered the church. The other man I sent round to watch the vestry door. You may catch a weasel asleep – but not your humble servant, Matthew Sharpin!

We stole up the gallery stairs, diverged to the organ loft and peered through the curtains in front. There they were all three, sitting in a pew below – yes, incredible as it may appear, sitting in a pew below!

Before I could determine what to do, a clergyman made his appearance in full canonicals, from the vestry door, followed by a clerk. My brain whirled, and my eyesight grew dim. Dark remembrances of robberies committed in vestries floated through my mind. I trembled for the excellent man in full canonicals – I even trembled for the clerk.

The clergyman placed himself inside the altar rails. The three desperadoes approached him. He opened his book, and began to read. What? – you will ask.

I answer, without the slightest hesitation, the first lines of the Marriage Service.

My subordinate had the audacity to look at me, and then to stuff his pocket-handkerchief into his mouth. I scorned to pay any attention to him. After I had discovered that the man 'Jack' was the bridegroom, and that the man Jay acted the part of father, and gave away the bride, I left the church, followed by my man, and joined the other subordinate outside the vestry door. Some people in my position would now have felt rather crestfallen, and would have begun to think that they had made a very foolish mistake. Not the faintest misgiving of any kind troubled me. I did not feel in the slightest degree depreciated in my own estimation. And even now, after a lapse of three hours, my mind remains, I am happy to say, in the same calm and hopeful condition.

As soon as I and my subordinates were assembled together outside the church, I intimated my intention of still following the other cab, in spite of what had occurred. My reason for deciding on this course will appear presently. The two subordinates were astonished at my resolution. One of them had the impertinence to say to me:–

'If you please, sir, who is it that we are after? A man who has stolen money, or a man who has stolen a wife?'

The other low person encouraged him by laughing. Both have deserved an official reprimand; and both, I sincerely trust, will be sure to get it.

When the marriage ceremony was over, the three got into their cab; and once more our vehicle (neatly hidden round the corner of the church, so that they could not suspect it to be near them) started to follow theirs.

We traced them to the terminus of the South-Western Railway. The newly-married couple took tickets for Richmond – paying their fare with a half-sovereign, and so depriving me of the pleasure of arresting them, which I should certainly have done, if they had offered a banknote. They parted from Mr. Jay, saying, 'Remember the address, – 14 Babylon Terrace. You dine with us tomorrow week.' Mr. Jay accepted the invitation, and added, jocosely, that he was going home at once to get off his clean clothes, and to be comfortable and dirty again for the rest of the day. I have to report that I saw him home safely, and that he is comfortable and dirty again (to use his own disgraceful language) at the present moment.

Here the affair rests, having by this time reached what I may call its first stage.

I know very well what persons of hasty judgment will be inclined to say of my proceedings thus far. They will assert that I have been deceiving myself all through, in the most absurd way; they will declare that the suspicious conversations which I have reported, referred solely to the difficulties and dangers of successfully carrying out a runaway match; and they will appeal to the scene in the church, as offering undeniable proof of the correctness of their assertions. So let it be. I dispute nothing up to this point. But I ask a question, out of the depths of my own sagacity as a man of the world, which the bitterest of my enemies will not, I think, find it particularly easy to answer.

Granted the fact of the marriage, what proof does it afford me of the innocence of the three persons concerned in that clandestine transaction? It gives me none. On the contrary, it strengthens my suspicions against Mr. Jay and his confederates, because it suggests a distinct motive for their stealing the money. A gentleman who is going to spend his honeymoon at Richmond wants money; and a gentleman who is in debt to all his tradespeople wants money. Is this an unjustifiable imputation of bad motives? In the name of outraged morality, I deny it. These men have combined together, and have stolen a woman. Why should they not combine together, and steal a cash-box? I take my stand on the logic of rigid virtue; and I defy all the sophistry of vice to move me an inch out of my position.

Speaking of virtue, I may add that I have put this view of the case to Mr. and Mrs. Yatman. That accomplished and charming woman found it difficult, at first, to follow the close chain of my reasoning. I am free to confess that she shook her head, and shed tears, and joined her husband in premature lamentation over the loss of the two hundred pounds. But a little careful explanation on my part, and a little attentive listening on hers, ultimately changed her opinion. She now agrees with me, that there is nothing in this unexpected circumstance of the clandestine marriage which absolutely tends to divert suspicion from Mr. Jay, or Mr. 'Jack', or the runaway lady. 'Audacious hussy' was the term my fair friend used in speaking of her, but let that pass. It is more to the purpose to record that Mrs. Yatman has not lost confidence in me and that Mr. Yatman promises to follow her example, and do his best to look hopefully for future results.

I have now, in the new turn that circumstances have taken, to wait advice from your office. I pause for fresh orders with all the composure of a man who has got two strings to his bow. When I traced the three confederates from the church door to the railway terminus, I had two motives for doing so. First, I followed them as a matter of official business, believing them still to have been guilty of the robbery. Secondly, I followed them as a matter of private speculation, with a view of discovering the place of refuge to which the runaway couple intended to retreat, and of making my information a marketable commodity to offer to the young lady's family and friends. Thus, whatever happens, I may congratulate myself beforehand on not having wasted my time. If the office approved of my conduct, I have my plan ready for further proceedings. If the office blames me, I shall take myself off, with my marketable information, to the genteel villa-residence in the neighbourhood of the Regent's Park. Any way, the affair puts money into my pocket, and does credit to my penetration as an uncommonly sharp man.

I have only one word more to add, and it is this:– if any individual ventures to assert that Mr. Jay and his confederates are innocent of all share in the stealing of the cash-box, I, in return, defy that individual – though he may even be Chief Inspector Theakstone himself – to tell me who has committed the robbery at Rutherford Street, Soho.

I have the honour to be,
Your very obedient servant,
Matthew Sharpin.

From Chief Inspector Theakstone to Sergeant Bulmer

Birmingham, July 9th.
Sergeant Bulmer, – That empty-headed puppy, Mr. Matthew Sharpin, has made a mess of the case at Rutherford Street, exactly as I expected he would. Business keeps me in this town; so I write to you to set the matter straight. I enclose, with this, the pages of feeble scribble-scrabble which the creature, Sharpin, calls a report. Look them over; and when you have made your way through all the gabble, I think you will agree with me that the conceited booby has looked for the thief in every direction but the right one. You can lay your hand on the guilty person in five minutes, now. Settle the case at once; forward your report to me at this place; and tell Mr. Sharpin that he is suspended till further notice.

Yours,
Francis Theakstone.

From Sergeant Bulmer to Chief Inspector Theakstone

London, July 10th.
Inspector Theakstone, – Your letter and enclosure came safe to

hand. Wise men, they say, may always learn something, even from a fool. By the time I had got through Sharpin's maundering report of his own folly, I saw my way clear enough to the end of the Rutherford Street case, just as you thought I should. In half an hour's time I was at the house. The first person I saw there was Mr. Sharpin himself.

'Have you come to help me?' says he.

'Not exactly,' says I. 'I've come to tell you that you are suspended till further notice.'

'Very good,' says he, not taken down, by so much as a single peg, in his own estimation. 'I thought you would be jealous of me. It's very natural; and I don't blame you. Walk in, pray, and make yourself at home. I'm off to do a little detective business on my own account, in the neighbourhood of the Regent's Park. Ta-ta, sergeant, ta-ta!' With those words he took himself out of the way – which was exactly what I wanted him to do.

As soon as the maid-servant had shut the door, I told her to inform her master that I wanted to say a word to him in private. She showed me into the parlour behind the shop; and there was Mr. Yatman, all alone, reading the newspaper.

'About this matter of the robbery, sir,' says I.

He cut me short, peevishly enough – being naturally a poor, weak, womanish sort of man. 'Yes, yes, I know,' says he. 'You have come to tell me that your wonderfully clever man, who has bored holes in my second-floor partition, has made a mistake, and is off the scent of the scoundrel who has stolen my money.'

'Yes, sir,' says I. 'That is one of the things I came to tell you. But I have got something else to say, besides that.'

'Can you tell me who the thief is?' says he, more pettish than ever.

'Yes, sir,' says I, 'I think I can.'

He put down the newspaper, and began to look rather anxious and frightened.

'Not my shopman?' says he. 'I hope, for the man's own sake, it's not my shopman.'

'Guess again, sir,' says I.

'That idle slut, the maid?' says he.

'She is idle, sir,' says I, 'and she is also a slut; my first inquiries about her proved as much as that. But she's not the thief.'

'Then in the name of heaven, who is?' says he.

'Will you please to prepare yourself for a very disagreeable surprise, sir?' says I. 'And in case you lose your temper, will you excuse my remarking that I am the stronger man of the two, and that, if you allow yourself to lay hands on me, I may unintentionally hurt you, in pure self-defence?'

He turned as pale as ashes, and pushed his chair two or three feet away from me.

'You have asked me to tell you, sir who has taken your money,' I went on. 'If you insist on my giving you an answer –'

'I do insist,' he said faintly. 'Who has taken it?'

'Your wife has taken it,' I said very quietly, and very positively at the same time.

He jumped out of the chair as if I had put a knife into him, and struck his fist on the table, so heavily that the wood cracked again.

'Steady, sir,' says I. 'Flying into a passion won't help you to the truth.'

'It's a lie!' says he, with another smack of his fist on the table – 'a base, vile, infamous lie! How dare you – '

He stopped, and fell back into the chair again, looked about him in a bewildered way, and ended by bursting out crying.

'When your better sense comes back to you, sir,' says I, 'I am sure you will be gentleman enough to make an apology for the language you have just used. In the meantime, please to listen, if you can, to a word of explanation. Mr. Sharpin has sent in a report to our inspector, of the most irregular and ridiculous kind; setting down, not only all his own foolish doings and sayings, but the doings and sayings of Mrs. Yatman as well. In most cases, such a document would have been fit for the wastepaper basket; but, in this particular case, it so happens that Mr. Sharpin's budget of nonsense leads to a certain conclusion, which the simpleton of a writer has been quite innocent of suspecting from the beginning to the end. Of that conclusion I am so sure, that I will forfeit my place, if it does not turn out that Mrs. Yatman has been practising upon the folly and conceit of this young man, and that she has tried to shield herself from discovery by purposely encouraging him to suspect the wrong persons. I tell you that confidently;

and I will even go further. I will undertake to give a decided opinion as to why Mrs. Yatman took the money, and what she has done with it, or with a part of it. Nobody can look at that lady, sir, without being struck by the great taste and beauty of her dress — '

As I said those last words, the poor man seemed to find his powers of speech again. He cut me short directly, as haughtily as if he had been a duke instead of a stationer.

'Try some other means of justifying your vile calumny against my wife,' says he. 'Her milliner's bill for the past year, is on my file of receipted accounts at this moment.'

'Excuse me, sir,' says I, 'but that proves nothing. Milliners, I must tell you, have a certain rascally custom which comes within the daily experience of our office. A married lady who wishes it, can keep two accounts at her dressmaker's; one is the account which her husband sees and pays; the other is the private account, which contains all the extravagant items, and which the wife pays secretly, by instalments, whenever she can. According to our usual experience, these instalments are mostly squeezed out of the housekeeping money. In your case, I suspect no instalments have been paid; proceedings have been threatened; Mrs. Yatman, knowing your altered circumstances, has felt herself driven into a corner; and she has paid her private account out of your cash-box.'

'I won't believe it,' says he. 'Every word you speak is an abominable insult to me and to my wife.'

'Are you man enough sir,' says I, taking him up short, in order to save time and words, 'to get that receipted bill you spoke of just now off the file, and come with me at once to the milliner's shop where Mrs. Yatman deals?'

He turned red in the face at that, got the bill directly, and put on his hat. I took out of my pocket-book the list containing the numbers of the lost notes, and we left the house together immediately.

Arrived at the milliner's (one of the expensive West End houses, as I expected), I asked for a private interview, on important business, with the mistress of the concern. It was not the first time that she and I had met over the same delicate investigation. The moment she set eyes on me, she sent for her husband. I mentioned who Mr. Yatman was, and what we wanted.

'This is strictly private?' inquires her husband. I nodded my head.

'And confidential?' says the wife. I nodded again.

'Do you see any objection, dear, to obliging the sergeant with a sight of the books?' says the husband.

'None in the world, love, if you approve of it,' says the wife.

All this while poor Mr. Yatman sat looking the picture of astonishment and distress, quite out of place at our polite conference. The books were brought – and one minute's look at the pages in which Mrs. Yatman's name figured was enough, and more than enough, to prove the truth of every word I had spoken.

There, in one book, was the husband's account, which Mr. Yatman had settled. And there, in the other, was the private account, crossed off also; the date of settlement being the very day after the loss of the cash-box. This said private account amounted to the sum of a hundred and seventy-five pounds, odd shillings; and it extended over a period of three years. Not a single instalment had been paid on it. Under the last line was an entry to this effect: 'Written to for the third time, June 23rd.' I pointed to it, and asked the milliner if that means 'last June.' Yes, it did mean last June; and she now deeply regretted to say that it had been accompanied by a threat of legal proceedings.

'I thought you gave good customers more than three years credit?' says I.

The milliner looks at Mr. Yatman, and whispers to me – 'Not when a lady's husband gets into difficulties.'

She pointed to the account as she spoke. The entries after the time when Mr. Yatman's circumstances became involved were just as extravagant, for a person in his wife's situation, as the entries for the year before that period. If the lady had economised in other things, she had certainly not economised in the matter of dress.

There was nothing left now but to examine the cash-book, for form's sake. The money had been paid in notes, the amounts and numbers of which exactly tallied with the figures set down in my list.

After that, I thought it best to get Mr. Yatman out of the house immediately. He was in such a pitiable condition, that I called a cab and accompanied him home in it. At first he cried and raved like a child: but I soon quieted him – and I must add, to his credit, that he made me a most handsome apology for his language, as the cab drew up at his house door. In return, I tried to give him some advice about how to set matters right, for the future, with his wife. He paid very little attention to me, and went upstairs muttering to himself about a separation. Whether Mrs. Yatman will come cleverly out of the scrape of not, seems doubtful. I should say, myself, that she will go into screeching hysterics, and so frighten the poor man into forgiving her. But this is no business of ours. So far as we are concerned, the case is now at an end; and the present report may come to a conclusion along with it.

I remain, accordingly, yours to command,

Thomas Bulmer.

P.S. – I have to add, that, on leaving Rutherford Street, I met Mr. Matthew Sharpin coming to pack up his things.

'Only think!' says he, rubbing his hands in great spirits, 'I've been to the genteel villa-residence; and the moment I mentioned my business, they kicked me out directly. There were two witnesses of the assault; and it's worth a hundred pounds to me, if it's worth a farthing.'

'I wish you joy of your luck,' says I.

'Thank you,' says he. 'When may I pay you the same compliment on finding the thief?'

'Whenever you like,' says I, 'for the thief is found.'

'Just what I expected,' says he. 'I've done all the work; and now you cut in, and claim all the credit – Mr. Jay of course?'

'No,' says I.

'Who is it then?' says he.

'Ask Mrs. Yatman,' says I. 'She's waiting to tell you.'

'All right! I'd much rather hear it from that charming woman than from you,' says he, and goes into the house in a mighty hurry.

What do you think of that, Inspector Theakstone? Would you like to stand in Mr. Sharpin's shoes? I shouldn't, I can promise you!

From Chief Inspector Theakstone to Mr. Matthew Sharpin

July 12th.

Sir, – Sergeant Bulmer has already told you to consider yourself suspended until further notice. I have now authority to add, that your services as a member of the Detective Police are positively declined. You will please to take this letter as notifying officially your dismissal from the force.

I may inform you, privately, that your rejection is not intended to cast any reflections on your character. It merely implies that you are not quite sharp enough for our purpose. If we *are* to have a new recruit among us, we should infinitely prefer Mrs. Yatman.

Your obedient servant,
    Francis Theakstone.

Note on the Preceding Correspondence, added by Mr. Theakstone

The Inspector is not in a position to append any explanations of importance to the last of the letters. It has been discovered that Mr. Matthew Sharpin left the house in Rutherford Street five minutes after his interview outside of it with Sergeant Bulmer – his manner expressing the liveliest emotions of terror and astonishment, and his left cheek displaying a bright patch of red, which might have been the result of a slap on the face from a female hand. He was also heard, by the shopman at Rutherford Street, to use a very shocking expression in reference to Mrs. Yatman; and was seen to clench his fist vindictively, as he ran round the corner of the street. Nothing more has been heard of him; and it is conjectured that he has left London with the intention of offering his valuable services to the provincial police.

On the interesting domestic subject of Mr. and Mrs. Yatman still less is known. It has, however, been positively ascertained that the medical attendant of the family was sent for in a great hurry, on the day when Mr. Yatman returned from the milliner's shop. The neighbouring chemist received, soon afterwards, a prescription of a soothing nature to make up for Mrs. Yatman. The day after, Mr. Yatman purchased some smelling-salts at the shop, and afterwards appeared at the circulating library to ask for a novel, descriptive of high life, that would amuse an invalid lady. It has been inferred from these circumstances, that he has not thought it desirable to carry out his threat of separating himself from his wife – at least in the present (presumed) condition of that lady's sensitive nervous system.

THE LADY OF GLENWITH GRANGE

THE LADY OF GLENWITH GRANGE

PROLOGUE

My practice in the art of portrait-painting, if it has done nothing else, has at least fitted me to turn my talents (such as they are) to a great variety of uses. I have not only taken the likenesses of men, women, and children, but have also extended the range of my brush, under stress of circumstances, to horses, dogs, houses, and in one case even to a bull – the terror and glory of his parish, and the most truculent sitter I ever had. The beast was appropriately named 'Thunder and Lightning,' and was the property of a gentleman-farmer named Garthwaite, a distant connexion of my wife's family.

How it was that I escaped being gored to death before I had finished my picture, is more than I can explain to this day. 'Thunder and Lightning' resented the very sight of me and my colour-box, as if he viewed the taking of his likeness in the light of a personal insult. It required two men to coax him, while a third held him by a ring in his nostrils, before I could venture on beginning to work. Even then he always lashed his tail, and jerked his huge head, and rolled his fiery eyes with a devouring anxiety to have me on his horns for daring to sit down quietly and look at him. Never, I can honestly say, did I feel more heartily grateful for the blessings of soundness of limb and wholeness of skin, than when I had completed the picture of the bull!

One morning, when I had but little more than half done my unwelcome task, my friend and I were met on our way to the bull's stable by the farm-bailiff, who informed us gravely that 'Thunder and Lightning' was just then in such an especially surly state of temper as to render it quite unsafe for me to think of painting him. I looked inquiringly at Mr. Garthwaite, who smiled with an air of comic resignation, and said:– 'Very well, then, we have nothing for it but to

35

wait till tomorrow. What do you say to a morning's fishing, Mr. Kerby, now that my bull's bad temper has given us a holiday?'

I replied, with perfect truth, that I knew nothing about fishing. But Mr. Garthwaite, who was as ardent an angler in his way as Izaak Walton himself, was not to be appeased even by the best of excuses. 'It is never too late to learn', cried he. 'I will make a fisherman of you in no time, if you will only attend to my directions.' It was impossible for me to make any more apologies, without the risk of appearing discourteous. So I thanked my host for his friendly intentions, and with some secret misgivings, accepted the first fishing rod that he put into my hands.

'We shall soon get there,' said Mr. Garthwaite. 'I am taking you to the best mill-stream in the neighbourhood.' It was all one to me whether we got there soon or late, and whether the stream was good or bad. However, I did my best to conceal my unsportsmanlike apathy; and tried to look quite happy and very impatient to begin, as we drew near to the mill, and heard louder and louder the gushing of many waters all around it.

Leading the way immediately to a place beneath the falling stream, where there was a deep, eddying pool, Mr. Garthwaite baited and threw in his line before I had fixed the joints of my fishing rod. This first difficulty overcome, I involuntarily plunged into some excellent, but rather embarrassing, sport with my line and hook. I caught every one of my garments, from head to foot; I angled for my own clothes with the dexterity and success of Izaak Walton himself. I caught my hat, my jacket, my waistcoat, my trousers, my fingers, and my thumbs – some devil possessed my hook; some more than eel-like vitality twirled and twisted in every inch of my line. By the time my host arrived to assist me, I had attached myself to my fishing rod, apparently for life. All difficulties yielded, however, to his patience and skill; my hook was baited for me, and thrown in; my rod was put into my hand; my friend went back to his place; and we began at last to angle in earnest.

We certainly caught a few fish (in my case, I mean, of course, that the fish caught themselves); but they were scanty in number and light in weight. Whether it was the presence of the miller's foreman – a gloomy personage, who stood staring disastrously upon us from a little flower-garden on the opposite bank – that cast an adverse influence over our sport; or whether my want of faith and earnestness as an angler acted retributively on my companion as well as myself, I know not; but it is certain that he got almost as little reward for his skill as I got for my patience. After nearly two hours of intense expectation on my part, and intense angling on his, Mr. Garthwaite jerked his line out of the water in a rage, and bade me follow him to another place, declaring that the stream must have been netted by poachers in the night, who had taken all the large fish away with them, and had thrown in the small ones to grow until their next visit. We moved away, further down the bank, leaving the imperturbable foreman still in the flower-garden, staring at us speechlessly on our departure, exactly as he had already stared at us on our approach.

'Stop a minute,' said Mr. Garthwaite suddenly, after we had walked some distance in silence by the side of the stream, 'I have an idea. Now we *are* out for a day's angling, we won't be baulked. Instead of trying the water here again, we will go where I know, by experience, that the fishing is excellent. And, what is more, you shall be introduced to a lady whose appearance is sure to interest you, and whose history, I can tell you beforehand, is a very remarkable one.'

'Indeed,' I said. 'May I ask in what way.'

'She is connected,' answered Mr. Garthwaite, 'with an extraordinary story, which relates to a family once settled in an old house in this neighbourhood. Her name is Miss Welwyn; but she is less formally known among the poor people about here, who love her dearly, and honour her almost superstitiously, as The Lady of Glenwith Grange. Wait till you have seen her before you ask me to say anything more. She lives in the strictest retirement: I am almost the only visitor who is admitted. Don't say you had rather not go in. Any friend of mine will be welcome at the Grange (the scene of the story, remember), for my sake – the more especially because I have never abused my privilege of introduction. The place is not above two miles from here, and the stream (which we call in our county dialect, Glenwith Beck), runs through the grounds.

As we walked on, Mr. Garthwaite's manner altered. He became unusually silent and thoughtful. The mention of Miss Welwyn's name had evidently called up some recollections which were not in harmony with his everyday mood. Feeling that to talk to him on any indifferent subject would be only to interrupt his thoughts to no purpose, I walked by his side in perfect silence, looking out already with some curiosity and impatience for a first view of Glenwith Grange. We stopped, at last, close by an old church, standing on the outskirts of a pretty village. The low wall of the churchyard was bounded on one side by a plantation, and was joined by a park paling, in which I noticed a small wicket-gate. Mr. Garthwaite opened it, and led me along a shrubbery-path, which conducted us circuitously to the dwelling-house.

We had evidently entered by a private way, for we approached the building by the back. I looked up at it curiously, and saw standing at one of the windows on the lower floor a little girl watching us as we advanced. She seemed to be about nine or ten years old. I could not help stopping a moment to look up at her, her clear complexion, and her long dark hair were so beautiful. And yet there was something in her expression – a dimness and vacancy in her large eyes, a changeless unmeaning smile on her parted lips – which seemed to jar with all that was naturally attractive in her face; which perplexed, disappointed, and even shocked me, though I hardly knew why. Mr. Garthwaite, who had been walking along thoughtfully, with his eyes on the ground, turned back when he found me lingering behind him; looked up where I was looking; started a little, I thought; and then took my arm, whispered rather impatiently, 'Don't say anything about having seen that poor child when you are introduced to Miss Welwyn; I'll tell you why afterwards,' and led me round hastily to the front of the building.

It was a very dreary old house, with a lawn in front thickly sprinkled with flowerbeds, and creepers of all sorts climbing in profusion about the heavy stone porch and the mullions of the lower windows. In spite of these prettiest of all ornaments clustering brightly round the building – in spite of the perfect repair in which it was kept from top to bottom – there was something repellent to me in the aspect of the whole place: a deathly stillness hung over it, which fell oppressively on my spirits. When my companion rang the loud, deep-toned bell, the sound startled me as if we had been committing a crime in disturbing the silence. And when the door was opened by an old female servant (while the hollow echo of the bell was still vibrating in the air), I could hardly imagine it possible that we should be let in. We were admitted, however, without the slightest demur. I remarked that there was the same atmosphere of dreary repose inside the house which I had already observed, or rather felt, outside it. No dogs barked at our approach – no doors banged in the servants' offices – no heads peeped over the banisters – not one of the ordinary domestic consequences of an unexpected visit in the country met either eye or ear. The large shadowy apartment, half library, half breakfast-room, into which we were ushered, was as solitary as the hall of entrance; unless I except such drowsy evidences of life as were here presented to us, in the shape of an Angola cat and a gray parrot – the first lying asleep in a chair, the second sitting ancient, solemn, and voiceless in a large cage. Mr. Garthwaite walked to the window when we entered, without saying a word. Determining to let his taciturn humour have its way, I asked him no questions, but looked around the room to see what information it would give me (and rooms often do give such information) about the character and habits of the owner of the house.

Two tables covered with books were the first objects that attracted me. On approaching them, I was surprised to find that the all-influencing periodical literature of the present day – whose sphere is already almost without limit; whose readers, even in our time, may be numbered by millions – was entirely unrepresented on Miss Welwyn's table. Nothing modern, nothing contemporary in the world of books, presented itself. Of all the volumes beneath my hand, not one bore the badge of the circulating library, or wore the flaring modern livery of gilt cloth. Every work that I took up had been written at least fifteen or twenty years since. The prints hanging round the walls (towards which I next looked) were all engraved from devotional subjects by the old masters: the music-stand con-

tained no music of later date than the compositions of Haydn
and Mozart. Whatever I examined besides, told me, with the
same consistency, the same strange tale. The owner of these
possessions lived in the bygone time; lived among old recollections and old associations – a voluntary recluse from all that
was connected with the passing day. In Miss Welwyn's house,
the stir, the tumult, the 'idle business' of the world, evidently
appealed in vain to sympathies which grew no longer with the
growing hour.

As these thoughts were passing through my mind, the door
opened, and the lady herself appeared.

She looked certainly past the prime of life; longer past it, as I
afterwards discovered, than she really was. But I never
remember, in any other face, to have seen so much of the
better part of the beauty of early womanhood still remaining,
as I saw in hers. Sorrow had evidently passed over the fair
calm countenance before me, but had left resignation there as
its only trace. Her expression was still youthful – youthful in
its kindness and its candour especially. It was only when I
looked at her hair, that was now growing gray – at her wan
thin hands – at the faint lines marked round her mouth – at the
sad serenity of her eyes, that I fairly detected the mark of age;
and, more than that, the token of some great grief, which had
been conquered; but not banished. Even from her voice alone
– from the peculiar uncertainty of its low calm tones when she
spoke – it was easy to conjecture that she must have passed
through sufferings, at some time of her life, which had tried to
the quick the noble nature that they could not subdue.

Mr. Garthwaite and she met each other almost like brother
and sister: it was plain that the friendly intimacy between them
had been of very long duration. Our visit was a short one. The
conversation never advanced beyond the commonplace topics
suited to the occasion: it was, therefore, from what I saw, and
not from what I heard, that I was enabled to form my
judgment of Miss Welwyn. Deeply as she had interested me –
far more deeply than I at all know how to explain in fitting
words – I cannot say that I was unwilling to depart when we
rose to take leave. Though nothing could be more courteous
and more kind than her manner towards me during the whole
interview, I could still perceive that it cost her some effort to

repress in my presence the shades of sadness and reserve which seemed often ready to steal over her. And I must confess that when I once or twice heard the half-sigh stifled, and saw the momentary relapse into thoughtfulness suddenly restrained, I felt an indefinable awkwardness in my position which made me ill at ease: which set me doubting whether, as a perfect stranger, I had done right in suffering myself to be introduced where no new faces could awaken either interest or curiosity; where no new sympathies could ever be felt, no new friendships ever be formed.

As soon as we had taken leave of Miss Welwyn, and were on our way to the stream in her grounds, I more than satisfied Mr. Garthwaite that the impression the lady had produced on me was of no transitory kind, by overwhelming him with questions about her – not omitting one or two incidental inquiries on the subject of the little girl whom I had seen at the back window. He only rejoined that his story would answer all my questions; and that he would begin to tell it as soon as we had arrived at Glenwith Beck, and were comfortably settled to fishing.

Five minutes more of walking brought us to the bank of the stream, and showed us the water running smoothly and slowly, tinged with the softest green lustre from the reflections of trees which almost entirely arched it over. Leaving me to admire the view at my ease, Mr. Garthwaite occupied himself with the necessary preparations for angling, baiting my hook as well as his own. Then, desiring me to sit near him on the bank, he at last satisfied my curiosity by beginning his story. I shall relate it in his own manner, and, as nearly as possible, in his own words.

THE LADY OF GLENWITH GRANGE

I have known Miss Welwyn long enough to be able to bear personal testimony to the truth of many of the particulars which I am now about to relate. I knew her father, and her younger sister Rosamond; and I was acquainted with the Frenchman who became Rosamond's husband. These are the persons of whom it will be principally necessary for me to speak; they are the only prominent characters in my story.

Miss Welwyn's father died some years since. I remember him very well – though he never excited in me, or in any one else that I ever heard of, the slightest feeling of interest. When I have said that he inherited a very large fortune, amassed during his father's time, by speculations of a very daring, very fortunate, but not always very honourable kind, and that he bought this old house with the notion of raising his social position, by making himself a member of our landed aristocracy in these parts, I have told you as much about him, I suspect, as you would care to hear. He was a thoroughly commonplace man, with no great virtues and no great vices in him. He had a little heart, a feeble mind, an amiable temper, a tall figure, and a handsome face. More than this need not, and cannot, be said on the subject of Mr. Welwyn's character.

I must have seen the late Mrs. Welwyn very often as a child; but I cannot say that I remember anything more of her than that she was tall and handsome, and very generous and sweet-tempered towards me when I was in her company. She was her husband's superior in birth, as in everything else; was a great reader of books in all languages; and possessed such admirable talents as a musician, that her wonderful playing on the organ is remembered and talked of to this day among the old people in our country houses about here. All her friends, as I have heard, were disappointed when she married Mr. Welwyn, rich as he was; and were afterwards astonished to find her preserving the appearance, at least, of being perfectly happy with a husband who, neither in mind nor heart, was worthy of her.

It was generally supposed (and I have no doubt correctly), that she found her great happiness and her great consolation in her little girl Ida – now the lady from whom we have just parted. The child took after her mother from the first – inheriting her mother's fondness for books, her mother's love of music, her mother's quick sensibilities, and, more than all, her mother's quiet firmness, patience, and loving-kindness of disposition. From Ida's earliest years, Mrs. Welwyn undertook the whole superintendence of her education. The two were hardly ever apart, within doors or without. Neighbours and friends said that the little girl was being brought up too fancifully, was not enough among other children, was sadly neglected as to all reasonable and practical teaching, and was perilously encouraged in those dreamy and imaginative tendencies of which she had naturally more than her due share. There was, perhaps, some truth in this; and there might have been still more, if Ida had possessed an ordinary character, or had been reserved for an ordinary destiny. But she was a strange child from the first, and a strange future was in store for her.

Little Ida reached her eleventh year without either brother or sister to be her playfellow and companion at home. Immediately after that period, however, her sister Rosamond was born. Though Mr. Welwyn's own desire was to have had a son, there were, nevertheless, great rejoicings yonder in the old house on the birth of this second daughter. But they were all turned, only a few months afterwards, to the bitterest grief and despair: the Grange lost its mistress. While Rosamond was still an infant in arms, her mother died.

Mrs. Welwyn had been afflicted with some disorder after the birth of her second child, the name of which I am not learned enough in medical science to be able to remember. I only know that she recovered from it, to all appearance, in an unexpectedly short time; that she suffered a fatal relapse, and that she died a lingering and a painful death. Mr. Welwyn (who, in after-years, had a habit of vaingloriously describing his marriage as 'a love-match on both sides') was really fond of his wife in his own frivolous feeble way, and suffered as acutely as such a man could suffer, during the latter days of her illness, and at the terrible time when the doctors, one and all, confessed that her life was a thing to be despaired of. He burst into irrepressible passions of tears, and was always obliged to leave the sick-room whenever Mrs. Welwyn spoke of her approaching end. The last solemn words of the dying woman, the tenderest messages that she could give, the dearest parting wishes that she could express, the most earnest commands that she could leave behind her, the gentlest reasons for consolation that she could suggest to the survivors among those who loved her, were not poured into her husband's ear, but into her child's. From the first period of her illness, Ida had persisted in remaining in the sick-room, rarely speaking, never showing outwardly any signs of terror or grief, except when she was removed from it; and then bursting into hysterical passions of weeping, which no expostulations, no arguments, no commands – nothing, in short, but bringing her back to the bedside – ever availed to calm. Her mother had been her playfellow, her companion, her dearest and most familiar friend; and there seemed something in the remembrance of this which, instead of overwhelming the child with despair, strengthened her to watch faithfully and bravely by her dying parent to the very last.

When the parting moment was over, and when Mr. Welwyn, unable to bear the shock of being present in the house of death at the time of his wife's funeral, left home and went to stay with one of his relations in a distant part of England, Ida, whom it had been his wish to take away with him, petitioned earnestly to be left behind. 'I promised mamma before she died that I would be as good to my little sister Rosamond as she had been to me,' said the child simply; 'and she told me in return that I might wait here and see her laid in her grave.' There happened to be an aunt of Mrs. Welwyn, and an old servant of the family, in the house at this time, who understood Ida much better than her father did, and they persuaded him not to take her away. I have heard my mother say that the effect of the child's appearance at the funeral on her, and on all who went to see it, was something that she could never think of without the tears coming into her eyes, and could never forget to the last day of her life.

It must have been very shortly after this period that I saw Ida for the first time.

I remember accompanying my mother on a visit to the old house we have just left, in the summer, when I was at home for the holidays. It was a lovely, sunshiny morning; there was nobody indoors, and we walked out into the garden. As we approached that lawn yonder, on the other side of the shrubbery, I saw, first, a young woman in mourning (apparently a servant) sitting reading; then a little girl, dressed all in black, moving towards us slowly over the bright turf, and holding up before her a baby whom she was trying to teach to walk. She looked, to my ideas, so very young to be engaged in such an occupation as this, and her gloomy black frock appeared to be such an unnaturally grave garment for a mere child of her age, and looked so doubly dismal by contrast with the brilliant sunny lawn on which she stood, that I quite started when I first saw her, and eagerly asked my mother who she was. The answer informed me of the sad family story, which I have just been relating to you. Mrs. Welwyn had then been buried about three months; and Ida, in her childish way, was trying, as she had promised, to supply her mother's place to her infant sister Rosamond.

I only mention this simple incident, because it is necessary, before I proceed to the eventful part of my narrative, that you should know exactly in what relation the sisters stood towards one another from the first. Of all the last parting words that Mrs. Welwyn had spoken to her child, none had been oftener repeated, none more solemnly urged, than those which had commended the little Rosamond to Ida's love and care. To other persons, the full, the all-trusting dependence which the dying mother was known to have placed in a child hardly eleven years old, seemed merely a proof of that helpless desire to cling even to the feeblest consolations which the approach of death so often brings with it. But the event showed that the trust so strangely placed had not been ventured vainly when it was committed to young and tender hands. The whole future existence of the child was one noble proof that she had been worthy of her mother's dying confidence when it was first reposed in her. In that simple incident which I have just mentioned, the new life of the two motherless sisters was all foreshadowed.

Time passed. I left school – went to college – travelled in Germany, and stayed there some time to learn the language. At every interval when I came home, and asked about the Welwyns, the answer was, in substance, almost always the same. Mr. Welwyn was giving his regular dinners, performing his regular duties as a county magistrate, enjoying his regular recreations as an amateur farmer and an eager sportsman. His two daughters were never separate. Ida was the same strange, quiet, retiring girl, that she had always been; and was still (as the phrase went) 'spoiling' Rosamond in every way in which it was possible for an elder sister to spoil a younger by too much kindness.

I myself went to the Grange occasionally, when I was in this neighbourhood, in holiday and vacation time; and was able to test the correctness of the picture of life there which had been drawn for me. I remember the two sisters, when Rosamond was four or five years old; and when Ida seemed to me, even then, to be more like the child's mother than her sister. She bore with her little caprices as sisters do not bear with one another. She was so patient at lesson-time, so anxious to conceal any weariness that might overcome her in play-hours, so proud when Rosamond's beauty was noticed, so grateful for Rosamond's kisses when the child thought of bestowing them, so quick to notice all that Rosamond did, and to attend to all that Rosamond said, even when visitors were in the room; that she seemed, to my boyish observations, altogether different from other elder sisters, in other family circles into which I was then received.

I remember them, again, when Rosamond was just growing to womanhood, and was in high spirits at the prospect of spending a season in London, and being presented at Court. She was very beautiful at that time – much handsomer than Ida. Her 'accomplishments' were talked of far and near in our country circles. Few, if any, of the people, however, who applauded her playing and singing, who admired her watercolour drawings, who were delighted at her fluency when she spoke French, and amazed at her ready comprehension when she read German, knew how little of all this elegant mental cultivation and nimble manual dexterity she owed to her governesses and masters, and how much to her elder sister. It was Ida who really found out the means of stimulating her when she was idle; Ida who helped her through all her worst difficulties; Ida who gently conquered her defects of memory over her books, her inaccuracies of ear at the piano, her errors of taste when she took the brush or pencil in hand. It was Ida alone who worked these marvels, and whose all-sufficient reward for her hardest exertions was a chance word of kindness from her sister's lips. Rosamond was not unaffectionate, and not ungrateful; but she inherited much of her father's commonness and frivolity of character. She became so accustomed to owe everything to her sister – to resign all her most trifling difficulties to Ida's ever-ready care – to have all her tastes consulted by Ida's ever watchful kindness – that she never appreciated, as it deserved the deep devoted love of which she was the object. When Ida refused two good offers of marriage, Rosamond was as much astonished as the veriest strangers, who wondered why the elder Miss Welwyn seemed bent on remaining single all her life.

When the journey to London, to which I have already alluded, took place, Ida accompanied her father and sister. If she had consulted her own tastes, she would have remained in the country; but Rosamond declared that she should feel quite lost and helpless twenty times a day, in town, without her sister. It was in the nature of Ida to sacrifice herself to any one whom she loved, on the smallest occasions as well as the greatest. Her affection was as intuitively ready to sanctify Rosamond's slightest caprices as to excuse Rosamond's most thoughtless faults. So she went to London cheerfully, to witness with pride all the little triumphs won by her sister's beauty; to hear, and never tire of hearing, all that admiring friends could say in her sister's praise.

At the end of the season, Mr. Welwyn and his daughters returned for a short time to the country; then left home again to spend the latter part of the autumn and the beginning of the winter in Paris.

They took with them excellent letters of introduction, and saw a great deal of the best society in Paris, foreign as well as English. At one of the first of the evening parties which they attended, the general topic of conversation was the conduct of a certain French nobleman, the Baron Franval, who had returned to his native country after a long absence, and who was spoken of in terms of high eulogy by the majority of the guests present. The history of who Franval was, and of what he had done, was readily communicated to Mr. Welwyn and his daughters, and was briefly this:—

The Baron inherited little from his ancestors besides his high rank and his ancient pedigree. On the death of his parents, he and his two unmarried sisters (their only surviving children) found the small territorial property of the Franvals, in Normandy, barely productive enough to afford a comfortable subsistence for the three. The Baron, then a young man of three-and-twenty, endeavoured to obtain such military or civil employment as might become his rank; but although the Bourbons were at that time restored to the throne of France, his efforts were ineffectual. Either his interest at Court was bad, or secret enemies were at work to oppose his advancement. He failed to obtain even the slightest favour; and, irritated by undeserved neglect, resolved to leave France, and seek occupation for his energies in foreign countries, where his rank would be no bar to his bettering his fortunes, if he pleased, by engaging in commercial pursuits.

An opportunity of the kind that he wanted unexpectedly offered itself. He left his sisters in care of an old male relative of the family at the château in Normandy, and sailed, in the first instance to the West Indies; afterwards extending his wanderings to the continent of South America, and there engaging in mining transactions on a very large scale. After fifteen years of absence (during the latter part of which time false reports of his death had reached Normandy), he had just returned to France; having realized a handsome independence, with which he proposed to widen the limits of his ancestral property, and to give his sisters (who were still, like himself, unmarried) all the luxuries and advantages that affluence could bestow. The Baron's independent spirit, and generous devotion to the honour of his family and the happiness of his surviving relatives, were themes of general admiration in most of the social circles of Paris. He was expected to arrive in the capital every day; and it was naturally enough predicted that his reception in society there could not fail to be of the most flattering and most brilliant kind.

The Welwyns listened to this story with some little interest; Rosamond, who was very romantic, being especially attracted by it, and openly avowing to her father and sister, when they got back to their hotel, that she felt as ardent a curiosity as anybody to see the adventurous and generous Baron. The desire was soon gratified. Franval came to Paris, as had been anticipated − was introduced to the Welwyns − met them constantly in society − made no favourable impression on Ida, but won the good opinion of Rosamond from the first; and was regarded with such high approval by their father, that when he mentioned his intention of visiting England in the spring of the new year, he was cordially invited to spend the hunting season at Glenwith Grange.

I came back from Germany about the same time that the Welwyns returned from Paris: and at once set myself to improve my neighbourly intimacy with the family. I was very fond of Ida; more fond, perhaps, than my vanity will now allow me to − but that is of no consequence. It is much more to the purpose to tell you, that I heard the whole of the Baron's story enthusiastically related by Mr. Welwyn and Rosamond; that he came to the Grange at the appointed time; that I was introduced to him; and that he produced as unfavourable an impression upon me as he had already produced upon Ida.

It was whimsical enough, but I really could not tell why I disliked him, though I could account very easily, according to my own notions, for his winning the favour and approval of Rosamond and her father. He was certainly a handsome man, as far as features went; he had a winning gentleness and graceful respect in his manner when he spoke to women; and he sang remarkably well, with one of the sweetest tenor voices I ever heard. These qualities alone were quite sufficient to attract any girl of Rosamond's disposition: and I certainly never wondered why he was a favourite of hers.

Then, as to her father, the Baron was not only fitted to win his sympathy and regard in the field, by proving himself an ardent sportsman and an excellent rider, but was also, in virtue of some of his minor personal peculiarities, just the man to gain the friendship of his host. Mr. Welwyn was as ridiculously prejudiced, as most weak-headed Englishmen are, on the subject of foreigners in general. In spite of his visit to Paris, the vulgar notion of a Frenchman continued to be his notion, both while he was in France and when he returned from it. Now, the Baron was as unlike the traditional 'Mounseer' of English songs, plays, and satires, as a man could well be; and it was on account of this very dissimilarity that Mr. Welwyn first took a violent fancy to him, and then invited him to his house. Franval spoke English remarkably well; wore neither beard, moustachios, or whiskers; kept his hair cut almost unbecomingly short; dressed in the extreme of plainness and modest good taste; talked little in general society; uttered his words, when he did speak, with singular calmness and deliberation; and, to crown all, had the greater part of his acquired property invested in English securities. In Mr. Welwyn's estimation, such a man as this was a perfect miracle of a Frenchman, and he admired and encouraged him accordingly.

I have said that I disliked him, yet could not assign a reason for my dislike; and I can only repeat it now. He was remarkably polite to me; we often rode together in hunting, and sat near each other at the Grange table; but I could never become familiar with him. He always gave me the idea of a man who had some mental reservation in saying the most trifling thing. There was a constant restraint, hardly perceptible to most people, but plainly visible, nevertheless, to me, which seemed to accompany his lightest words, and to hang about his most familiar manner. This, however, was no just reason for my secretly disliking and distrusting him as I did. Ida said as much to me, I remember, when I confessed to her what my feelings towards him were, and tried (but vainly) to induce her to be equally candid with me in return. She seemed to shrink from the tacit condemnation of Rosamond's opinion which such a confidence on her part would have implied. And yet she watched the growth of that opinion, or, in other words, the growth of her sister's liking for the Baron, with an apprehension and sorrow which she tried fruitlessly to conceal. Even her father began to notice that her spirits were not so good as usual, and to suspect the cause of her melancholy. I remember he jested, with all the dense insensibility of a stupid man, about Ida having invariably been jealous, from a child, if

Rosamond looked kindly upon anybody except her elder sister.

The spring began to get far advanced towards summer. Franval paid a visit to London; came back in the middle of the season to Glenwith Grange; wrote to put off his departure for France; and, at last (not at all to the surprise of anybody who was intimate with the Welwyns) proposed to Rosamond, and was accepted. He was candour and generosity itself when the preliminaries of the marriage settlement were under discussion. He quite overpowered Mr. Welwyn and the lawyers with references, papers, and statements of the distribution and extent of his property, which were found to be perfectly correct. His sisters were written to, and returned the most cordial answers: saying that the state of their health would not allow them to come to England for the marriage; but adding a warm invitation to Normandy for the bride and her family. Nothing, in short, could be more straightforward and satisfactory than the Baron's behaviour, and the testimonies to his worth and integrity which the news of the approaching marriage produced from his relatives and his friends.

The only joyless face at the Grange now was Ida's. At any time it would have been a hard trial to her to resign that first and foremost place, which she had held since childhood in her sister's heart, as she knew she must resign it when Rosamond married. But, secretly disliking and distrusting Franval as she did, the thought that he was soon to become the husband of her beloved sister filled her with a vague sense of terror which she could not explain to herself, which it was imperatively necessary that she should conceal, and which, on those very accounts, become a daily and hourly torment to her that was almost more than she could bear.

One consolation alone supported her: Rosamond and she were not to be separated. She knew that the Baron secretly disliked her as much as she disliked him; she knew that she must bid farewell to the brighter and happier part of her life on the day when she went to live under the same roof with her sister's husband; but, true to the promise made years and years ago, by her dying mother's bed, true to the affection which was the ruling and beautiful feeling of her whole existence, she never hesitated about indulging Rosamond's wish, when the girl, in her bright light-hearted way, said that she could never get on comfortably in the marriage state unless she had Ida to live with her and help her just the same as ever. The Baron was too polite a man even to look dissatisfied when he heard of the proposed arrangement; and it was therefore settled from the beginning that Ida was always to live with her sister.

The marriage took place in the summer, and the bride and bridegroom went to spend their honeymoon in Cumberland. On their return to Glenwith Grange, a visit to the Baron's sisters, in Normandy, was talked of; but the execution of this project was suddenly and disastrously suspended by the death of Mr. Welwyn from an attack of pleurisy.

In consequence of this calamity, the projected journey was of course deferred: and when autumn and the shooting season came, the Baron was unwilling to leave the well-stocked preserves of the Grange. He seemed, indeed, to grow less and less inclined, as time advanced, for the trip to Normandy; and wrote excuse after excuse to his sisters, when letters arrived from them urging him to pay the promised visit. In the winter-time, he said he would not allow his wife to risk a long journey. In the spring, his health was pronounced to be delicate. In the genial summertime, the accomplishment of the proposed visit would be impossible; for at that period the Baroness expected to become a mother. Such were the apologies which Franval seemed almost glad to be able to send to his sisters in France.

The marriage was, in the strictest sense of the term, a happy one. The Baron, though he never altogether lost the strange restraint and reserve of his manner, was, in his quiet, peculiar way, the fondest and kindest of husbands. He went to town occasionally on business, but always seemed glad to return to the Baroness; he never varied in the politeness of his bearing towards his wife's sister; he behaved with the most courteous hospitality towards all the friends of the Welwyns: in short, he thoroughly justified the good opinion which Rosamond and her father had formed of him when they first met at Paris. And yet no experience of his character thoroughly reassured Ida. Months passed on quietly and pleasantly; and still that secret sadness, that indefinable, unreasonable apprehension on Rosamond's account, hung heavily on her sister's heart.

At the beginning of the first summer months, a little domestic inconvenience happened, which showed the Baroness, for the first time, that her husband's temper could be seriously ruffled – and that by the veriest trifle. He was in the habit of taking in two French provincial newspapers – one published at Bordeaux, and the other at Havre. He always opened these journals the moment they came, looked at one particular column of each with the deepest attention for a few minutes, then carelessly threw them aside into his wastepaper basket. His wife and her sister were at first rather surprised at the manner in which he read his two papers; but they thought no more of it when he explained that he only took them in to consult them about French commercial intelligence, which might be, occasionally, of importance to him.

These papers were published weekly. On the occasion to which I have just referred, the Bordeaux paper came on the proper day, as usual; but the Havre paper never made its appearance. This trifling circumstance seemed to make the Baron seriously uneasy. He wrote off directly to the country post office, and to the newspaper agent in London. His wife, astonished to see his tranquillity so completely overthrown by so slight a cause, tried to restore his good humour by jesting with him about the missing newspaper. He replied by the first angry and unfeeling words that she had heard issue from his lips. She was then within about six weeks of her confinement, and very unfit to bear harsh answers from anybody – least of all from her husband.

On the second day no answer came. On the afternoon of the third, the Baron rode off to the post-town to make inquiries. About an hour after he had gone, a strange gentleman came to the Grange, and asked to see the Baroness. On being informed that she was not well enough to receive visitors, he sent up a message that his business was of great importance, and that he would wait down stairs for a second answer.

On receiving this message, Rosamond turned, as usual to her elder sister for advice. Ida went down stairs immediately to see the stranger. What I am now about to tell you of the extraordinary interview which took place between them, and of the shocking events that followed it, I have heard from Miss Welwyn's own lips.

She felt unaccountably nervous when she entered the room. The stranger bowed very politely, and asked, in a foreign accent, if she were the Baroness Franval. She set him right on this point, and told him she attended to all matters of business for the Baroness; adding, that, if his errand at all concerned her sister's husband, the Baron was not then at home.

The stranger answered that he was aware of it when he called, and that the unpleasant business on which he came could not be confided to the Baron – at least in the first instance.

She asked why. He said he was there to explain; and expressed himself as feeling greatly relieved at having to open his business to her, because she would doubtless, be best able to prepare her sister for the bad news that he was, unfortunately, obliged to bring. The sudden faintness which overcame her, as he spoke those words, prevented her from addressing him in return. He poured out some water for her from a bottle which happened to be standing on the table, and asked if he might depend on her fortitude. She tried to say 'Yes;' but the violent throbbing of her heart seemed to choke her. He took a foreign newspaper from his pocket, saying that he was a secret agent of the French police – that the paper was the *Havre Journal* for the past week, and that it had been expressly kept from reaching the Baron, as usual, through his (the agent's) interference. He then opened the newspaper, and begged that she would nerve herself sufficiently (for her sister's sake) to read certain lines, which would give her some hint of the business that brought him there. He pointed to the passage as he spoke. It was among the 'Shipping Entries,' and was thus expressed:–

'Arrived, the *Berenice*, from San Francisco, with a valuable cargo of hides. She brings one passenger, the Baron Franval, of Chateau Franval, in Normandy.'

As Miss Welwyn read the entry, her heart, which had been throbbing violently but the moment before, seemed suddenly to cease from all action, and she began to shiver, though it was a warm June evening. The agent held the tumbler to her lips, and made her drink a little of the water, entreating her very earnestly to take courage and listen to him. He then sat down, and referred again to the entry; every word he uttered seeming to burn itself in for ever (as she expressed it) on her memory and her heart.

He said: 'It has been ascertained beyond the possibility of doubt that there is no mistake about the name in the lines you have just read. And it is as certain as that we are here, that there is only one Baron Franval now alive. The question, therefore, is, whether the passenger by the *Berenice* is the true Baron, or – I beg you most earnestly to bear with me and to compose yourself – or the husband of your sister. The person who arrived last week at Havre was scouted as an impostor by the ladies at the château, the moment he presented himself there as their brother, returning to them after sixteen years of absence. The authorities were communicated with, and I and my assistants were instantly sent for from Paris.

'We wasted no time in questioning the supposed impostor. He either was, or affected to be, in a perfect frenzy of grief and indignation. We just ascertained, from competent witnesses, that he bore an extraordinary resemblance to the real Baron, and that he was perfectly familiar with places and persons in and about the château; we just ascertained that, and then proceeded to confer with the local authorities, and to examine their private entries of suspected persons in their jurisdiction, ranging back over a past period of twenty years or more. One of the entries thus consulted contained these particulars:– "Hector Auguste Monbrun, son of a respectable proprietor in Normandy. Well educated; gentlemanlike manners. On bad terms with his family. Character: bold, cunning, unscrupulous, self-possessed. Is a clever mimic. May be easily recognised by his striking likeness to the Baron Franval. Imprisoned at twenty for theft and assault."'

Miss Welwyn saw the agent look up at her after he had read this extract from the police-book, to ascertain if she was still able to listen to him. He asked, with some appearance of alarm, as their eyes met, if she would like some more water. She was just able to make a sign in the negative. He took a second extract from his pocket-book, and went on.

He said: 'The next entry under the same name was dated four years later, and ran thus: "H. A. Monbrun, condemned to the galleys for life, for assassination, and other crimes not officially necessary to be here specified. Escaped from custody at Toulon. Is known, since the expiration of his first term of imprisonment, to have allowed his beard to grow, and to have worn his hair long, with the intention of rendering it impossible for those acquainted with him in his native province to recognise him, as heretofore, by his likeness to the Baron Franval." There were more particulars added, not important enough for extract. We immediately examined the supposed impostor: for, if he was Monbrun, we knew that we should find on his shoulder the two letters of the convict brand, "T.F." (standing for *Travaux Forces*). After the minutest examination with the mechanical and chemical tests used on such occasions, not the slightest trace of the brand was to be found. The moment this astounding discovery was made, I started to lay an embargo on the forthcoming numbers of the *Havre Journal* for that week, which were about to be sent to the English agent in London. I arrived at Havre on Saturday (the morning of publication), in time to execute my design. I waited there long enough to communicate by telegraph with my superiors in Paris, then hastened to this place. What my errand here is, you may —'

He might have gone on speaking for some moments longer; but Miss Welwyn heard no more.

Her first sensation of returning consciousness was the feeling that water was being sprinkled on her face. Then she saw that all the windows in the room had been set wide open, to give her air; and that she and the agent were still alone. At first, she felt bewildered, and hardly knew who he was; but he soon recalled to her mind the horrible realities that had brought him there, by apologizing for not having summoned assistance when she fainted. He said it was of the last importance, in Franval's absence, that no one in the house should imagine that anything unusual was taking place in it. Then, after giving her an interval of a minute or two to collect what little strength she had left, he added that he would not increase her sufferings by saying anything more, just then, on the shocking subject of the investigation which it was his duty to make – that he would leave her to recover herself, and to consider what was the best course to be taken with the Baroness in the present terrible emergency – and that he would privately return to the house between eight and nine o'clock that evening, ready to act as Miss Welwyn wished, and to afford her and her sister any aid and protection of which they might stand in need. With these words he bowed, and noiselessly quitted the room.

For the first few awful minutes after she was left alone, Miss Welwyn sat helpless and speechless; utterly numbed in heart, and mind, and body – then a sort of instinct (she was incapable of thinking) seemed to urge her to conceal the fearful news from her sister as long as possible. She ran up stairs to Rosamond's sitting-room, and called through the door (for she dared not trust herself in her sister's presence) that the visitor had come on some troublesome business from their late father's lawyers, and that she was going to shut herself up, and write some long letters in connexion with that business. After she had got into her own room, she was never sensible of how time was passing – never conscious of any feeling within her, except a baseless, helpless hope that the French police might yet be proved to have made some terrible mistake – until she heard a violent shower of rain come on a little after sunset. The noise of the rain, and freshness it brought with it in the air, seemed to awaken her as if from a painful and fearful sleep. The power of reflection returned to her; her heart heaved and bounded with an overwhelming terror, as the thought of Rosamond came back vividly to it; her memory recurred despairingly to the long past day of her mother's death, and to the farewell promise she had made by her mother's bedside. She burst into an hysterical passion of weeping that seemed to be tearing her to pieces. In the midst of it she heard the clatter of a horse's hoofs in the courtyard, and knew that Rosamond's husband had come back.

Dipping her handkerchief in cold water, and passing it over her eyes as she left the room, she instantly hastened to her sister.

Fortunately, the daylight was fading in the old-fashioned chamber that Rosamond occupied. Before they could say two words to each other, Franval was in the room. He seemed violently irritated; said that he had waited for the arrival of the mail – that the missing newspaper had not come by it – that he had got wet through – that he felt a shivering fit coming on – and that he believed he had caught a violent cold. His wife anxiously suggested some simple remedies. He roughly interrupted her, saying there was but one remedy, the remedy of going to bed; and so left them without another word. She just put her handkerchief to her eyes, and said softly to her sister, 'How he is changed!' – then spoke no more. They sat silent for half an hour or longer. After that, Rosamond went affectionately and forgivingly to see how her husband was. She returned, saying that he was in bed, and in a deep, heavy sleep; and predicting hopefully that he would wake up quite well the next morning. In a few minutes more the clock struck nine, and Ida heard the servant's step ascending the stairs. She suspected what his errand was, and went out to meet him. Her presentiment had not deceived her; the police agent had arrived, and was waiting for her downstairs.

He asked her if she had said anything to her sister, or had thought of any plan of action, the moment she entered the room; and, on receiving a reply in the negative, inquired further if 'the Baron' had come home yet. She answered that he had; that he was ill and tired, and vexed, and that he had gone to bed. The agent asked in an eager whisper if she knew that he was asleep, and alone in bed? and, when he received her reply, said that he must go up into the bedroom directly.

She began to feel the faintness coming over her again, and with it sensations of loathing and terror that she could neither express to others nor define to herself. He said that if she hesitated to let him avail himself of this unexpected opportunity, her scruples might lead to fatal results. He reminded her that if 'the Baron' were really the convict Monbrun, the claims of society and of justice demanded that he should be discovered by the first available means; and that if he were not – if some inconceivable mistake had really been committed – then, such a plan for getting immediately at the truth as was now proposed, would ensure the delivery of an innocent man from suspicion, and at the same time spare him the knowledge that he had ever been suspected. This last argument had its effect on Miss Welwyn. The baseless, helpless hope that the French authorities might yet be proved to be in error, which she had already felt in her own room, returned to her now. She suffered the agent to lead her up stairs.

He took the candle from her hand when she pointed to the door; opened it softly; and, leaving it ajar, went into the room.

She looked through the gap, with a feverish, horrorstruck curiosity. Franval was lying on his side in a profound sleep, with his back turned towards the door. The agent softly placed the candle upon a small reading-table between the door and the bedside, softly drew down the bed-clothes a little way from the sleeper's back, then took a pair of scissors from the toilette table, and very gently and slowly began to cut away, first the loose folds, then the intervening strips of linen from the part of Franval's nightgown, that was over his shoulders. When the upper part of his back had been bared in this way, the agent took the candle and held it near the flesh. Miss Welwyn heard him ejaculate some word under his breath, then saw him looking round to where she was standing, and beckoning to her to come in.

Mechanically she obeyed; mechanically she looked down where his finger was pointing. It was the convict Monbrun – there, just visible under the bright light of the candle, were the fatal letters 'T.F.' branded on the villain's shoulder!

Though she could neither move nor speak, the horror of this discovery did not deprive her of her consciousness. She saw the agent softly draw up the bed-clothes again into their proper position, replace the scissors on the toilet-table, and take from it a bottle of smelling-salts. She felt him removing her from the bedroom, and helping her quickly downstairs, giving her the salts to smell by the way. When they were alone again, he said, with the first appearance of agitation that he had yet exhibited, 'Now, madam, for God's sake, collect all your courage, and be guided by me. You and your sister had better leave the house immediately. Have you any relatives in the neighbourhood, with whom you could take refuge?' They had none. 'What is the name of the nearest town where you could get good accommodation for the night?' Harleybrook (he wrote the name down on his tablets). 'How far off is it?' Twelve miles. 'You had better have the carriage out at once, to go there with as little delay as possible: leaving me to pass the night here. I will communicate with you tomorrow at the principal hotel. Can you

compose yourself sufficiently to be able to tell the head-
servant, if I ring for him, that he is to obey my orders till
further notice?'

The servant was summoned, and received his instructions,
the agent going out with him to see that the carriage was got
ready quietly and quickly. Miss Welwyn went up stairs to her
sister.

How the fearful news was first broken to Rosamond, I
cannot relate to you. Miss Welwyn has never confided to me,
has never confided to anybody, what happened at the interview between her sister and herself that night. I can tell you
nothing of the shock they both suffered, except that the
younger and the weaker died under it; that the elder and the
stronger has never recovered from it, and never will.

They went away the same night, with one attendant, to
Harleybrook, as the agent had advised. Before daybreak
Rosamond was seized with the pains of premature labour. She
died three days after, unconscious of the horror of her
situation; wandering in her mind about past times, and singing
old tunes that Ida had taught her, as she lay in her sister's arms.

The child was born alive, and lives still. You saw her at the
window as we came in at the back way to the Grange. I
surprised you, I dare say, by asking you not to speak of her to
Miss Welwyn. Perhaps you noticed something vacant in the
little girl's expression. I am sorry to say that her mind is more
vacant still. If 'idiot' did not sound like a mocking word,
however tenderly and pityingly one may wish to utter it, I
should tell you that the poor thing had been an idiot from her
birth.

You will, doubtless, want to hear now what happened at
Glenwith Grange, after Miss Welwyn and her sister had left it.
I have seen the letter which the police agent sent the next
morning to Harleybrook; and, speaking from my recollection
of that, I shall be able to relate all you can desire to know.

First, as to the history of the scoundrel Monbrun, I need
only tell you that he was identical with an escaped convict,
who, for a long term of years, had successfully eluded the
vigilance of the authorities all over Europe, and in America as
well. In conjunction with two accomplices, he had succeeded
in possessing himself of large sums of money by the most

criminal means. He also acted secretly as the 'banker' of his convict brethren, whose dishonest gains were all confided to his hands for safe keeping. He would have been certainly captured, on venturing back to France, along with his two associates, but for the daring imposture in which he took refuge; and which, if the true Baron Franval had really died abroad, as was reported, would, in all probability never have been found out.

Besides his extraordinary likeness to the Baron, he had every other requisite for carrying on his deception successfully. Though his parents were not wealthy he had received a good education He was so notorious for his gentlemanlike manners among the villainous associates of his crimes and excesses, that they nicknamed him 'the Prince.' All his early life had been passed in the neighbourhood of the Château Franval. He knew what were the circumstances which had induced the Baron to leave it. He had been in the country to which the Baron had emigrated. He was able to refer familiarly to persons and localities, at home and abroad, with which the Baron was sure to be acquainted. And, lastly, he had an expatriation of fifteen years to plead for him as his all-sufficient excuse, if he made any slight mistakes before the Baron's sisters, in his assumed character of their long-absent brother. It will be, of course, hardly necessary for me to tell you, in relation to this part of the subject, that the true Franval was immediately and honourably reinstated in the family rights of which the impostor had succeeded for a time in depriving him.

According to Monbrun's own account, he had married poor Rosamond purely for love; and the probabilities certainly are, that the pretty innocent English girl had really struck the villain's fancy for the time; and that the easy, quiet life he was leading at the Grange pleased him, by contrast with his perilous and vagabond existence of former days. What might have happened if he had had time enough to grow wearied of his ill-fated wife and his English home, it is now useless to inquire. What really did happen on the morning when he awoke after the flight of Ida and her sister can be briefly told.

As soon as his eyes opened they rested on the police-agent, sitting quietly by the bedside, with a loaded pistol in his hand.

Monbrun knew immediately that he was discovered; but he never for an instant lost the self-possession for which he was famous. He said he wished to have five minutes allowed him to deliberate quietly in bed, whether he should resist the French authorities on English ground, and so gain time by obliging the one government to apply specially to have him delivered up by the other – or whether he should accept the terms officially offered to him by the agent, if he quietly allowed himself to be captured. He chose the latter course – it was suspected, because he wished to communicate personally with some of his convict associates in France, whose fraudulent gains were in his keeping, and because he felt boastfully confident of being able to escape again, whenever he pleased. Be his secret motives, however, what they might, he allowed the agent to conduct him peaceably from the Grange; first writing a farewell letter to poor Rosamond, full of heartless French sentiment, and glib sophistries about Fate and Society. His own fate was not long in overtaking him. He attempted to escape again, as it had been expected he would, and was shot by the sentinel on duty at the time. I remember hearing that the bullet entered his head and killed him on the spot.

My story is done. It is ten years now since Rosamond was buried in the churchyard yonder; and it is ten years also since Miss Welwyn returned to be the lonely inhabitant of Glenwith Grange. She now lives but in the remembrances that it calls up before her of her happier existence of former days. There is hardly an object in the old house which does not tenderly and solemnly remind her of the mother, whose last wishes she lived to obey; of the sister, whose happiness was once her dearest earthly care. Those prints that you noticed on the library walls, Rosamond used to copy in the past time, when her pencil was often guided by Ida's hand. Those music-books that you were looking over, she and her mother have played from together, through many a long and quiet summer's evening. She has no ties now to bind her to the present but the poor child whose affliction it is her constant effort to lighten, and the little peasant population around her, whose humble cares and wants and sorrows she is always ready to relieve. Far and near her modest charities have penetrated among us; and far and near she is heartily beloved and blessed in many a labourer's household. There is no poor man's hearth, not in this village only, but for miles away from it as well, at which you would not be received with the welcome given to an old friend, if you only told the cottagers that you knew the Lady of Glenwith Grange!

GABRIEL'S MARRIAGE

GABRIEL'S MARRIAGE

CHAPTER I

One night, during the period of the first French Revolution, the family of François Sarzeau, a fisherman of Brittany, were all waking and watching at a late hour in their cottage on the peninsula of Quiberon. François had gone out in his boat that evening, as usual, to fish. Shortly after his departure, the wind had risen, the clouds had gathered; and the storm, which had been threatening at intervals throughout the whole day, burst forth furiously about nine o'clock. It was now eleven; and the raging of the wind over the barren, heathy peninsula still seemed to increase with each fresh blast that tore its way out upon the open sea; the crashing of the waves on the beach was awful to hear; the dreary blackness of the sky terrible to behold. The longer they listened to the storm, the oftener they looked out at it, the fainter grew the hopes which the fisherman's family still strove to cherish for the safety of François Sarzeau and of his younger son who had gone with him in the boat.

There was something impressive in the simplicity of the scene that was now passing within the cottage.

On one side of the great rugged black fireplace crouched two little girls; the younger half asleep, with her head in her sister's lap. These were the daughters of the fisherman; and opposite to them sat their eldest brother Gabriel. His right arm had been badly wounded in a recent encounter at the national game of *Soule,* a sport resembling our English football; but played on both sides in such savage earnest by the people of Brittany as to end always in bloodshed, often in mutilation, sometimes in loss of life. On the same bench with Gabriel sat his betrothed wife – a girl of eighteen – clothed in the plain, almost monastic black and white costume of her native district. She was the daughter of a small farmer living at some

67

little distance from the coast. Between the groups formed on either side of the fireplace, the vacant space was occupied by the foot of a truckle bed. In this bed lay a very old man, the father of François Sarzeau. His haggard face was covered with deep wrinkles; his long white hair flowed over the coarse lump of sacking which served him for a pillow, and his light grey eyes wandered incessantly, with a strange expression of terror and suspicion, from person to person, and from object to object, in all parts of the room. Whenever the wind and sea whistled and roared at their loudest, he muttered to himself and tossed his hands fretfully on his wretched coverlid. On these occasions his eyes always fixed themselves intently on a little Delft image of the Virgin placed in a niche over the fireplace. Every time they saw him look in this direction Gabriel and the young girls shuddered and crossed themselves; and even the child, who still kept awake, imitated their example. There was one bond of feeling at least between the old man and his grandchildren, which connected his age and their youth unnaturally and closely together. This feeling was reverence for the superstitions which had been handed down to them by their ancestors from centuries and centuries back, as far even as the age of the Druids. The spirit-warnings of disaster and death which the old man heard in the wailing of the wind, in the crashing of the waves, in the dreary monotonous rattling of the casement, the young man and his affianced wife and the little child who cowered by the fireside, heard too. All differences in sex, in temperament, in years, Superstition was strong enough to strike down to its own dread level, in the fisherman's cottage, on the stormy night.

Besides the benches by the fireside and the bed the only piece of furniture in the room was a coarse wooden table, with a loaf of black bread, a knife, and pitcher of cider placed on it. Old nets, coils of rope, tattered sails, hung about the walls and over the wooden partition which separated the room into two compartments. Wisps of straw and ears of barley drooped down through the rotten rafters and gaping boards that made the floor of the granary above.

These different objects, and the persons in the cottage, who composed the only surviving members of the fisherman's family, were strangely and wildly lit up by the blaze of the fire and by the still brighter glare of the resin torch stuck into a block of wood in the chimney-corner. The red and yellow light played full on the wierd face of the old man as he lay opposite to it, and glanced fitfully on the figures of the young girl, Gabriel, and the two children; the great gloomy shadows rose and fell, and grew and lessened in bulk about the walls like visions of darkness, animated by a supernatural spectre-life, while the dense obscurity outside spreading before the curtainless window seemed as a wall of solid darkness that had closed in for ever around the fisherman's house. The night-scene within the cottage was almost as wild and as dreary to look upon as the night-scene without.

For a long time the different persons in the room sat together without speaking, even without looking at each other. At last, the girl turned and whispered something into Gabriel's ear.

'Perrine, what were you saying to Gabriel?' asked the child opposite, seizing the first opportunity of breaking the desolate silence – doubly desolate at her age – which was preserved by all around her.

'I was telling him,' answered Perrine simply, 'that it was time to change the bandages on his arm; and I also said to him, what I have often said before, that he must never play that terrible game of the *Soule* again.'

The old man had been looking intently at Perrine and his grandchild as they spoke. His harsh, hollow voice mingled with the last soft tones of the young girl, repeating over and over again the same terrible words; 'Drowned! drowned! Son and grandson, both drowned! both drowned!'

'Hush! grandfather,' said Gabriel, 'we must not lose all hope for them yet. God and the Blessed Virgin protect them!' He looked at the little Delft image, and crossed himself; the others imitated him, except the old man. He still tossed his hands over the coverlid, and still repeated 'Drowned! drowned!'

'Oh that accursed *Soule!*' groaned the young man. 'But for this wound I should have been with my father. The poor boy's life might at least have been saved; for we should then have left him here.'

'Silence!' exclaimed the harsh voice from the bed. 'The wail of dying men rises louder than the loud sea; the devil's psalm-singing roars higher than the roaring wind! Be silent, and listen! Francois drowned! Pierre drowned! Hark! Hark!'

A terrific blast of wind burst over the house as he spoke, shaking it to its centre, overpowering all other sounds, even to the deafening crash of waves. The slumbering child awoke, and uttered a scream of fear. Perrine, who had been kneeling before her lover binding the fresh bandages on his wounded arm, paused in her occupation, trembling from head to foot. Gabriel looked towards the window: his experience told him what must be the hurricane fury of that blast of wind out at sea, and he sighed bitterly as he murmured to himself, 'God help them both – man's help will be as nothing to them now!'

'Gabriel!' cried the voice from the bed in altered tones – very faint and trembling.

He did not hear, or did not attend to the old man. He was trying to soothe and encourage the young girl at his feet.

'Don't be frightened, love,' he said, kissing her very gently and tenderly on the forehead. 'You are as safe here as anywhere. Was I not right in saying that it would be madness to attempt taking you back to the farmhouse this evening? You can sleep in that room, Perrine, when you are tired – you can sleep with the two girls.'

'Gabriel! brother Gabriel!' cried one of the children. 'O! look at grandfather!'

Gabriel ran to the bedside. The old man had raised himself into a sitting position; his eyes were dilated, his whole face was rigid with terror, his hands were stretched out convulsively towards his grandson. 'The White Women!' he screamed. 'The White Women! the grave-diggers of the drowned are out on the sea!'

The children, with cries of terror, flung themselves into Perrine's arms; even Gabriel uttered an exclamation of horror, and started back from the bedside.

Still the old man reiterated, 'The White Women! The White Women! Open the door, Gabriel! look out westward, where the ebb-tide has left the sand dry. You'll see them bright as lightning in the darkness, mighty as the angels in stature, sweeping like the wind over the sea, in their long white garments, with their white hair trailing far behind them! Open the door, Gabriel! You'll see them stop and hover over the

place where your father and your brother have been drowned;
you'll see them come on till they reach the sand; you'll see
them dig in it with their naked feet, and beckon awfully to the
raging sea to give up its dead. Open the door, Gabriel – or,
though it should be the death of me, I will get up and open it
myself!'

Gabriel's face whitened even to his lips, but he made a sign
that he would obey. It required the exertion of his whole
strength to keep the door open against the wind while he
looked out.

'Do you see them, grandson Gabriel? Speak the truth, and
tell me if you see them,' cried the old man.

'I see nothing but darkness – pitch darkness,' answered
Gabriel, letting the door close again.

'Ah! woe! woe!' groaned his grandfather, sinking back
exhausted on the pillow. 'Darkness to *you*; but bright as
lightning to the eyes that are allowed to see them. Drowned!
drowned! Pray for their souls, Gabriel – *I* see the White
Women even where I lie, and dare not pray for them. Son and
grandson drowned! both drowned!'

The young man went back to Perrine and the children.

'Grandfather is very ill tonight,' he whispered. 'You had
better all go into the bedroom, and leave me alone to watch by
him.'

They rose as he spoke, crossed themselves before the image
of the Virgin, kissed him one by one, and, without uttering a
word, softly entered the little room on the other side of the
partition. Gabriel looked at his grandfather, and saw that he
lay quiet now, with his eyes closed as if he were already
dropping asleep. The young man then heaped some fresh logs
on the fire, and sat down by it to watch till morning.

Very dreary was the moaning of the night-storm; but it was
not more dreary than the thoughts which now occupied him
in his solitude – thoughts darkened and distorted by the
terrible superstitions of his country and his race. Ever since the
period of his mother's death he had been oppressed by the
conviction that some curse hung over the family. At first they
had been prosperous, they had got money, a little legacy had
been left them. But this good fortune had availed only for a
time; disaster on disaster strangely and suddenly succeeded.

Losses, misfortunes, poverty, want itself had overwhelmed them; his father's temper had become so soured, that the oldest friends of François Sarzeau declared he was changed beyond recognition. And now, all this past misfortune – the steady, withering, household blight of many years – had ended in the last worst misery of all – in death. The fate of his father and his brother admitted no longer of a doubt – he knew it, as he listened to the storm, as he reflected on his grand-father's words, as he called to mind his own experience of the perils of the sea. And this double bereavement had fallen on him just as the time was approaching for his marriage with Perrine; just when misfortune was most ominous of evil, just when it was hardest to bear! Forebodings which he dared not realize began now to mingle with the bitterness of his grief, whenever his thoughts wandered from the present to the future; and as he sat by the lonely fireside, murmuring from time to time the Church prayer for the repose of the dead, he almost involuntarily mingled it with another prayer, expressed only in his own simple words, for the safety of the living – for the young girl whose love was his sole earthly treasure; for the motherless children who must now look for protection to him alone.

He had sat by the hearth a long, long time, absorbed in his thoughts, not once looking round towards the bed, when he was startled by hearing the sound of his grandfather's voice once more.

'Gabriel,' whispered the old man, trembling and shrinking as he spoke, 'Gabriel, do you hear a dripping of water – now slow, now quick again – on the floor at the foot of my bed?'

'I hear nothing, grandfather, but the crackling of the fire, and the roaring of the storm outside.'

'Drip, drip, drip! Faster and faster; plainer and plainer. Take the torch, Gabriel; look down on the floor – look with all your eyes. Is the place wet there? Is it the rain from heaven that is dripping through the roof?'

Gabriel took the torch with trembling fingers, and knelt down on the floor to examine it closely. He started back from the place, as he saw that it was quite dry – the torch dropped upon the hearth – he fell on his knees before the statue of the Virgin and hid his face.

'Is the floor wet? Answer me, I command you – Is the floor wet?' asked the old man quickly and breathlessly.

Gabriel rose, went back to the bedside, and whispered to him that no drop of rain had fallen inside the cottage. As he spoke the words, he saw a change pass over his grandfather's face – the sharp features seemed to wither up on a sudden; the eager expression to grow vacant and death-like in an instant. The voice too altered; it was harsh and querulous no more; its tones became strangely soft, slow, and solemn, when the old man spoke again.

'I hear it still,' he said, 'drip! drip! faster and plainer than ever. That ghostly dropping of water is the last and the surest of the fatal signs which have told of your father's and your brother's deaths tonight, and I know from the place where I hear it – the foot of the bed I lie on – that it is a warning to me of my own approaching end. I am called where my son and grandson have gone before me: my weary time in this world is over at last. Don't let Perrine and the children come in here, if they should awake – they are too young to look at death.'

Gabriel's blood curdled, when he heard these words – when he touched his grandfather's hand, and felt the chill that it struck to his own – when he listened to the raging wind, and knew that all help was miles and miles away from the cottage. Still, in spite of the storm, the darkness, and the distance, he thought not for a moment of neglecting the duty that had been taught him from his childhood – the duty of summoning the priest to the bedside of the dying. 'I must call Perrine,' he said, 'to watch by you while I am away.'

'Stop!' cried the old man, 'Stop, Gabriel; I implore, I command you not to leave me!'

'The priest, grandfather – your confession – '

'It must be made to you. In this darkness and this hurricane no man can keep the path across the heath. Gabriel! For the love of the Blessed Virgin, stop here with me till I die – my time is short – I have a terrible secret that I must tell to somebody before I draw my last breath! Your ear to my mouth – quick! quick!'

As he spoke the last words, a slight noise was audible on the other side of the partition, the door half opened, and Perrine appeared at it, looking affrightedly into the room. The vigilant eyes of the old man – suspicious even in death – caught sight of her directly.

'Go back!' he exclaimed faintly, before she could utter a word, 'go back – push her back, Gabriel, and nail down the latch in the door, if she won't shut it of herself!'

'Dear Perrine! go in again,' implored Gabriel. 'Go in and keep the children from disturbing us. You will only make him worse – you can be of no use here!'

She obeyed without speaking, and shut the door again.

While the old man clutched him by the arm, and repeated, 'Quick! quick! – your ear close to my mouth,' Gabriel heard her say to the children (who were both awake), 'Let us pray for grandfather.' And as he knelt down by the bedside, there stole on his ear the sweet, childish tones of his little sisters, and the soft subdued voice of the young girl who was teaching them the prayer, mingling divinely with the solemn wailing of wind and sea, rising in a still and awful purity over the hoarse, gasping whispers of the dying man.

'I took an oath not to tell it, Gabriel – lean down closer! I'm weak, and they mustn't hear a word in that room – I took an oath not to tell it; but death is a warrant to all men for breaking such an oath as that. Listen; don't lose a word I'm saying! Don't look away into the room: the stain of blood-guilt has defiled it for ever! – Hush! Hush! Hush! Let me speak. Now your father's dead, I can't carry the horrid secret with me into the grave. Just remember, Gabriel – try if you can't remember the time before I was bedridden – ten years ago and more – it was about six weeks, you know, before your mother's death; you can remember it by that. You and all the children were in that room with your mother; you were all asleep, I think; it was night, not very late – only nine o'clock. Your father and I were standing at the door, looking out at the heath in the moonlight. He was so poor at that time, he had been obliged to sell his own boat, and none of the neighbours would take him out fishing with them – your father wasn't liked by any of the neighbours. Well; we saw a stranger coming towards us; a very young man, with a knapsack on his back. He looked like a gentleman, though he was but poorly dressed. He came up, and told us he was dead tired, and didn't think he could reach the town that night, and asked if we would give him shelter till morning. And your father said yes, if he would make no noise, because the wife was ill, and the children were asleep. So he said all he wanted was to go to sleep himself before the fire. We had nothing to give him but black bread. He had better food with him than that, and undid his knapsack to get at it – and – and – Gabriel! I'm sinking – drink! something to drink – I'm parched with thirst.'

Silent and deadly pale, Gabriel poured some of the cider from the pitcher on the table into a drinking-cup, and gave it to the old man. Slight as the stimulant was, its effect on him was almost instantaneous. His dull eyes brightened a little, and he went on in the same whispering tone as before.

'He pulled the food out of his knapsack rather in a hurry, so that some of the other small things in it fell on the floor. Among these was a pocket-book, which your father picked up and gave him back; and he put it in his coat pocket – there was a tear in one of the sides of the book, and through the hole some banknotes bulged out. I saw them, and so did your father (don't move away, Gabriel; keep close, there's nothing in me to shrink from). Well, he shared his food, like an honest fellow, with us; and then put his hand in his pocket, and gave me four or five livres, and then lay down before the fire to go to sleep. As he shut his eyes, your father looked at me in a way I didn't like. He'd been behaving very bitterly and desperately towards us for some time past; being soured about poverty, and your mother's illness, and the constant crying out of you children for more to eat. So when he told me to go and buy some wood, some bread, and some wine with the money I had got, I didn't like, somehow, to leave him alone with the stranger; and so made excuses, saying (which was true) that it was too late to buy things in the village that night. But he told me in a rage to go and do as he bid me, and knock the people up if the shop was shut. So I went out, being dreadfully afraid of your father – as indeed we all were at that time – but I couldn't make up my mind to go far from the house: I was afraid of something happening, though I didn't dare to think what. I don't know how it was; but I stole back in about ten minutes on tiptoe to the cottage; and looked in at the window; and saw – O! God forgive him! O, God forgive me! – I saw – I – more to drink, Gabriel! I can't speak again – more to drink!'

The voices in the next room had ceased; but in the minute of silence which now ensued, Gabriel heard his sisters kissing Perrine, and wishing her good night. They were all three trying to go to sleep again.

'Gabriel, pray yourself, and teach your children after you to pray, that your father may find forgiveness where he is now gone. I saw him as plainly as I now see you, kneeling with his knife in one hand over the sleeping man. He was taking the little book with the notes in it out of the stranger's pocket. He got the book into his possession, and held it quite still in his hand for an instant, thinking. I believe – oh, no! no! – I'm sure he was repenting; I'm sure he was going to put the book back; but just at that moment the stranger moved, and raised one of his arms, as if he was waking up. Then, the temptation of the devil grew too strong for your father – I saw him lift the hand with the knife in it – but saw nothing more. I couldn't look in at the window – I couldn't move away – I couldn't cry out; I stood with my back turned towards the house, shivering all over, though it was a warm summer-time, and hearing no cries, no noises at all, from the room behind me. I was too frightened to know how long it was before the opening of the cottage door made me turn round; but when I did, I saw your father standing before me in the yellow moonlight, carrying in his arms the bleeding body of the poor lad who had shared his food with us and slept on our hearth. Hush! hush! Don't groan and sob in that way! Stifle it with the bed-clothes. Hush! you'll wake them in the next room!'

'Gabriel – Gabriel!' exclaimed a voice from behind the partition. 'What has happened? Gabriel! let me come out and be with you?'

'No! no!' cried the old man, collecting the last remains of his strength in the attempt to speak above the wind, which was just then howling at the loudest; 'stay where you are – don't speak – don't come out, I command you! – Gabriel' (his voice dropped to a faint whisper), 'raise me up in bed – you must hear the whole of it, now – raise me; I'm choking so that I can hardly speak. Keep close and listen – I can't say much more. Where was I? – Ah, your father! He threatened to kill me if I didn't swear to keep it secret; and in terror of my life I swore. He made me help him to carry the body – we took it all across the heath – oh! horrible, horrible, under the bright moon – (lift me higher, Gabriel). You know the great stones yonder, set up by the heathens; you know the hollow place under the stones they call 'The Merchant's Table' – we had plenty of room to lay him in that, and hide him so; and then we ran back to the cottage. I never dared go near the place afterwards; no, nor your father either! (Higher, Gabriel! I'm choking again.) We burnt the pocket-book and the knapsack – never knew his name – we kept the money to spend. (You're not lifting me! you're not listening close enough!) Your father said it was a legacy, when you and your mother asked about the money, (You hurt me, you shake me to pieces, Gabriel, when you sob like that.) It brought a curse on us, the money; the curse drowned your father and your brother; the curse is killing me; but I've confessed – tell the priest I confessed before I died. Stop her; stop Perrine! I hear her getting up. Take his bones away from The Merchant's Table, and bury them for the love of God! – and tell the priest – (lift me higher: lift me till I'm on my knees) – if your father was alive, he'd murder me – but tell the priest – because of my guilty soul – to pray – and remember The Merchant's Table – to bury, and to pray – to pray always for –'

As long as Perrine heard faintly the whispering of the old man – though no word that he said reached her ear – she shrank from opening the door in the partition. But, when the whispering sounds – which terrified her she knew not how or why – first faltered, then ceased altogether; when she heard the sobs that followed them; and when her heart told her who was weeping in the next room – then, she began to be influenced by a new feeling which was stronger than the strongest fear, and she opened the door without hesitating – almost without trembling.

The coverlid was drawn up over the old man; Gabriel was kneeling by the bedside, with his face hidden. When she spoke to him, he neither answered nor looked at her. After a while, the sobs that shook him ceased; but still he never moved – except once when she touched him, and then he shuddered – shuddered under *her* hand! She called in his little sisters, and they spoke to him, and still he uttered no word in reply. They wept. One by one, often and often, they entreated him with loving words; but the stupor of grief which held him speech-less and motionless was beyond the power of human tears, stronger even then the strength of human love.

It was near daybreak, and the storm was lulling – but still no change occurred at the bedside. Once or twice, as Perrine knelt near Gabriel, still vainly endeavouring to arouse him to a sense of her presence, she thought she heard the old man breathing feebly, and stretched out her hand towards the coverlid; but she could not summon courage to touch him or to look at him. This was the first time she had ever been present at a deathbed; the stillness in the room, the stupor of despair that had seized on Gabriel, so horrified her, that she was almost as helpless as the two children by her side. It was not till the dawn looked in at the cottage window – so coldly, so drearily, and yet so reassuringly – that she began to recover her self-possession at all. Then she knew that her best resource would be to summon assistance immediately from the nearest house. While she was trying to persuade the two children to remain alone in the cottage with Gabriel during her temporary absence, she was startled by the sound of footsteps outside the door. It opened; and a man appeared on the threshold, standing still there for a moment in the dim uncertain light.

She looked closer – looked intently at him. It was François Sarzeau himself!

CHAPTER II

The fisherman was dripping with wet; but his face – always pale and inflexible – seemed to be but little altered in express-ion by the perils through which he must have passed during the night. Young Pierre lay almost insensible in his arms. In the astonishment and fright of the first moment, Perrine screamed as she recognised him.

'There! there! there!' he said, peevishly, advancing straight to the hearth with his burden; 'don't make a noise. You never expected to see us alive again, I dare say. We gave ourselves up as lost, and only escaped after all by a miracle.'

He laid the boy down where he could get the full warmth of the fire; and then, turning round, took a wicker-covered bottle

from his pocket, and said, 'If it hadn't been for the brandy! — '
He stopped suddenly — started — put down the bottle on the
bench near him — and advanced quickly to the bedside.

Perrine looked after him as he went; and saw Gabriel, who
had risen when the door was opened, moving back from the
bed as François approached. The young man's face seemed to
have been suddenly struck to stone — its blank ghastly
whiteness was awful to look at. He moved slowly backward
and backward till he came to the cottage wall — then stood
quite still, staring on his father with wild vacant eyes, moving
his hands to and fro before him, muttering but never pronouncing one audible word.

François did not appear to notice his son; he had the coverlid
of the bed in his hand.

'Anything the matter here?' he asked, as he drew it down.

Still Gabriel could not speak. Perrine saw it, and answered
for him.

'Gabriel is afraid that his poor grandfather is dead,' she
whispered nervously.

'Dead!' There was no sorrow in the tone as he echoed the
word. 'Was he very bad in the night before his death happened? Did he wander in his mind? He has been rather light-
headed lately.'

'He was very restless, and spoke of the ghostly warnings
that we all know of: he said he saw and heard many things
which told him from the other world that you and Pierre —
Gabriel!' she screamed, suddenly interrupting herself. 'Look at
him! Look at his face! Your grandfather is not dead!'

At that moment, François was raising his father's head to
look closely at him. A faint spasm had indeed passed over the
deathly face; the lips quivered, the jaw dropped. François
shuddered as he looked, and moved away hastily from the
bed. At the same instant Gabriel started from the wall: his
expression altered, his pale cheeks flushed suddenly, as he
snatched up the wicker-cased bottle, and poured all the little
brandy that was left in it down his grandfather's throat.

The effect was nearly instantaneous; the sinking vital forces
rallied desperately. The old man's eyes opened again, wandered round the room, then fixed themselves intently on
François, as he stood near the fire. Trying and terrible as his

position was at that moment, Gabriel still retained self-possesion enough to whisper a few words in Perrine's ear. 'Go back again into the bedroom, and take the children with you,' he said. 'We may have something to speak about which you had better not hear.'

'Son Gabriel, your grandfather is trembling all over,' said François. 'If he is dying at all, he is dying of cold: help me to lift him, bed and all, to the hearth.'

'No, no! don't let him touch me!' gasped the old man. 'Don't let him look at me in that way! Don't let him come near me, Gabriel! Is it his ghost? or is it himself?'

As Gabriel answered, he heard a knocking at the door. His father opened it; and disclosed to view some people from the neighbouring fishing-village, who had come – more out of curiosity than sympathy – to inquire whether François and the boy Pierre had survived the night. Without asking any one to enter, the fisherman surlily and shortly answered the various questions addressed to him, standing in his own doorway. While he was thus engaged, Gabriel heard his grandfather muttering vacantly to himself – 'Last night – how about last night, grandson? What was I talking about last night? Did I say your father was drowned? Very foolish to say he was drowned, and then to see him come back alive again! But it wasn't that – I'm so weak in my head, I can't remember! What was it, Gabriel? Something too horrible to speak of? Is that what you're whispering and trembling about? I said nothing horrible. A crime? Bloodshed? I know nothing of any crime or bloodshed here – I must have been frightened out of my wits to talk in that way! The Merchant's Table? Only a big heap of old stones! What with the storm, and thinking I was going to die, and being afraid about your father, I must have been light-headed. Don't give another thought to that nonsense, Gabriel! I'm better now. We shall all live to laugh at poor grandfather for talking nonsense about crime and bloodshed in his sleep. Ah! poor old man – last night – light-headed – fancies and nonsense of an old man – why don't you laugh at it? I'm laughing – so light-headed – so light —'

He stopped suddenly. A low cry, partly of terror and partly of pain, escaped him; the look of pining anxiety and imbecile cunning which had distorted his face while he had been speaking, faded from it for ever. He shivered a little – breathed heavily once or twice – then became still.

Had he died with a falsehood on his lips?

Gabriel looked round and saw that the cottage door was closed, and that his father was standing against it. How long he had occupied that position, how many of the old man's last words he had heard, it was impossible to conjecture, but there was a lowering suspicion in his harsh face as he now looked away from the corpse to his son, which made Gabriel shudder; and the first question that he asked, on once more approaching the bedside, was expressed in tones which, quiet as they were, had a fearful meaning in them.

'What did your grandfather talk about last night?' he asked.

Gabriel did not answer. All that he had heard, all that he had seen, all the misery and horror that might yet be to come, had stunned his mind. The unspeakable dangers of his present position were too tremendous to be realized. He could only feel them vaguely in the weary torpor that oppressed his heart: while in every other direction the use of his faculties, physical and mental, seemed to have suddenly and totally abandoned him.

'Is your tongue wounded, son Gabriel, as well as your arm?' his father went on with a bitter laugh. 'I come back to you, saved by a miracle; and you never speak to me. Would you rather I had died than the old man there? He can't hear you now – why shouldn't you tell me what nonsense he was talking last night? – You won't? I say you shall!' (He crossed the room and put his back to the door.) 'Before either of us leave this place, you shall confess it! You know that my duty to the Church bids me to go at once and tell the priest of your grandfather's death. If I leave that duty unfulfilled, remember it is through your fault! *You* keep me here – for here I stop till I am obeyed. Do you hear that, idiot? Speak! Speak instantly, or you shall repent it to the day of your death! I ask again – what did your grandfather say to you when he was wandering in his mind, last night?'

'He spoke of a crime, committed by another, and guiltily kept secret by him,' answered Gabriel slowly and sternly. 'And this morning he denied his own words with his last living breath. But last night, if he spoke the truth – '

'The truth!' echoed François. 'What truth?'

He stopped, his eyes fell, then turned towards the corpse. For a few minutes he stood steadily contemplating it; breathing quickly, and drawing his hand several times across his forehead. Then he faced his son once more. In that short interval he had become in outward appearance a changed man: expression, voice, and manner, all were altered.

'Heaven forgive me!' he went on, 'but I could almost laugh at myself, at this solemn moment, for having spoken and acted just now so much like a fool! Denied his words, did he? Poor old man! they say sense often comes back to light-headed people just before death; and he is a proof of it. The fact is, Gabriel, my own wits must have been a little shaken – and no wonder – by what I went through last night and what I have come home to this morning. As if you, or anybody, could ever really give serious credit to the wandering speeches of a dying old man! (Where is Perrine? Why did you send her away?) I don't wonder at your still looking a little startled, and feeling low in your mind, and all that – for you've had a trying night of it; trying in every way. He must have been a good deal shaken in his wits last night, between fears about himself and fears about me. (To think of my being angry with you, Gabriel, for being a little alarmed – very naturally – by an old man's queer fancies!) Come out, Perrine – come out of the bedroom whenever you are tired of it: you must learn sooner or later to look at death calmly. Shake hands, Gabriel; and let us make it up, and say no more about what has passed. You won't? Still angry with me for what I said to you just now? – Ah! you'll think better about it by the time I return. Come out, Perrine, we've no secrets here.'

'Where are you going to?' asked Gabriel, as he saw his father hastily open the door.

'To tell the priest that one of his congregation is dead, and to have the death registered,' answered François. 'These are *my* duties, and must be performed before I take any rest.'

He went out hurriedly as he said these words. Gabriel almost trembled at himself, when he found that he breathed more freely, that he felt less horribly oppressed both in mind and body, the moment his father's back was turned. Fearful as thought was now, it was still a change for the better to be

capable of thinking at all. Was the behaviour of his father
compatible with innocence? Could the old man's confused
denial of his own words in the morning and in the presence of
his son, be set for one instant against the circumstantial
confession that he had made during the night alone with his
grandson? These were the terrible questions which Gabriel
now asked himself; and which he shrank involuntarily from
answering. And yet that doubt, the solution of which would
one way or the other irrevocably affect the whole future of his
life, must sooner or later be solved at any hazard!

Was there any way of setting it at rest? Yes, one way:– to go
instantly while his father was absent, and examine the hollow
place under the Merchant's Table. If his grandfather's confession had really been made while he was in possession of his
senses, this place (which Gabriel knew to be covered in from
wind and weather) had never been visited since the commission of the crime by the perpetrator, or by his unwilling
accomplice: though time had destroyed all besides, the hair
and the bones of the victim would still be left to bear witness
to the truth – if truth had indeed been spoken. As this
conviction grew on him, the young man's cheek paled; and he
stopped irresolute half-way between the hearth and the door.
Then he looked down doubtfully at the corpse on the bed; and
then there came upon him suddenly a revulsion of feeling. A
wild feverish impatience to know the worst without another
instant of delay possessed him. Only telling Perrine that he
should be back soon, and that she must watch by the dead in
his absence, he left the cottage at once, without waiting to hear
her reply, even without looking back as he closed the door
behind him.

There were two tracks to the Merchant's Table. One, the
longer of the two, by the coast cliffs; the other across the
heath. But this latter path was also, for some little distance, the
path which led to the village and the church. He was afraid of
attracting his father's attention here, so he took the direction
of the coast. At one spot the track trended inland, winding
round some of the many Druid monuments scattered over the
country. This place was on high ground, and commanded a
view, at no great distance, of the path leading to the village,
just where it branched off from the heathy ridge which ran in

the direction of the Merchant's Table. Here Gabriel described
the figure of a man standing with his back towards the coast.

This figure was too far off to be identified with absolute
certainty, but it looked like, and might well be, François
Sarzeau. Whoever he was, the man was evidently uncertain
which way he should proceed. When he moved forward, it
was first to advance several paces towards the Merchant's
Table – then he went back again towards the distant cottages
and the church. Twice he hesitated thus: the second time
pausing long before he appeared finally to take the way that
led to the village.

Leaving the post of observation among the stones, at which
he had instinctively halted for some minutes past, Gabriel now
proceeded on his own path. Could this man really be his
father? And if it were so, why did François Sarzeau only
determine to go to the village where his business lay, after
having twice vainly attempted to persevere in taking the
exactly opposite direction of the Merchant's Table? Did he
really desire to go there. Had he heard the name mentioned,
when the old man referred to it in his dying words? And had
he failed to summon courage enough to make all safe by
removing – ? This last question was too horrible to be
pursued: Gabriel stifled it affrightedly in his own heart as he
went on.

He reached the great Druid monument without meeting a
living soul on his way. The sun was rising, and the mighty
storm-clouds of the night were parting asunder wildly over
the whole eastward horizon. The waves still leapt and foamed
gloriously: but the gale had sunk to a keen fresh breeze. As
Gabriel looked up, and saw how brightly the promise of a
lovely day was written in the heavens, he trembled as he
thought of the search which he was now about to make. The
sight of the fair fresh sunrise jarred horribly with the suspicions of committed murder that were rankling foully in his
heart. But he knew that his errand must be performed and he
nerved himself to go through with it; for he dared not return
to the cottage until the mystery had been cleared up at once
and for ever.

The Merchant's Table was formed by two huge stones
resting horizontally on three others. In the troubled times of

more than half a century ago, regular tourists were unknown among the Druid monuments of Brittany; and the entrance to the hollow place under the stones – since often visited by strangers – was at this time nearly choked up by brambles and weeds. Gabriel's first look at this tangled nook of briars convinced him that the place had not been entered – perhaps for years – by any living being. Without allowing himself to hesitate (for he felt that the slightest delay might be fatal to his resolution), he passed as gently as possible through the brambles, and knelt down at the low, dusky, irregular entrance of the hollow place under the stones.

His heart throbbed violently, his breath almost failed him; but he forced himself to crawl a few feet into the cavity, and then groped with his hand on the ground about him.

He touched something! Something which it made his flesh creep to handle; something which he would fain have dropped, but which he grasped tight in spite of himself. He drew back into outer air and sunshine. Was it a human bone? No! he had been in the dupe of his own morbid terror – he had only taken up a fragment of dried wood!

Feeling shame at such self-deception as this, he was about to throw the wood from him before he re-entered the place, when another idea occurred to him.

Though it was dimly lighted through one or two chinks in the stones, the far part of the interior of the cavity was still too dusky to admit of perfect examination by the eye, even on a bright sunshiny morning. Observing this, he took out the tinder-box and matches, which – like the other inhabitants of the district – he always carried about with him for the purpose of lighting his pipe, determining to use the piece of wood as a torch which might illuminate the darkest corner of the place when he next entered it. Fortunately the wood had remained so long and had been preserved so dry in its sheltered position, that it caught fire almost as easily as a piece of paper. The moment it was fairly aflame Gabriel went into the cavity – penetrating at once – this time – to its farthest extremity.

He remained among the stones long enough for the wood to burn down nearly to his hand. When he came out, and flung the burning fragment from him, his face was flushed deeply, his eyes sparkled. He leaped carelessly on to the heath, over the bushes through which he had threaded his way so warily but a few minutes before, exclaiming, 'I may marry Perrine with a clear conscience now – I am the son of as honest a man as there is in Brittany!'

He had closely examined the cavity in every corner, and not the slightest sign that any dead body had ever been laid there was visible in the hollow place under the Merchant's Table.

CHAPTER III

'I may marry Perrine with a clear conscience now!'

There are some parts of the world where it would be drawing no natural picture of human nature to represent a son as believing conscientiously that an offence against life and the laws of hospitality, secretly committed by his father, rendered him, though innocent of all participation in it, unworthy to fulfil his engagement with his affianced wife. Among the simple inhabitants of Gabriel's province, however, such acuteness of conscientious sensibility as this was no extraordinary exception to all general rules. Ignorant and superstitious as they might be, the people of Brittany practised the duties of hospitality as devoutly as they practised the duties of the national religion. The presence of the stranger-guest, rich or poor, was a sacred presence at their hearths. His safety was their especial charge – his property their especial responsibility. They might be half-starved, but they were ready to share the last crust with him nevertheless, as they would share it with their own children.

Any outrage on the virtue of hospitality, thus born and bred in the people, was viewed by them with universal disgust, and punished with universal execration. This ignominy was uppermost in Gabriel's thoughts by the side of his grandfather's bed; the dread of this worst dishonour, which there was no wiping out, held him speechless before Perrine, shamed and horrified him so that he felt unworthy to look her in the face; and when the result of his search at the Merchant's Table proved the absence there of all evidence of the crime spoken of by the old man, the blessed relief, the absorbing triumph of that discovery, was expressed entirely in the one thought which had prompted his first joyful words:– He could marry Perrine with a clear conscience, for he was the son of an honest man!

When he returned to the cottage, François had not come back. Perrine was astonished at the change in Gabriel's manner; even Pierre and the children remarked it. Rest and warmth had by this time so far recovered the younger brother, that he was able to give some account of the perilous adventures of the night at sea. They were still listening to the boy's narrative when François at last returned. It was now Gabriel who held out his hand, and made the first advances towards reconciliation.

To his utter amazement, his father recoiled from him. The variable temper of François had evidently changed completely during his absence at the village. A settled scowl of distrust darkened his face as he looked at his son.

'I never shake hands with people who have once doubted me,' he exclaimed loudly and irritably; 'for I always doubt them for ever after. You are a bad son! You have suspected your father of some infamy that you dare not openly charge him with, on no other testimony than the rambling nonsense of a half-witted, dying old man. Don't speak to me! I won't hear you! An innocent man and a spy are bad company. Go and denounce me, you Judas in disguise! I don't care for your secret or for you. What's that girl Perrine doing here still? Why hasn't she gone home long ago? The priest's coming; we don't want strangers in the house of death. Take her back to the farmhouse, and stop there with her, if you like: nobody wants you here!'

There was something in the manner and look of the speaker as he uttered these words, so strange, so sinister, so indescribably suggestive of his meaning much more than he said, that Gabriel felt his heart sink within him instantly; and almost at the same moment this fearful question forced itself irresistably on his mind – might not his father have followed him to the Merchant's Table?

Even if he had been desired to speak, he could not have spoken now, while that question and the suspicion that it brought with it were utterly destroying all the reassuring hopes and convictions of the morning. The mental suffering produced by the sudden change from pleasure to pain in all his thoughts, reacted on him physically. He felt as if he were stifling in the air of the cottage, in the presence of his father; and when Perrine hurried on her walking attire, and with a face which alternately flushed and turned pale with every moment, approached the door, he went out with her as hastily as if he had been flying from his home. Never had the fresh air and the free daylight felt like heavenly and guardian influences to him until now!

He could comfort Perrine under his father's harshness, he could assure her of his own affection which no earthly influence could change, while they walked together towards the farmhouse; but he could do no more. He durst not confide to her the subject that was uppermost in his mind: of all human beings she was the last to whom he could reveal the terrible secret that was festering at his heart. As soon as they got within sight of the farmhouse, Gabriel stopped; and, promising to see her again soon, took leave of Perrine with assumed ease in his manner and with real despair in his heart. Whatever the poor girl might think of it, he felt, at that moment, that he had not courage to face her father, and hear him talk happily and pleasantly, as his custom was, of Perrine's approaching marriage.

Left to himself, Gabriel wandered hither and thither over the open heath, neither knowing nor caring in what direction he turned his steps. The doubts about his father's innocence which had been dissipated by his visit to the Merchant's Table, that father's own language and manner had now revived – had even confirmed, though he dared not yet acknowledge so much to himself. It was terrible enough to be obliged to admit that the result of his morning's search was, after all, not conclusive – that the mystery was in very truth not yet cleared up. The violence of his father's last words of distrust; the extraordinary and indescribable changes in his father's manner while uttering them – what did these things mean? Guilt or innocence? Again, was it any longer reasonable to doubt the deathbed confession made by his grandfather? Was it not, on the contrary, far more probable that the old man's denial in the morning of his own words at night had been made under the influence of a panic terror, when his moral consciousness was bewildered, and his intellectual faculties were sinking? – The longer Gabriel thought of these questions, the less competent – possibly also the less willing – he felt to answer them. Should he seek advice from others wiser than he? No: not while the thousandth part of a chance remained that his father was innocent.

This thought was still in his mind, when he found himself once more in sight of his home. He was still hesitating near the door, when he saw it opened cautiously. His brother Pierre looked out, and then came running towards him. 'Come in, Gabriel; oh, do come in!' said the boy earnestly. 'We are afraid to be alone with father. He's been beating us for talking of you.'

Gabriel went in. His father looked up from the hearth where he was sitting, muttered the word 'Spy!' and made a gesture of contempt – but did not address a word directly to his son. The hours passed on in silence; afternoon waned into evening, and evening into night; and still he never spoke to any of his children. Soon after it was dark, he went out, and took his net with him – saying that it was better to be alone on the sea than in the house with a spy.

When he returned the next morning, there was no change in him. Days passed – weeks, months even elapsed, and still, though his manner insensibly became what it used to be towards his other children, it never altered towards his eldest son. At the rare periods when they now met, except when absolutely obliged to speak, he preserved total silence in his intercourse with Gabriel. He would never take Gabriel out with him in the boat; he would never sit alone with Gabriel in the house; he would never eat a meal with Gabriel; he would never let the other children talk to him about Gabriel; and he would never hear a word in expostulation, a word in reference to anything his dead father had said or done on the night of the storm, from Gabriel himself.

The young man pined and changed so that even Perrine hardly knew him again, under this cruel system of domestic excommunication; under the wearing influence of the one unchanging doubt which never left him; and, more than all, under the incessant reproaches of his own conscience, aroused by the sense that he was evading a responsibility which it was his solemn, his immediate duty to undertake. But no sting of conscience, no ill-treatment at home, and no self-reproaches for failing in his duty of confession as a good Catholic, were powerful enough to make him disclose the secret, under the oppression of which his very life was wasting away. He knew that if he once revealed it, whether his father was ultimately proved to be guilty or innocent, there would remain a slur and a suspicion on the family, and on Perrine besides, from her approaching connexion with it, which in their time and in their generation could never be removed. The reproach of the world is terrible even in the crowded city, where many of the dwellers in our abiding-place are strangers to us – but it is far more terrible in the country, where none near us are strangers, where all talk of us and the tyranny of the evil tongue. Gabriel had not courage to face this, and dare the fearful chance of lifelong ignominy – no, not even to serve the sacred interests of justice, of atonement, and of truth.

CHAPTER IV

While Gabriel still remained prostrated under the affliction that was wasting his energies of body and mind, Brittany was visited by a great public calamity, in which all private misfortunes were overwhelmed for a while.

It was now the time when the ever-gathering storm of the French Revolution had risen to its hurricane climax. Those chiefs of the new republic were in power, whose last, worst madness it was to decree the extinction of religion and the overthrow of everything that outwardly symbolized it throughout the whole of the country that they governed. Already this decree had been executed to the letter in and around Paris; and now the soldiers of the republic were on their way to Brittany, headed by commanders whose commission was to root out the Christian religion in the last and the surest of the strongholds still left to it in France.

These men began their work in a spirit worthy of the worst of their superiors who had sent them to do it. They gutted churches, they demolished chapels, they overthrew roadside crosses wherever they found them. The terrible guillotine devoured human lives in the villages of Brittany, as it had devoured them in the streets of Paris; the musket and the sword, in highway and byway, wreaked havoc on the people – even on women and children kneeling in the act of prayer; the priests were tracked night and day from one hiding-place where they still offered up worship to another, and were killed as soon as overtaken – every atrocity was committed in every district; but the Christian religion still spread wider than the widest bloodshed; still sprang up with ever-renewed vitality from under the very feet of the men whose vain fury was powerless to trample it down. Everywhere the people remained true to their Faith; everywhere the priests stood firm by them in their sorest need. The executioners of the republic had been sent to make Brittany a country of apostates: they did their worst and left it a country of martyrs.

One evening while this frightful persecution was still raging, Gabriel happened to be detained unusually late at the cottage of Perrine's father. He had lately spent much of his time at the farmhouse: it was his only refuge now from that place of suffering, of silence, and of secret shame, which he had once called home! Just as he had taken leave of Perrine for the night, and was about to open the farmhouse door, her father stopped him, and pointed to a chair in the chimney-corner. 'Leave us alone, my dear,' said the old man to his daughter; 'I want to speak to Gabriel. You can go to your mother in the next room.'

The words which Père Bonan – as he was called by the neighbours – had now to say in private, were destined to lead to very unexpected events. After referring to the alteration which had appeared of late in Gabriel's manner, the old man began by asking him, sorrowfully but not suspiciously, whether he still preserved his old affection for Perrine. On receiving an eager answer in the affirmative, Père Bonan then referred to the persecution still raging through the country, and to the consequent possibility that he, like others of his countrymen, might yet be called to suffer and perhaps to die for the cause of his religion. If this last act of self-sacrifice were required of him, Perrine would be left unprotected, unless her affianced husband performed his promise to her, and assumed, without delay, the position of her lawful guardian. 'Let me know that you will do this,' concluded the old man. 'I shall be resigned to all that may be required of me, if I can only know that I shall not die leaving Perrine unprotected.' Gabriel gave the promise – gave it with his whole heart. As he took leave of Père Bonan, the old man said to him:–

'Come here tomorrow; I shall know more then than I know now – I shall be able to fix with certainty the day for the fulfillment of your engagement with Perrine.'

Why did Gabriel hesitate at the farmhouse door, looking back on Père Bonan as though he would fain say something and yet not speaking a word? Why, after he had gone out and had walked onward several paces, did he suddenly stop, return quickly to the farmhouse, stand irresolute before the gate, and then retrace his steps sighing heavily as he went, but never pausing again on his homeward way? Because the torment of his horrible secret had grown harder to bear than ever, since he had given the promise that had been required of him. Because, while a strong impulse moved him frankly to lay bare his hidden dread and doubt to the father whose beloved daughter was soon to be his wife, there was a yet stronger passive influence which paralysed on his lips the terrible confession that he knew not whether he was the son of an honest man, or the son of an assassin and a robber. Made desperate by his situation, he determined, while he hastened homeward, to risk the worst and ask that fatal question of his father in plain words. But this supreme trial for parent and child was not to be. When he entered the cottage, François was absent. He had told the younger children that he should not be home again before noon on the next day.

Early in the morning Gabriel repaired to the farmhouse, as he had been bidden. Influenced by his love for Perrine, blindly confiding in the faint hope (which in despite of heart and conscience he still forced himself to cherish) that his father might be innocent, he now preserved the appearance at least of perfect calmness. 'If I tell my secret to Perrine's father, I risk disturbing in him that confidence in the future safety of his child, for which I am his present and only warrant' – Something like this thought was in Gabriel's mind, as he took the hand of Père Bonan, and waited anxiously to hear what was required of him on that day.

'We have a short respite from danger, Gabriel,' said the old man. 'News has come to me that the spoilers of our churches and the murderers of our congregations, have been stopped on their way hitherward by tidings which have reached them from another district. This interval of peace and safety will be a short one – we must take advantage of it while it it ours. My name is among the names on the list of the denounced. If the soldiers of the Republic find me here! – but we will say nothing more of this: it is of Perrine and of you that I must now speak. On this very evening, your marriage may be solemnized with all the wonted rites of our holy religion, and the blessing may be pronounced over you by the lips of a priest. This evening, therefore, Gabriel, you must become the husband and the protector of Perrine. Listen to me attentively, and I will tell you how.'

This was the substance of what Gabriel now heard from Père Bonan:–

Not very long before the persecutions broke out in Brittany, a priest, known generally by the name of Father Paul, was appointed to a curacy in one of the northern districts of the province. He fulfilled all the duties of his station in such a manner as to win the confidence and affection of every member of his congregation, and was often spoken of with respect, even in parts of the country distant from the scene of his labours. It was not, however, until the troubles broke out, and the destruction and bloodshed began, that he became renowned far and wide, from one end of Brittany to another. From the date of the very first persecutions the name of Father Paul was a rallying cry of the hunted peasantry; he was their great encouragement under oppression, their example in danger, their last and only consoler in the hour of death. Wherever havoc and ruin raged most fiercely, wherever the pursuit was hottest and the slaughter most cruel, there the intrepid priest was sure to be seen pursuing his sacred duties in defiance of every peril. His hairbreadth escapes from death; his extraordinary re-appearances in parts of the country where no one ever expected to see him again, were regarded by the poorer classes with superstitious awe. Wherever Father Paul appeared, with his black dress, his calm face, and the ivory crucifix which he always carried in his hand, the people reverenced him as more than mortal; and grew at last to believe that, single-handed, he would successfully defend his religion against the armies of the republic. But their simple confidence in his powers of resistance was soon destined to be shaken. Fresh reinforcements arrived in Brittany, and overran the whole province from one end to the other. One morning, after celebrating service in a dismantled church, and after narrowly escaping with his life from those who pursued him, the priest disappeared. Secret inquiries were made after him in all directions; but he was heard of no more.

Many weary days had passed, and the dispirited peasantry had already mourned him as dead, when some fishermen on the northern coast observed a ship of light burden in the offing, making signals to the shore. They put off to her in their boats; and on reaching the deck saw standing before them the well-remembered figure of Father Paul.

The priest had returned to his congregations; and had founded the new altar that they were to worship at on the deck of a ship! Razed from the face of the earth, their church had not been destroyed – for Father Paul and the priests who acted with him had given that church a refuge on the sea. Henceforth, their children could still be baptized, their sons and daughters could still be married, the burial of their dead could still be solemnized, under the sanction of the old religion for which, not vainly, they had suffered so patiently and so long.

Throughout the remaining time of trouble, the services were uninterrupted on board the ship. A code of signals was established by which those on shore were always enabled to direct their brethren at sea towards such parts of the coast as happened to be uninfested by the enemies of their worship. On the morning of Gabriel's visit to the farmhouse, these signals had shaped the course of the ship towards the extremity of the peninsula of Quiberon. The people of the district were all prepared to expect the appearance of the vessel some time in the evening, and had their boats ready at a moment's notice to put off and attend the service. At the conclusion of this service Père Bonan had arranged that the marriage of his daughter and Gabriel was to take place.

They waited for evening at the farmhouse. A little before sunset the ship was signalled as in sight; and then Père Bonan and his wife, followed by Gabriel and Perrine, set forth over the heath to the beach. With the solitary exception of François Sarzeau, the whole of the neighbourhood was already assembled there; Gabriel's brother and sisters being among the number.

It was the calmest evening that had been known for months. There was not a cloud in the lustrous sky – not a ripple on the still surface of the sea. The smallest children were suffered by their mothers to stray down on the beach as they pleased; for the waves of the great ocean slept as if they had been changed into the waters of an inland lake. Slow, almost imperceptible, was the approach of the ship – there was hardly a breath of wind to carry her on – she was just drifting gently with the landward set of the tide at that hour, while her sails hung idly against the masts. Long after the sun had gone down, the congregation still waited and watched on the beach. The moon and stars were arrayed in their glory of the night, before the ship dropped anchor. Then the muffled tolling of a bell came solemnly across the quiet waters; and then, from every creek along the shore, as far as the eye could reach, the black forms of the fishermen's boats shot out swift and stealthy into the shining sea.

By the time the boats had arrived alongside of the ship, the lamp had been kindled before the altar, and its flame was gleaming red and dull in the radiant moonlight. Two of the priests on board were clothed in their robes of office, and were waiting in their appointed places to begin the service. But there was a third, dressed only in the ordinary attire of his calling, who mingled with the congregation, and spoke a few words to each of the persons composing it, as, one by one, they mounted the sides of the ship. Those who had never seen him before knew by the famous ivory crucifix in his hand that the priest who received them was Father Paul. Gabriel looked at this man, whom he now beheld for the first time, with a mixture of astonishment and awe; for he saw that the renowned chief of the Christians of Brittany was, to all appearances, but little older than himself.

The expression on the pale calm face of the priest was so gentle and kind, that children just able to walk tottered up to him, and held familiarly by the skirts of his black gown, whenever his clear blue eyes rested on theirs, while he beckoned them to his side. No one would ever have guessed from the countenance of Father Paul what deadly perils he had confronted but for the scar of a sabre-wound, as yet hardly healed, which ran across his forehead. That wound had been dealt while he was kneeling before the altar, in the last church in Brittany which had escaped spoliation. He would have died where he knelt, but for the peasants who were praying with him, and who, unarmed as they were, threw themselves like tigers on the soldiery, and at awful sacrifice of their own lives saved the life of their priest. There was not a man now on board the ship who would have hesitated, had the occasion called for it again, to have rescued him in the same way.

The service began. Since the days when the primitive Christians worshipped amid the caverns of the earth, can any service be imagined nobler in itself, or sublimer in the circumstances surrounding it, than that which was now offered up? Here was no artificial pomp, no gaudy profusion of ornament, no attendant grandeur of man's creation. All around this church spread the hushed and awful majesty of the tranquil sea. The roof of this cathedral was the immeasurable heaven, the pure moon its one great light, the countless glories of the stars its only adornment. Here were no hired singers or rich priest-princes; no curious sightseers, or careless lovers of sweet sounds. This congregation and they who had gathered it together, were all poor alike, all persecuted alike, all worshipping alike, to the overthrow of their worldly interests, and at the imminent peril of their lives. How brightly and tenderly the moonlight shone upon the altar and the people before it! – how solemnly and divinely the deep harmonies, as they chanted the penitential Psalms, mingled with the hoarse singing of the freshening night-breeze in the rigging of the ship! – how sweetly the still rushing murmur of many voices, as they uttered the responses together, now died away and now rose again softly into the mysterious night!

Of all the members of the congregation – young or old – there was but one over whom that impressive service exercised no influence of consolation or of peace: that one was Gabriel. Often, throughout the day, his reproaching conscience had spoken within him again and again. Often, when he joined the little assembly on the beach, he turned away his face in secret shame and apprehension from Perrine and her father. Vainly, after gaining the deck of the ship, did he try to meet the eye of Father Paul as frankly, as readily, and as affectionately as others met it. The burden of concealment seemed too heavy to be borne in the presence of the priest – and yet, torment as it was, he still bore it! But when he knelt with the rest of the congregation and saw Perrine kneeling by his side – when he felt the calmness of the solemn night and the still sea filling his heart – when the sounds of the first prayers spoke with a dread spiritual language of their own to his soul – then, the remembrance of the confession which he had neglected, and the terror of receiving unprepared the sacrament which he knew would be offered to him – grew too vivid to be endured: the sense that he merited no longer though once worthy of it, the confidence in his perfect truth and candour placed in him by the woman with whom he was soon to stand before the altar, overwhelmed him with shame: the mere act of kneeling among that congregation, the passive accomplice by his silence and secrecy, for aught he knew to the contrary, of a crime which it was his bounden duty to denounce, appalled him as if he had already committed sacrilege that could never be forgiven. Tears flowed down his cheeks, though he strove to repress them: sobs burst forth from him, though he tried to stifle them. He knew that others besides Perrine were looking at him in astonishment and alarm; but he could neither control himself, nor move to leave his place, nor raise his eyes even – until suddenly he felt a hand on his shoulder. That touch, slight as it was, ran through him instantly. He looked up, and saw Father Paul standing by his side.

Beckoning him to follow, and signing to the congregation not to suspend their devotions, he led Gabriel out of the assembly – then paused for a moment, reflecting – then beckoning again, took him into the cabin of the ship, and closed the door carefully.

'You have something on your mind,' he said, simply and quietly, taking the young man by the hand. 'I may be able to relieve you, if you tell me what it is.'

As Gabriel heard these gentle words, and saw, by the light of a lamp which burned before a cross fixed against the wall, the sad kindness of expression with which the priest was regarding him, the oppression that had lain so long on his heart seemed to leave it in an instant. The haunting fear of ever divulging his fatal suspicions and his fatal secret had vanished, as it were, at the touch of Father Paul's hand. For the first time, he now repeated to another ear – the sounds of prayer and praise rising grandly the while from the congregation above – his grandfather's deathbed confession, word for word almost, as he had heard it in the cottage on the night of the storm.

Once, and once only, did Father Paul interrupt the narrative, which in whispers was addressed to him. Gabriel had hardly repeated the first two or three sentences of his grandfather's confession, when the priest, in quick altered tones, abruptly asked him his name and place of abode.

As the question was answered, Father Paul's calm face became suddenly agitated; but the next moment, resolutely resuming his self-possession, he bowed his head, as a sign that Gabriel was to continue; clasped his trembling hands, and raising them as if in silent prayer, fixed his eyes intently on the cross. He never looked away from it while the terrible narrative proceeded. But when Gabriel described his search at the Merchant's Table; and, referring to his father's behaviour since that time, appealed to the priest to know whether he might, even yet, in defiance of appearances, be still filially justified in doubting whether the crime had really been perpetrated – then Father Paul moved near to him once more, and spoke again.

'Compose yourself, and look at me,' he said with his former sad kindness of voice and manner. 'I can end your doubts for ever. Gabriel, your father was guilty in intention and in act; but the victim of his crime still lives. I can prove it.'

Gabriel's heart beat wildly; a deadly coldness crept over him, as he saw Father Paul loosen the fastening of his cassock round the throat.

At that instant the chanting of the congregation above ceased; and then, the sudden and awful stillness was deepened rather than interrupted by the faint sound of one voice praying. Slowly and with trembling fingers the priest removed the band round his neck – paused a little – sighed heavily – and pointed to a scar which was now plainly visible on one side of his throat. He said something at the same time; but the bell above tolled while he spoke. It was the signal of the elevation of the Host. Gabriel felt an arm passed round him, guiding him to his knees, and sustaining him from sinking to the floor. For one moment longer he was conscious that the bell had stopped, that there was dead silence, that Father Paul was kneeling by him beneath the cross, with bowed head – then all objects around vanished; and he saw and knew nothing more.

When he recovered his senses, he was still in the cabin – the man whose life his father had attempted was bending over him, and sprinkling water on his face – and the clear voices of the women and children of the congregation were joining the voices of the men in singing the *Agnus Dei*.

'Look up at me without fear, Gabriel,' said the priest. 'I desire not to avenge injuries: I visit not the sins of the father on the child. Look up, and listen! I have strange things to speak of; and I have a sacred mission to fulfill before the morning, in which you must be my guide.'

Gabriel attempted to kneel and kiss his hand, but Father Paul stopped him, and said, pointing to the cross: 'Kneel to that – not to me: not to your fellow mortal, and your friend – for I will be your friend, Gabriel; believing that God's mercy has ordered it so. And now listen to me,' he proceeded, with a brotherly tenderness in his manner which went to Gabriel's heart. 'The service is nearly ended. What I have to tell you must be told at once; the errand on which you will guide me must be performed before tomorrow dawns. Sit here near me; and attend to what I now say!'

Gabriel obeyed: Father Paul then proceeded thus:–

'I believe the confession made to you by your grandfather to have been true in every particular. One the evening to which he referred you, I approached your cottage, as he said, for the purpose of asking shelter for the night. At that period I had been studying to qualify myself for the holy calling which I now pursue; and, on the completion of my studies, had indulged in the recreation of a tour on foot through Brittany, by way of innocently and agreeably occupying the leisure time then at my disposal, before I entered the priesthood.

When I accosted your father I had lost my way, had been walking for many hours, and was glad of any rest that I could get for the night. It is unnecessary to pain you now, by reference to the events which followed my entrance under your father's roof. I remember nothing that happened from the time when I lay down to sleep before the fire, until the time when I recovered my senses at the place which you call the Merchant's Table. My first sensation was that of being moved into the cold air: when I opened my eyes I saw the great Druid stones rising close above me, and two men on either side of me rifling my pockets. They found nothing valuable there, and were about to leave me where I lay, when I gathered strength enough to appeal to their mercy through their cupidity. Money was not scarce with me then, and I was able to offer them a rich reward (which they ultimately received as I had promised) if they would take me to any place where I could get shelter and medical help. I suppose they inferred by my language and accent – perhaps also by the linen I wore, which they examined closely – that I belonged to the higher ranks of the community, in spite of the plainness of my outer garments; and might therefore be in a position to make good my promise to them. I heard one say to the other, 'Let us risk it;' and then they took me in their arms, carried me down to a boat on the beach, and rowed to a vessel in the offing. The next day they disembarked me at Paimbœuf, where I got the assistance which I so much needed. I learnt through the confidence they were obliged to place in me, in order to give me the means of sending them their promised reward, that these men were smugglers, and that they were in the habit of using the cavity in which I had been laid, as a place of concealment for goods, and for letters of advice to their accomplices. This accounted for their finding me. As to my wound, I was informed by the surgeon who attended me, that it had missed being inflicted in a mortal part by less than a quarter of an inch, and that, as it was, nothing but the action of the night air in coagulating the blood over the place had, in the first instance, saved my life. To be brief, I recovered after a long illness, returned to Paris, and was called to the priesthood. The will of my superiors obliged me to perform the first duties of my vocation in the great city; but my own wish was to be appointed to a cure of souls in your province, Gabriel. Can you imagine why?'

The answer to this question was in Gabriel's heart; but he was still too deeply awed and affected by what he had heard to give it utterance.

'I must tell you then what my motive was,' said Father Paul. 'You must know first that I uniformly abstained from disclosing to any one where and by whom my life had been attempted. I kept this a secret from the men who rescued me – from the surgeon – from my own friends even. My reason for such a proceeding was, I would fain believe, a Christian reason. I hope I had always felt a sincere and humble desire to prove myself, by the help of God, worthy of the sacred vocation to which I was destined. But my miraculous escape from death made an impression on my mind, which gave me another and an infinitely higher view of this vocation – the view which I have since striven, and shall always strive for the future, to maintain. As I lay, during the first days of my recovery, examining my own heart, and considering in what manner it would be my duty to act towards your father when I was restored to health, a thought came into my mind which calmed, comforted, and resolved all my doubts. I said within myself – 'In a few months more I shall be called to be one of the chosen ministers of God. If I am worthy of my vocation, my first desire towards this man who has attempted to take my life, should be, not to know that human justice has overtaken him, but to know that he has truly and religiously repented and made atonement for his guilt. To such repentance and atonement let it be my duty to call him; if he reject that appeal, and be hardened only the more against me because I have forgiven him my injuries, then it will be time enough to denounce him for his crimes to his fellow men. Surely it must be well for me here and hereafter, if I begin my career in the holy priesthood by helping to save from hell the soul of the man who, of all others, has most cruelly wronged me.' It was for this reason, Gabriel – it was because I desired to go straightway to your father's cottage, and reclaim him after he had believed me to be dead – that I kept the secret and entreated of my superiors that I might be sent to Brittany. But this, as I have said, was not to be at first, and when my desire was granted, my place was assigned me in a far district. The persecution under which we still suffer broke out; the designs of my life were changed; my own will became no longer mine to guide me. But, through sorrow and suffering, and danger and bloodshed, I am now led after many days to the execution of that first purpose which I formed on entering the priesthood. Gabriel! when the service is over, and the congregation dispersed, you must guide me to the door of your father's cottage.'

He held up his hand, in sign of silence, as Gabriel was about to answer. Just then, the officiating priests above were pronouncing the final benediction. When it was over, Father Paul opened the cabin door. As he ascended the steps, followed by Gabriel, Père Bonan met them. The old man looked doubtfully and searchingly on his future son-in-law, as he respectfully whispered a few words in the ear of the priest. Father Paul listened attentively, answered in a whisper, and then turned to Gabriel, first begging the few people near them to withdraw a little.

'I have been asked whether there is any impediment to your marriage,' he said, 'and have answered that there is none. What you have said to me has been said in confession, and is a secret between us two. Remember that; and forget not, at the same time, the service which I shall require of you tonight, after the marriage ceremony is over. Where is Perrine Bonan?' he added aloud, looking round him. Perrine came forward. Father Paul took her hand, and placed it in Gabriel's. 'Lead her to the altar steps,' he said, 'and wait there for me.'

It was more than an hour later; the boats had left the ship's side; the congregation had dispersed over the face of the country – but still the vessel remained at anchor. Those who were left in her watched the land more anxiously than usual; for they knew that Father Paul had risked meeting the soldiers of the republic by trusting himself on shore. A boat was awaiting his return on the beach; half of the crew, armed, being posted as scouts in various directions on the high land of the heath. They would have followed and guarded the priest to the place of his destination; but he forbade it; and, leaving them abruptly, walked swiftly onward with one young man only for his companion.

Gabriel had committed his brother and his sisters to the charge of Perrine. They were to go to the farmhouse that night with his newly married wife and her father and mother. Father Paul had desired that this might be done. When Gabriel and he were left alone to follow the path which led to the fisherman's cottage, the priest never spoke while they walked on – never looked aside either to the right or the left – always held his ivory crucifix clasped to his breast. They arrived at the door.

'Knock,' whispered Father Paul to Gabriel, 'and then wait here with me.'

The door was opened. On a lovely moonlight night François Sarzeau had stood on that threshold, years since, with a bleeding body in his arms. On a lovely moonlight night, he now stood there again, confronting the very man whose life he had attempted, and knowing him not.

Father Paul advanced a few paces, so that the moonlight fell fuller on his features, and removed his hat.

François Sarzeau looked, started, moved one step back, then stood motionless and perfectly silent, while all traces of expression of any kind suddenly vanished from his face. Then the calm, clear tones of the priest stole gently on the dead silence. 'I bring a message of peace and forgiveness from a guest of former years,' he said; and pointed, as he spoke, to the place where he had been wounded in the neck.

For one moment, Gabriel saw his father trembling violently from head to foot – then his limbs steadied again – stiffened suddenly, as if struck by catalepsy. His lips parted, but without quivering; his eyes glared, but without moving their orbits. The lovely moonlight itself looked ghastly and horrible, shining on the supernatural panic-deformity of that face! Gabriel turned away his head in terror. He heard the voice of Father Paul saying to him: 'Wait here till I come back,' – then a low groaning sound, that seemed to articulate the name of God; a sound unlike his father's voice, unlike any human voice he had ever heard – and then the noise of a closing door. He looked up, and saw that he was standing alone before the cottage.

Once, after an interval, he approached the window.

He just saw through it the hand of the priest holding on high the ivory crucifix; but stopped not to see more, for he heard such words, such sounds, as drove him back to his former place. There he stayed, until the noise of something falling heavily within the cottage, struck on his ear. Again he advanced towards the door; heard Father Paul praying; listened for several minutes; then heard a moaning voice, now joining itself to the voice of the priest, now choked in sobs and bitter wailing. Once more he went back out of hearing, and stirred not again from his place. He waited a long and a weary time there – so long that one of the scouts on the look-out came towards him, evidently suspicious of the delay in the priest's return. He waved the man back, and then looked again towards the door. At last, he saw it open – saw Father Paul approach him, leading François Sarzeau by the hand.

The fisherman never raised his downcast eyes to his son's face; tears trickled silently over his cheeks; he followed the hand that led him, as a little child might follow it, listening anxiously and humbly at the priest's side to every word that he spoke.

'Gabriel,' said Father Paul, in a voice which trembled a little for the first time that night – 'Gabriel, it has pleased God to grant the perfect fulfillment of the purpose which brought me to this place; I tell you this, as all that you need – as all, I believe, that you would wish – to know of what has passed while you have been left waiting for me here. Such words as I have now to speak to you, are spoken by your father's earnest desire. It is his own wish that I should communicate to you his confession of having secretly followed you to the Merchant's Table, and of having discovered (as you discovered) that no evidence of his guilt remained there. This admission he thinks will be enough to account for his conduct towards yourself from that time to this. I have to tell you (also at your father's desire) that he has promised in my presence, and now promises again in yours, sincerity of repentance in this manner:– When the persecution of our religion has ceased – as cease it will, and that speedily, be assured of it! – he solemnly pledges himself henceforth to devote his life, his strength, and what worldly possessions he may have, or may acquire, to the task of re-erecting and restoring the roadside crosses which have been sacrilegiously overthrown and destroyed in his native province, and to doing good, good where he may. I have now said all that is required of me, and may bid you farewell – bearing with me the happy remembrance that I have left a father and son reconciled and restored to each other. May God bless and prosper you, and those dear to you, Gabriel! May God accept your father's repentance, and bless him also throughout his future life!'

He took their hands, pressed them long and warmly, then turned and walked quickly down the path which led to the beach. Gabriel dared not trust himself yet to speak; but he raised his arm, and put it gently round his father's neck. The two stood together so, looking out dimly through the tears that filled their eyes, to the sea. They saw the boat put off in the bright track of the moonlight, and reach the vessel's side; they watched the spreading of the sails, and followed the slow course of the ship till she disappeared past a distant headland from sight.

After that, they went into the cottage together. They knew it not then, but they had seen the last, in this world, of Father Paul.

CHAPTER V

The events foretold by the good priest happened sooner even than he anticipated. A new government ruled the destinies of France, and the persecution ceased in Brittany.

Among other propositions which were then submitted to the parliament, was one advocating the restoration of the roadside crosses throughout the province. It was found, however, on inquiry, that these crosses were to be counted by thousands, and that the mere cost of the wood required to re-erect them necessitated an expenditure of money which the bankrupt nation could ill afford to spare. While this project was under discussion, and before it was finally rejected, one man had undertaken the task which the government shrank from attempting. When Gabriel left the cottage, taking his brother and sisters to live with his wife and himself at the farmhouse, François Sarzeau left it also, to perform in highway and byway his promise to Father Paul. For months and months he laboured without intermission at his task; still, always doing good, and rendering help and kindness and true charity to all whom he could serve. He walked many a weary mile, toiled through many a hard day's work, humbled himself even to beg of others, to get wood enough to restore a single cross. No one ever heard him complain, ever saw him impatient, ever detected him in faltering at his task. The shelter in an outhouse, the crust of bread and drink of water, which he could always get from the peasantry, seemed to suffice him. Among the people who watched his perseverance, a belief began to gain ground that his life would be miraculously prolonged until he had completed his undertaking from one end of Brittany to the other. But this was not to be.

He was seen one cold autumn evening, silently and steadily at work as usual, setting up a new cross on the site of one which had been shattered to splinters in the troubled times. In the morning he was found lying dead beneath the sacred symbol which his own hands had completed and erected in its place during the night. They buried him where he lay; and the priest who consecrated the ground allowed Gabriel to engrave his father's epitaph in the wood of the cross. It was simply the initial letters of the dead man's name, followed by this inscription:– *'Pray for the repose of his soul: he died penitent, and the doer of good works.'*

Once, and once only, did Gabriel hear anything of Father Paul. The good priest showed, by writing to the farmhouse, that he had not forgotten the family so largely indebted to him for their happiness. The letter was dated 'Rome'. Father Paul said that such services as he had been permitted to render to the Church in Brittany, had obtained for him a new and far more glorious trust than any he had yet held. He had been recalled from his curacy, and appointed to be at the head of a mission which was shortly to be despatched to convert the inhabitants of a savage and a far distant land to the Christian faith. He now wrote, as his brethren with him were writing, to take leave of all friends for ever in this world, before setting out – for it was well known to the chosen persons entrusted with the new mission, that they could only hope to advance its object by cheerfully risking their own lives for the sake of their religion. He gave his blessing to François Sarzeau, to Gabriel, and to his family; and bade them affectionately farewell for the last time.

There was a postscript to the letter, which was addressed to Perrine, and which she often read afterwards with tearful eyes. The writer begged that, if she should have any children, she would show her friendly and Christian remembrance of him by teaching them to pray (as he hoped she herself would pray) that a blessing might attend Father Paul's labours in the distant land.

The priest's loving petition was never forgotten. When Perrine taught its first prayer to her first child, the little creature was instructed to end the few simple words pronounced at its mother's knees, with:– 'God bless Father Paul.'

In those words the nun concluded her narrative. After it was ended, she pointed to the old wooden cross, and said to me:–

'That was one of the many that he made. It was found, a few years since, to have suffered so much from exposure to the weather, that it was unfit to remain any longer in its old place. A priest in Brittany gave it to one of the nuns in this convent. Do you wonder now that the Mother-Superior always calls it a Relic?'

'No,' I answered. 'And I should have small respect indeed for the religious convictions of any one who could hear the story of that wooden cross, and not feel that the Mother-Superior's name for it is the very best that could have been chosen.'

MAD MONKTON

MAD MONKTON

CHAPTER I

The Monktons of Wincot Abbey bore a sad character for want of sociability in our county. They held no friendly intercourse with their neighbours; and, excepting my father, and a lady and her daughter living near them, they never received anyone under their own roof.

Proud as they all were, it was not pride but dread which kept them thus apart from their neighbours. The family had suffered for generations past from the horrible affliction of hereditary insanity, and the members of it shrank from exposing their calamity to others, as they must have exposed it if they had mingled with the busy little world around them. There is a frightful story of crime committed in past times by two of the Monktons, near relatives, from which the first appearance of the insanity was always supposed to date, but it is needless for me to shock anyone by repeating it. It is enough to say that at intervals almost every form of madness appeared in the family; monomania being the most frequent manifestation of the affliction among them. I have these particulars, and one or two yet to be related, from my father.

At the period of my youth but three of the Monktons were left at the Abbey: Mr. and Mrs. Monkton, and their only child, Alfred, heir to the property. The one other member of this, the elder, branch of the family who was then alive, was Mr. Monkton's younger brother, Stephen. He was an unmarried man, possessing a fine estate in Scotland; but he lived almost entirely on the Continent, and bore the reputation of being a shameless profligate. The family at Wincot held almost as little communication with him as with their neighbours.

I have already mentioned my father, and a lady and her daughter, as the only privileged people who were admitted into Wincot Abbey.

My father had been an old school and college friend of Mr. Monkton, and accident had brought them so much together in later life, that their continued intimacy at Wincot was quite intelligible. I am not so well able to account for the friendly terms on which Mrs. Elmslie (the lady to whom I have alluded) lived with the Monktons. Her late husband had been distantly related to Mrs. Monkton, and my father was her daughter's guardian. But even these claims to friendship and regard never seemed to me strong enough to explain the intimacy between Mrs. Elmslie and the inhabitants of the Abbey. Intimate, however, they certainly were, and one result of the constant interchange of visits between the two families in due time declared itself – Mr. Monkton's son and Mrs. Elmslie's daughter became attached to each other.

I had no opportunities of seeing much of the young lady; I only remember her at that time as a delicate, gentle, lovable girl, the very opposite in appearance, and apparently in character also, to Alfred Monkton. But perhaps that was one reason why they fell in love with each other. The attachment was soon discovered, and was far from being disapproved by the parents on either side. In all essential points, except that of wealth, the Elmslies were nearly the equals of the Monktons, and want of money in a bride was of no consequence to the heir of Wincot. Alfred, it was well known, would succeed to thirty thousand a year on his father's death.

Thus, though the parents on both sides thought the young people not old enough to be married at once, they saw no reason why Ada and Alfred should not be engaged to each other, with the understanding that they should be united when young Monkton came of age, in two years' time. The person to be consulted in the matter, after the parents, was my father in his capacity of Ada's guardian. He knew that the family misery had shown itself many years ago in Mrs. Monkton, who was her husband's cousin. The *illness*, as it was significantly called, had been palliated by careful treatment, and was reported to have passed away. But my father was not to be deceived. He knew where the hereditary taint still lurked; he viewed with horror the bare possibility of its reappearing one day in the children of his friend's only daughter; and he positively refused his consent to the marriage engagement.

The result was that the doors of the Abbey and the doors of Mrs. Elmslie's house were closed to him. This suspension of friendly intercourse had lasted but a very short time, when Mrs. Monkton died. Her husband, who was fondly attached to her, caught a violent cold while attending her funeral. The cold was neglected, and settled on his lungs. In a few months' time, he followed his wife to the grave, and Alfred was left master of the grand old Abbey, and the fair lands that spread all around it.

At this period Mrs. Elmslie had the indelicacy to endeavour a second time to procure my father's consent to the marriage engagement. He refused it again more positively than before. More than a year passed away. The time was approaching fast when Alfred would be of age. I returned from college to spend the long vacation at home, and made some advances towards bettering my acquaintance with young Monkton. They were evaded – certainly with perfect politeness, but still in such a way as to prevent me from offering my friendship to him again. Any mortification I might have felt at this petty repulse, under ordinary circumstances, was dismissed from my mind by the occurrence of a real misfortune in our household. For some months past my father's health had been failing, and, just at the time of which I am now writing, his sons had to mourn the irreparable calamity of his death.

This event (through some informality or error in the late Mr. Elmslie's will) left the future of Ada's life entirely at her mother's disposal. The consequence was the immediate ratification of the marriage engagement to which my father had so steadily refused his consent. As soon as the fact was publicly announced, some of Mrs. Elmslie's more intimate friends, who were acquainted with the reports affecting the Monkton family, ventured to mingle with their formal congratulations one or two significant references to the late Mrs. Monkton, and some searching inquiries as to the disposition of her son.

Mrs. Elmslie always met these polite hints with one bold form of answer. She first admitted the existence of those reports about the Monktons which her friends were unwilling to specify distinctly; and then declared that they were infamous calumnies. The hereditary taint had died out of the family generations back. Alfred was the best, the kindest, the sanest of human beings. He loved study and retirement; Ada sympathised with his tastes, and had made her choice unbiassed; if any more hints were dropped about sacrificing her by her marriage, those hints would be viewed as so many insults to her mother, whose affection for her it was monstrous to call in question. This way of talking silenced people, but did not convince them. They began to suspect, what was indeed the actual truth, that Mrs. Elmslie was a selfish, worldly, grasping woman, who wanted to get her daughter well married, and cared nothing for consequences as long as she saw Ada mistress of the greatest establishment in the whole county.

It seemed, however, as if there was some fatality at work to prevent the attainment of Mrs. Elmslie's great object in life. Hardly was one obstacle to the ill-omened marriage removed by my father's death, before another succeeded it, in the shape of anxieties and difficulties caused by the delicate state of Ada's health. Doctors were consulted in all directions, and the result of their advice was that the marriage must be deferred, and that Miss Elmslie must leave England for a certain time, to reside in a warmer climate; the South of France, if I remember rightly. Thus it happened that just before Alfred came of age, Ada and her mother departed for the Continent, and the union of the two young people was understood to be indefinitely postponed.

Some curiosity was felt in the neighbourhood as to what Alfred Monkton would do under these circumstances. Would he follow his lady-love? Would he go yachting? Would he throw open the doors of the old Abbey at last, and endeavour to forget the absence of Ada, and the postponement of his marriage, in a round of gaieties? He did none of these things. He simply remained at Wincot, living as suspiciously strange and solitary a life as his father had lived before him. Literally, there was now no companion for him at the Abbey but the old priest (the Monktons, I should have mentioned before, were Roman Catholics) who had held the office of tutor to Alfred from his earliest years. He came of age, and there was not even so much as a private dinner party at Wincot to celebrate the event. Families in the neighbourhood determined to forget the offence which his father's reserve had given them, and invited him to their houses. The invitations were politely declined. Civil visitors called resolutely at the Abbey, and were resolutely bowed away from the doors as soon as they had left their cards. Under this combination of sinister and aggravating circumstances, people in all directions took to shaking their heads mysteriously when the name of Mr. Alfred Monkton was mentioned, hinting at the family calamity, and wondering peevishly or sadly, as their tempers inclined them, what he could possibly do to occupy himself month after month in the lonely old house.

The right answer to this question was not easy to find. It was quite useless, for example, to apply to the priest for it. He was a very quiet, polite old gentleman; his replies were always excessively ready and civil, and appeared at the time to convey a reasonable amount of information; but when they were tested by after-reflection, it was universally observed that nothing tangible could be extracted from them. The housekeeper, a weird old woman, with a very abrupt and repelling manner, was too fierce and taciturn to be safely approached. The few indoor servants had all been long enough in the family to have learnt to hold their tongues in public as a regular habit. It was only from the farm-servant who supplied the table at the Abbey, that any information could be obtained; and vague enough it was when they came to communicate it.

Some of them had observed the 'young master' walking about the library with heaps of dusty papers in his hands. Others had heard odd noises in the uninhabited parts of the Abbey, had looked up, and had seen him forcing open old windows, as if to let light and air into rooms supposed to have been shut close for years and years; or had discovered him standing on the perilous summit of one of the crumbling turrets, never ascended before within their memories, and popularly considered to be inhabited by the ghosts of the monks who had once possessed the building. The result of these observations and discoveries, when they were communicated to others, was of course to impress every one with a firm belief that 'poor young Monkton was going the way that the rest of the family had gone before him': which opinion always appeared to be immensely strengthened in the popular mind by a conviction – founded on no particle of evidence – that the priest was at the bottom of all the mischief.

Thus far I have spoken from hearsay evidence mostly. What I have next to tell will be the result of my own personal experience.

CHAPTER II

About five months after Alfred Monkton came of age I left college, and resolved to amuse and instruct myself a little by travelling abroad.

At the time when I quitted England, young Monkton was still leading his secluded life at the Abbey, and was, in the opinion of everybody, sinking rapidly, if he had not already succumbed, under the hereditary curse of his family. As to the Elmslies, report said that Ada had benefited by her sojourn abroad, and that mother and daughter were on their way back to England to resume their old relations with the heir of Wincot. Before they returned, I was away on my travels, and wandered half over Europe, hardly ever planning whither I should shape my course beforehand. Chance, which thus led me everywhere, led me at last to Naples. There I met with an old school friend, who was one of the *attachés* at the English embassy; and there began the extraordinary events in connection with Alfred Monkton which form the main interest of the story I am now relating.

I was idling away the time one morning with my friend the *attaché*, in the garden of the Villa Reale, when we were passed by a young man, walking alone, who exchanged bows with my friend.

I thought I recognised the dark eager eyes, the colourless cheeks, the strangely-vigilant, anxious expression which I remembered in past times as characteristic of Alfred Monkton's face, and was about to question my friend on the subject, when he gave me unasked the information of which I was in search.

'That is Alfred Monkton,' said he; 'he comes from your part of England. You ought to know him.'

'I do know a little of him,' I answered; 'he was engaged to

Miss Elmslie when I was last in the neighbourhood of Wincot.
Is he married to her yet?'

'No; and he never ought to be. He has gone the way of the
rest of the family; or, in plainer words, he has gone mad.'

'Mad! But I ought not to be surprised at hearing that, after
the reports about him in England.'

'I speak from no reports; I speak from what he has said and
done here before me, and before hundreds of other people.
Surely you must have heard of it?'

'Never. I have been out of the way of news from Naples or
England for months past.'

'Then I have a very extraordinary story to tell you. You
know, of course, that Alfred had an uncle, Stephen Monkton.
Well, some time ago, this uncle fought a duel in the Roman
states, with a Frenchman who shot him dead. The seconds and
the Frenchman (who was unhurt) took to flight in different
directions, as it is supposed. We heard nothing here of the
details of the duel till a month after it happened, when one of
the French journals published an account of it, taken from
papers left by Monkton's second, who died at Paris of
consumption. These papers stated the manner in which the
duel was fought, and how it terminated, but nothing more.
The surviving second and the Frenchman have never been
traced from that time to this. All that anybody knows,
therefore, of the duel is that Stephen Monkton was shot; an
event which nobody can regret, for a greater scoundrel never
existed. The exact place where he died, and what was done
with his body, are still mysteries not to be penetrated.'

'But what has all this to do with Alfred?'

'Wait a moment, and you will hear. Soon after the news of
his uncle's death reached England, what do you think Alfred
did? He actually put off his marriage with Miss Elmslie, which
was then about to be celebrated, to come out here in search of
the burial-place of his wretched scamp of an uncle. And no
power on earth will now induce him to return to England and
to Miss Elmslie, until he has found the body and can take it
back with him to be buried with all the other dead Monktons,
in the vault under Wincot Abbey Chapel. He has squandered
his money, pestered the police, exposed himself to the ridicule
of the men and the indignation of the women for the past three

months, in trying to achieve his insane purpose, and is now as far from it as ever. He will not assign to anybody the smallest motive for his conduct. You can't laugh him out of it, or reason him out of it. When we met him just now, I happen to know that he was on his way to the office of the police minister, to send out fresh agents to search and inquire through the Roman states for the place where his uncle was shot. And mind, all this time he professes to be passionately in love with Miss Elmslie, and to be miserable at his separation from her. Just think of that! And then think of his self-imposed absence from her here, to hunt after the remains of a wretch who was a disgrace to the family, and whom he never saw but once or twice in his life. Of all the "Mad Monktons," as they used to call them in England, Alfred is the maddest. He is actually our principal excitement in this dull opera season, though, for my own part, when I think of the poor girl in England, I am a great deal more ready to despise him than to laugh at him.'

'You know the Elmslies, then?'

'Intimately. The other day, my mother wrote to me from England, after having seen Ada. This escapade of Monkton's has outraged all her friends. They have been entreating her to break off the match, which it seems she could do if she liked. Even her mother, sordid and selfish as she is, has been obliged at last, in common decency, to side with the rest of the family; but the good faithful girl won't give Monkton up. She humours his insanity, declares he gave her a good reason, in secret, for going away; says she could always make him happy when they were together in the old Abbey, and can make him still happier when they are married; in short, she loves him dearly, and will therefore believe in him to the last. Nothing shakes her; she has made up her mind to throw away her life on him, and she will do it.'

'I hope not. Mad as his conduct looks to us, he may have some sensible reason for it that we cannot imagine. Does his mind seem at all disordered when he talks on ordinary topics?'

'Not in the least. When you can get him to say anything, which is not often, he talks like a sensible, well-educated man. Keep silence about his precious errand here, and you would fancy him the gentlest and most temperate of human beings.

But touch the subject of his vagabond of an uncle and the Monkton madness comes out directly. The other night a lady asked him, jestingly of course, whether he had ever seen his uncle's ghost. He scowled at her like a perfect fiend, and said that he and his uncle would answer her question together some day, if they came from hell to do it. We laughed at his words, but the lady fainted at his looks, and we had a scene of hysterics and hartshorn in consequence. Any other man would have been kicked out of the room for nearly frightening a pretty woman to death that way; but "Mad Monkton," as we have christened him, is a privileged lunatic in Neapolitan society, because he is English, good-looking, and worth thirty thousand a year. He goes out everywhere, under the impression that he may meet with somebody who has been let into the secret place where the mysterious duel was fought. If you are introduced to him, he is sure to ask you whether you know anything about it; but beware of following up the subject after you have answered him, unless you want to make sure that he is out of his senses. In that case, only talk of his uncle, and the result will rather more than satisfy you.'

A day or two after this conversation with my friend the *attaché*, I met Monkton at an evening party.

The moment he heard my name mentioned, his face flushed up; he drew me away into a corner, and referring to his cool reception of my advance, years ago, towards making his acquaintance, asked my pardon for what he termed his inexcusable ingratitude, with an earnestness and an agitation which utterly astonished me. His next proceeding was to question me, as my friend had said he would, about the place of the mysterious duel.

An extraordinary change came over him while he interrogated me on this point. Instead of looking into my face as they had looked hitherto, his eyes wandered away, and fixed themselves intensely, almost fiercely, either on the perfectly empty wall at our side, or on the vacant space between the wall and ourselves – it was impossible to say which. I had come to Naples from Spain by sea, and briefly told him so, as the best way of satisfying him that I could not assist his inquiries. He pursued them no further; and mindful of my friend's warning, I took care to lead the conversation to general topics. He looked back at me directly, and as long as we stood in our corner, his eyes never wandered away again to the empty wall or the vacant space at our side.

Though more ready to listen than to speak, his conversation, when he did talk, had no trace of anything the least like insanity about it. He had evidently read, not generally only, but deeply as well, and could apply his reading with singular felicity to the illustration of almost any subject under discussion, neither obtruding his knowledge absurdly, nor concealing it affectedly. His manner was in itself a standing protest against such a nickname as 'Mad Monkton.' He was so shy, so quiet, so composed and gentle in all his actions, that at times I should have been almost inclined to call him effeminate. We had a long talk together on the first evening of our meeting; we often saw each other afterwards, and never lost a single opportunity of bettering our acquaintance. I felt that he had taken a liking to me; and in spite of what I had heard about his behaviour to Miss Elmslie, in spite of the suspicions which the history of his family and his own conduct had arrayed against him, I began to like 'Mad Monkton' as much as he liked me. We took many a quiet ride together in the country, and sailed often along the shores of the Bay on either side. But for two eccentricities in his conduct, which I could not at all understand, I should soon have felt as much at my ease in his society as if he had been my own brother.

The first of these eccentricities consisted in the reappearance on several occasions of the odd expression in his eyes, which I had first seen when he asked me whether I knew anything about the duel. No matter what we were talking about, or where we happened to be, there were times when he would suddenly look away from my face, now on one side of me, now on the other, but always where there was nothing to see, and always with the same intensity and fierceness in his eyes. This looked so like madness – or hypochondria, at the least – that I felt afraid to ask him about it, and always pretended not to observe him.

The second peculiarity in his conduct was that he never referred while in my company, to the reports about his errand at Naples, and never once spoke of Miss Elmslie, or of his life at Wincot Abbey. This not only astonished me, but amazed those who had noticed our intimacy, and who had made sure that I must be the depositary of all his secrets. But the time was near at hand when this mystery, and some other mysteries of which I had no suspicion at that period, were all to be revealed.

I met him one night at a large ball, given by a Russian nobleman, whose name I could not pronounce then, and cannot remember now. I had wandered away from reception-room, ballroom, and card-room to a small apartment at one extremity of the palace, which was half conservatory, half boudoir, and which had been prettily illuminated for the occasion with Chinese lanthorns. Nobody was in the room when I got there. The view over the Mediterranean, bathed in the bright softness of Italian moonlight, was so lovely, that I remained for a long time at the window, looking out, and listening to the dance music which faintly reached me from the ballroom. My thoughts were far away with the relations I had left in England, when I was startled out of them by hearing my name softly pronounced.

I looked round directly, and saw Monkton standing in the room. A livid paleness overspread his face, and his eyes were turned away from me with the same extraordinary expression in them to which I have already alluded.

'Do you mind leaving the ball early tonight?' he asked, still not looking at me.

'Not at all,' said I. 'Can I do anything for you? Are you ill?'

'No, at least nothing to speak of. Will you come to my rooms?'

'At once, if you like.'

'No, not at once. *I* must go home directly; but don't you come to me for half an hour yet. You have not been at my rooms before, I know; but you will easily find them out, they are close by. There is a card with my address. I *must* speak to you tonight; my life depends on it. Pray come! for God's sake come when the half hour is up!'

I promised to be punctual, and he left me directly.

Most people will be easily able to imagine the state of nervous impatience and vague expectation in which I passed the allotted period of delay, after hearing such words as those Monkton had spoken to me. Before the half hour had quite expired, I began to make my way out through the ballroom.

At the head of the staircase, my friend the *attaché* met me. 'What! going away already?' said he.

'Yes; and on a very curious expedition. I am going to Monkton's rooms, by his own invitation.'

'You don't mean it! Upon my honour, you're a bold fellow to trust yourself alone with "Mad Monkton" when the moon is at the full.'

'He is ill, poor fellow. Besides, I don't think him half as mad as you do.'

'We won't dispute about that; but mark my words, he has not asked you to go where no visitor has ever been admitted before, without a special purpose. I predict that you will see or hear something tonight which you will remember for the rest of your life.'

We parted. When I knocked at the courtyard gate of the house where Monkton lived, my friend's last words on the palace staircase occurred to me; and though I had laughed at him when he had spoken them, I began to suspect even then that his prediction would be fulfilled.

CHAPTER III

The porter who let me into the house where Monkton lived, directed me to the floor on which his rooms were situated. On getting upstairs, I found his door on the landing ajar. He heard my footsteps, I suppose, for he called to me to come in before I could knock.

I entered, and found him sitting by the table, with some loose letters in his hand, which he was just tying together in a packet. I noticed, as he asked me to sit down, that his expression looked more composed, though the paleness had not yet left his face. He thanked me for coming; repeated that he had something very important to say to me; and then stopped short, apparently too much embarrassed to proceed. I tried to set him at ease by assuring him that if my assistance or advice could be of any use, I was ready to place myself and my time heartily and unreservedly at his service.

As I said this, I saw his eyes beginning to wander away from my face – to wander slowly, inch by inch as it were, until they stopped at a certain point, with the same fixed stare into vacancy which had so often startled me on former occasions. The whole expression of his face altered as I had never yet seen it alter; he sat before me, looking like a man in a death-trance.

'You are very kind,' he said, slowly and faintly, speaking, not to me, but in the direction in which his eyes were still fixed – 'I know you can help me; but – '

He stopped; his face whitened horribly, and the perspiration broke out all over it. He tried to continue; said a word or two, then stopped again. Seriously alarmed about him, I rose from my chair, with the intention of getting him some water from a jug which I saw standing on a side table.

He sprang up at the same moment. All the suspicions I had ever heard whispered against his sanity flashed over my mind in an instant; and I involuntarily stepped back a pace or two.

'Stop,' he said, seating himself again; 'don't mind me; and don't leave your chair. I want – I wish, if you please, to make a little alteration, before we say anything more. Do you mind sitting in a strong light?'

'Not in the least.'

I had hitherto been seated in the shade of his reading-lamp, the only light in the room.

As I answered him, he rose again; and going into another apartment, returned with a large lamp in his hand; then took two candles from the side table, and two others from the chimney-piece; placed them all, to my amazement, together, so as to stand exactly between us; and then tried to light them. His hand trembled so, that he was obliged to give up the attempt, and allow me to come to his assistance. By his direction I took the shade off the reading lamp, after I had lit the other lamp and the four candles. When he sat down again, with this concentration of light between us, his better and gentler manner began to return: and while he now addressed me, he spoke without the slightest hesitation.

'It is useless to ask whether you have heard the reports about me,' he said; 'I know that you have. My purpose tonight is to give you some reasonable explanation of the conduct which has produced those reports. My secret has been hitherto confided to one person only; I am now about to trust it to your keeping, with a special object which will appear as I go on.

First, however, I must begin by telling you exactly what the great difficulty is which obliges me to be still absent from England. I want your advice and your help; and, to conceal nothing from you, I want also to test your forbearance and your friendly sympathy, before I can venture on thrusting my miserable secret into your keeping. Will you pardon this apparent distrust of your frank and open character – this apparent ingratitude for your kindness towards me ever since we first met?'

I begged him not to speak of these things, but to go on.

'You know,' he proceeded, 'that I am here to recover the body of my Uncle Stephen, and to carry it back with me to our family burial-place in England; and you must also be aware that I have not yet succeeded in discovering his remains. Try to pass over for the present whatever may seem extraordinary and incomprehensible in such a purpose as mine is; and read this newspaper article, where the ink-line is traced. It is the only evidence hitherto obtained on the subject of the fatal duel in which my uncle fell: and I want to hear what course of proceeding the perusal of it may suggest to you as likely to be best on my part.'

He handed me an old French newspaper. The substance of what I read there is still so firmly impressed on my memory, that I am certain of being able to repeat correctly at this distance of time, all the facts which it is necessary for me to communicate to the reader.

The article began, I remember, with editorial remarks on the great curiosity then felt in regard to the fatal duel between the Count St. Lo and Mr. Stephen Monkton, an English gentleman. The writer proceeded to dwell at great length on the extraordinary secrecy in which the whole affair had been involved from first to last; and to express a hope that the publication of a certain manuscript, to which his introductory observations referred, might lead to the production of fresh evidence from other and better informed quarters. The manuscript had been found among the papers of Monsieur Foulton, Mr. Monkton's second, who had died at Paris of a rapid decline, shortly after returning to his home in that city from the scene of the duel. The document was unfinished, having been left incomplete at the very place where the reader would

most wish to find it continued. No reason could be discovered for this, and no second manuscript bearing on the all-
important subject had been found, after the strictest search
among the papers left by the deceased.

The document itself then followed.

It purported to be an agreement privately drawn up
between Mr. Monkton's second, Monsieur Foulon, and the
Count St. Lo's second, Monsieur Dalville; and contained a
statement of all the arrangements for concluding the duel.
The paper was dated 'Naples, February 22nd'; and was
divided into some seven or eight clauses.

The first clause described the origin and nature of the
quarrel – a very disgraceful affair on both sides, worth
neither remembering nor repeating. The second clause stated
that the challenged man having chosen the pistol as his
weapon, and the challenger (an excellent swordsman) having,
on his side, thereupon insisted that the duel should be fought
in such a manner as to make the first fire decisive in its
results, the seconds, seeing that fatal consequences must
inevitably follow the hostile meeting, determined, first of all,
that the duel should be kept a profound secret from everybody, and that the place where it was to be fought should not
be made known beforehand, even to the principals themselves. It was added that this excess of precaution had been
rendered absolutely necessary, in consequence of a recent
address from the Pope to the ruling powers in Italy, com-
menting on the scandalous frequency of the practice of
duelling, and urgently desiring that the laws against duellists
should be enforced for the future with the utmost rigour.

The third clause detailed the manner in which it had been
arranged that the duel should be fought.

The pistols having been loaded by the seconds on the
ground, the combatants were to be placed thirty paces apart,
and were to toss up for the first fire. The man who won was
to advance ten paces – marked out for him beforehand – and
was then to discharge his pistol. If he missed, or failed to
disable his opponent, the latter was free to advance, if he
chose, the whole remaining twenty paces before he fired in
his turn. This arrangement ensured the decisive termination
of the duel at the first discharge of the pistols, and both

principals and seconds pledged themselves on either side to abide by it.

The fourth clause stated that the seconds had agreed that the duel should be fought *out* of the Neapolitan states, but left themselves to be guided by circumstances as to the exact locality in which it should take place. The remaining clauses, so far as I remember them, were devoted to detailing the different precautions to be adopted for avoiding discovery. The duellists and their seconds were to leave Naples in separate parties; were to change carriages several times; were to meet at a certain town, or, failing that, at a certain post-house on the high road from Naples to Rome; were to carry drawing-books, colour-boxes, and camp-stools, as if they had been artists out on a sketching tour; and were to proceed to the place of the duel on foot, employing no guides, for fear of treachery. Such general arrangements as these, and others for facilitating the flight of the survivors after the affair was over, formed the conclusion of this extraordinary document, which was signed, in initials only, by both the seconds.

Just below the initials, appeared the beginning of a narrative, dated 'Paris,' and evidently intended to describe the duel itself with extreme minuteness. The handwriting was that of the deceased second.

Monsieur Foulon, the gentleman in question, stated his belief that circumstances might transpire which would render an account by an eye-witness of the hostile meeting between St. Lo and Mr. Monkton an important document. He proposed, therefore, as one of the seconds, to testify that the duel had been fought in exact accordance with the terms of the agreement, both the principals conducting themselves like men of gallantry and honour(!). And he further announced that, in order not to compromise any one, he should place the paper containing his testimony in safe hands, with strict directions that it was on no account to be opened, except in a case of the last emergency.

After this preamble, Monsieur Foulon related that the duel had been fought two days after the drawing up of the agreement, in a locality to which accident had conducted the duelling party. (The name of the place was not mentioned, nor even the neighbourhood in which it was situated.) The men having been placed according to previous arrangement, the Count St. Lo had won the toss for the first fire, had advanced his ten paces, and had shot his opponent in the body. Mr. Monkton did not immediately fall, but staggered forward some six or seven paces, discharged his pistol ineffectually at the Count, and dropped to the ground a dead man. Monsieur Foulon then stated that he tore a leaf from his pocket-book, wrote on it a brief description of the manner in which Mr. Monkton had died, and pinned the paper to his clothes; this proceeding having been rendered necessary by a peculiar nature of the plan organised on the spot for safely disposing of the dead body. What this plan was, or what was done with the corpse, did not appear, for at this important point the narrative abruptly broke off.

A footnote in the newspaper merely stated the manner in which the document had been obtained for publication, and repeated the announcement contained in the editor's introductory remarks, that no continuation had been found by the persons entrusted with the care of Monsieur Foulon's papers. I have now given the whole substance of what I read, and have mentioned all that was then known of Mr. Stephen Monkton's death.

When I gave the newspaper back to Alfred, he was too much agitated to speak; but he reminded me by a sign that he was anxiously waiting to hear what I had to say. My position was a very trying and very painful one. I could hardly tell what consequences might not follow any want of caution on my part, and could think at first of no safer plan than questioning him carefully before I committed myself either one way or the other.

'Will you excuse me if I ask you a question or two before I give you my advice?' I said.

He nodded impatiently.

'Yes, yes; any questions you like.'

'Were you at any time in the habit of seeing your uncle frequently?'

'I never saw him more than twice in my life; on each occasion, when I was a mere child.'

'Then you could have had no very strong personal regard for him?'

'Regard for him! I should have been ashamed to feel any regard for him. He disgraced us wherever he went.'

'May I ask if any family motive is involved in your anxiety to recover his remains?'

'Family motives may enter into it among others – but why do you ask?'

'Because, having heard that you employ the police to assist your search, I was anxious to know whether you had stimulated their superiors to make them do their best in your service, by giving some strong personal reasons at headquarters for the very unusual project which has brought you here.'

'I give no reasons. I pay for the work I want done, and in return for my liberality I am treated with the most infamous indifference on all sides. A stranger in the country, and badly acquainted with the language, I can do nothing to help myself. The authorities, both at Rome and in this place, pretend to assist me, pretend to search and inquire as I would have them search and inquire, and do nothing more. I am insulted, laughed at, almost to my face.'

'Do you not think it possible – mind, I have no wish to excuse the misconduct of the authorities, and do not share in any such opinion myself – but do you not think it likely that the police may doubt whether you are in earnest?'

'Not in earnest!' he cried, starting up and confronting me fiercely, with wild eyes and quickened breath. 'Not in earnest! *You* think I'm not in earnest, too. I know you think it, though you tell me you don't. Stop! before we say another word, your own eyes shall convince you. Come here – only for a minute – only for one minute!'

I followed him into his bedroom, which opened out of the sitting-room. At one side of his bed stood a large packing-case of plain wood, upwards of seven feet in length.

'Open the lid, and look in,' he said, 'while I hold the candle so that you can see.'

I obeyed his directions, and discovered, to my astonishment, that the packing-case contained a leaden coffin, magnificently emblazoned with the arms of the Monkton family, and inscribed in old-fashioned letters with the name of 'Stephen Monkton,' his age and the manner of his death being added underneath.

'I keep his coffin ready for him,' whispered Alfred, close at my ear. 'Does that look like earnest?'

It looked more like insanity – so like, that I shrank from answering him.

'Yes! yes! I see you are convinced,' he continued quickly; 'we may go back into the next room, and may talk without restraint on either side now.'

On returning to our places, I mechanically moved my chair away from the table. My mind was by this time in such a state of confusion and uncertainty about what it would be best for me to say or do next, that I forgot for the moment the position he had assigned to me when we lit the candles. He reminded me of this directly.

'Don't move away,' he said, very earnestly; 'keep on sitting in the light; pray do! I'll soon tell you why I am so particular about that. But first give me your advice; help me in my great distress and suspense. Remember, you promised me you would.'

I made an effort to collect my thoughts and succeeded. It was useless to treat the affair otherwise than seriously in his presence; it would have been cruel not to have advised him as I best could.

'You know,' I said, 'that two days after the drawing up of the agreement at Naples, the duel was fought out of the Neapolitan States. This fact has of course led you to the conclusion that all inquiries about localities had better be confined to the Roman territory?'

'Certainly: the search, such as it is, has been made there, and there only. If I can believe the police, they and their agents have inquired for the place where the duel was fought (offering a large reward in my name to the person who can discover it), all along the highroad from Naples to Rome. They have also circulated – at least, so they tell me – descriptions of the duellists and their seconds; have left an agent to superintend investigations at the post-house, and another at the town mentioned as meeting-points in the agreement; and have endeavoured by correspondence with foreign authorities to trace the Count St. Lo and Monsieur Dalville to their place or places of refuge. All these efforts, supposing them to have been really made, have hitherto proved utterly fruitless.'

'My impression is,' said I, after a moment's consideration, 'that all inquiries made along the highroad, or anywhere near Rome, are likely to be in vain. As to the discovery of your uncle's remains, that is, I think, identical with the discovery of the place where he was shot; for those engaged in the duel would certainly not risk detection by carrying a corpse any distance with them in their flight. The place, then, is all that we want to find out. Now, let us consider for a moment. The duelling-party changed carriages; travelled separately, two and two; doubtless took roundabout roads; stopped at the post-house and the town as a blind; walked, perhaps, a considerable distance unguided. Depend upon it, such precautions as these (which we know they must have employed) left them very little time out of two days – though they might start at sunrise, and not stop at nightfall – for straightforward travelling. My belief therefore is, that the duel was fought somewhere near the Neapolitan frontier; and if I had been the police agent who conducted the search, I should only have pursued it parallel with the frontier, starting from west to east till I got up among the lonely places in the mountains. That is my idea: do you think it worth anything?'

His face flushed all over in an instant. 'I think it an inspiration!' he cried. 'Not a day is to be lost in carrying out our plan. The police are not to be trusted with it. I must start myself, tomorrow morning; and you —'

He stopped; his face grew suddenly pale; he sighed heavily; his eyes wandered once more into the fixed look at vacancy; and the rigid, deathly expression fastened again upon all his features.

'I must tell you my secret before I talk of tomorrow,' he proceeded, faintly. 'If I hesitated any longer at confessing everything, I should be unworthy of your past kindness, unworthy of the help which it is my last hope that you will gladly give me when you have heard all.'

I begged him to wait until he was more composed, until he was better able to speak; but he did not appear to notice what I said. Slowly, and struggling as it seemed against himself, he turned a little away from me; and bending his head over the table, supported it on his hand. The packet of letters with which I had seen him occupied when I came in, lay just beneath his eyes. He looked down on it steadfastly when he next spoke to me.

CHAPTER IV

'You were born, I believe, in our county,' he said; 'perhaps therefore you may have heard at some time of a curious old prophecy about our family, which is still preserved among the traditions of Wincot Abbey?'

'I have heard of such a prophecy,' I answered; 'but I never knew in what terms it was expressed. It professed to predict the extinction of your family, or something of that sort, did it not?'

'No inquiries,' he went on, 'have traced back that prophecy to the time when it was first made; none of our family records tell us anything of its origin. Old servants and old tenants of ours remember to have heard it from their fathers and grandfathers. The monks, whom we succeeded in the Abbey in Henry VIII's time, got knowledge of it in some way; for I myself discovered the rhymes in which we know the prophecy to have been preserved from a very remote period, written on a blank leaf of one of the Abbey manuscripts. These are the verses, if verses they deserve to be called:

> When in Wincot vault a place
> Waits for one of Monkton's race;
> When that one forlorn shall lie
> Graveless under open sky,
> Beggared of six feet of earth,
> Though lord of acres from his birth—
> That shall be a certain sign
> Of the end of Monkton's line.
> Dwindling ever faster, faster,
> Dwindling to the last-left master;
> From mortal ken, from light of day,
> Monkton's race shall pass away.

'The prediction seems almost vague enough to have been uttered by an ancient oracle,' said I, observing that he waited, after repeating the verses, as if expecting me to say something.

'Vague or not, it is being accomplished,' he returned. 'I am now the "Last-left Master" – the last of that elder line of our family at which the prediction points; and the corpse of Stephen Monkton is not in the vaults of Wincot Abbey. Wait, before you exclaim against me! I have more to say about this. Long before the Abbey was ours, when we lived in the ancient manor-house near it (the very ruins of which have long since disappeared), the family burying place was in the vault under the Abbey chapel. Whether in those remote times the prediction against us was known and dreaded or not, this much is certain: every one of the Monktons (whether living at the Abbey or on the smaller estate in Scotland) was buried in Wincot vault, no matter at what risk or what sacrifice. In the fierce fighting days of the olden time, the bodies of my ancestors who fell in foreign places were recovered and brought back to Wincot, though it often cost, not heavy ransom only but desperate bloodshed as well, to obtain them. This superstition, if you please to call it so, has never died out of the family from that time to the present day; for centuries the succession of the dead in the vault at the Abbey has been unbroken – absolutely unbroken – until now. The place mentioned in the prediction as waiting to be filled, is Stephen Monkton's place; the voice that cries vainly to the earth for shelter is the voice of the dead. As surely as if I saw it, I know that they have left him unburied on the ground where he fell!'

He stopped me before I could utter a word in remonstrance, by slowly rising to his feet, and pointing in the same direction towards which his eyes had wandered a short time since.

'I can guess what you want to ask me,' he exclaimed, sternly and loudly; 'you want to ask me how I can be mad enough to believe in a doggerel prophecy, uttered in an age of superstition to awe the most ignorant hearers. I answer' (at those words his voice sank suddenly to a whisper), 'I answer, because *Stephen Monkton himself stands there at this moment, confirming me in my belief.'*

Whether it was the awe and horror that looked out ghastly from his face as he confronted me, whether it was that I had never hitherto fairly believed in the reports about his madness, and that the conviction of their truth now forced itself upon me on a sudden I know not; but I felt my blood curdling as he spoke, and I knew in my own heart, as I sat there speechless, that I dare not turn round and look where he was still pointing close at my side.

'I see there,' he went on in the same whispering voice, 'the figure of a dark-complexioned man, standing up with his head uncovered. One of his hands, still clutching a pistol, has fallen to his side; the other presses a bloody handkerchief over his mouth. The spasm of mortal agony convulses his features; but I know them for the features of a swarthy man, who twice frightened me by taking me up in his arms when I was a child, at Wincot Abbey. I asked the nurses at the time who that man was, and they told me it was my uncle, Stephen Monkton. Plainly, as if he stood there living, I see him now at your side, with the death-glare in his great black eyes; and so have I ever seen him since the moment when he was shot; at home and abroad, waking or sleeping, day and night, we are always together wherever I go!'

His whispering tones sank into almost inaudible murmuring as he pronounced these last words. From the direction and expression of his eyes, I suspected that he was speaking to the apparition. If I had beheld it myself at that moment, it would have been, I think, a less horrible sight to witness than to see him, as I saw him now, muttering inarticulately at vacancy. My own nerves were more shaken than I could have thought possible by what had passed. A vague dread of being near him in his present mood came over me, and I moved back a step or two.

He noticed the action instantly.

'Don't go! – pray, pray don't go! Have I alarmed you? Don't you believe me? Do the lights make your eyes ache? I only asked you to sit in the glare of the candles because I could not bear to see the light that always shines from the phantom there at dusk, shining over you as you sat in the shadow. Don't go – don't leave me yet!'

There was an utter forlornness, an unspeakable misery in his face as he said those words, which gave me back my self-possession by the simple process of first moving me to pity. I resumed my chair, and said that I would stay with him as long as he wished.

'Thank you a thousand times! You are patience and kindness itself,' he said, going back to his former place, and resuming his former gentleness of manner. 'Now that I have got over my first confession of the misery that follows me in secret wherever I go, I think I can tell you calmly all that remains to be told. You see, as I said, my uncle Stephen,' – he turned away his head quickly, and looked down at the table as the name passed his lips – 'my uncle Stephen came twice to Wincot while I was a child, and on both occasions frightened me dreadfully. He only took me up in his arms, and spoke to me – very kindly, as I afterwards heard, for *him* – but he terrified me, nevertheless. Perhaps I was frightened at his great stature, his swarthy complexion, and his thick black hair and moustache, as other children might have been; perhaps the mere sight of him had some strange influence on me which I could not then understand, and cannot now explain. However it was, I used to dream of him long after he had gone away; and to fancy that he was stealing on me to catch me up in his arms, whenever I was left in the dark. The servants who took care of me found this out, and used to threaten me with my uncle Stephen whenever I was perverse and difficult to manage. As I grew up, I still retained my vague dread and abhorrence of our absent relative. I always listened intently, yet without knowing why, whenever his name was mentioned by my father or my mother – listened with an unaccountable presentiment that something terrible had happened to him, or was about to happen to me. This feeling only changed when I was left alone in the Abbey; and then it seemed to merge into the eager curiosity which had begun to grow on me rather before that time, about the origin of the ancient prophecy predicting the extinction of our race. Are you following me?'

'I follow every word with the closest attention.'

'You must know, then, that I had first found out some fragments of the old rhyme, in which the prophecy occurs, quoted as a curiosity in an antiquarian book in the library. On the page opposite this quotation, had been pasted a rude old woodcut, representing a dark-haired man, whose face was so strangely like what I remembered of my uncle Stephen, that the portrait absolutely startled me. When I asked my father about this – it was then just before his death – he either knew, or pretended to know, nothing of it; and when I afterwards mentioned the prediction he fretfully changed the subject. It was just the same with our chaplain when I spoke to him. He said the portrait had been done centuries before my uncle was born; and called the prophecy doggerel and nonsense. I used to argue with him on the latter point, asking why we Catholics, who believed that the gift of working miracles had never departed from certain favoured persons, might not just as well believe that the gift of prophecy had never departed either? He would not dispute with me; he would only say that I must not waste time in thinking of such trifles, that I had more imagination than was good for me, and must suppress instead of exciting it. Such advice as this only irritated my curiosity. I determined secretly to search through the oldest uninhabited part of the Abbey, and to try if I could not find out from forgotten family records what the portrait was, and when the prophecy had been first written or uttered. Did you ever pass a day alone in the long-deserted chambers of an ancient house?'

'Never; such solitude as that is not at all to my taste.'

'Ah! what a life it was when I began my search. I should like to live it over again! Such tempting suspense, such strange discoveries, such wild fancies, such enthralling terrors, all belonged to that life! Only think of breaking open the door of a room which no living soul had entered before you for nearly a hundred years! think of the first step forward into a region of airless, awful stillness, where the light falls faint and sickly through closed windows and rotting curtains! think of the ghostly creaking of the old floor that cries out on you for treading on it, step as softly as you will! think of arms, helmets, weird tapestries of bygone days, that seem to be moving out on you from the walls as you first walk up to them in the dim light! think of prying into great cabinets and iron-clasped chests, not knowing what horrors may appear when you tear them open! or poring over their contents till twilight stole on you, and darkness grew terrible in the lonely place! of trying to leave it, and not being able to go, as if something held you; of wind wailing outside; of shadows darkening round you, and closing you up in obscurity within. Only think of these things, and you may imagine the fascination of suspense and terror in such a life as mine was in those past days!'

(I shrunk from imagining that life: it was bad enough to see its results, as I saw them before me now.)

'Well, my search lasted months and months; then it was suspended a little, then resumed. In whatever direction I pursued it, I always found something to lure me on. Terrible confessions of past crimes, shocking proofs of secret wickedness that had been hidden securely from all eyes but mine, came to light. Sometimes these discoveries were associated with particular parts of the Abbey, which have had a horrible interest of their own for me ever since. Sometimes with certain old portraits in the picture-gallery, which I actually dreaded to look at, after what I had found out. There were periods when the results of this search of mine so horrified me, that I determined to give it up entirely; but I never could persevere in my resolution, the temptation to go on seemed at certain intervals to get too strong for me, and then I yielded to it again and again. At last I found the book that had belonged to the monks, with the whole of the prophecy written in the blank leaf. This first success encouraged me to get back further yet in the family records. I had discovered nothing hitherto of the identity of the mysterious portrait, but the same intuitive conviction which had assured me of its extraordinary resemblance to my uncle Stephen, seemed also to assure me that he must be more closely connected with the prophecy, and must know more of it than anyone else. I had no means of holding any communication with him, no means of satisfying myself whether this strange idea of mine were right or wrong, until the day when my doubts were settled for ever, by the same terrible proof which is now present to me in this very room.'

He paused for a moment, and looked at me intently and suspiciously; then asked if I believed all he had said to me so far. My instant reply in the affirmative seemed to satisfy his doubts, and he went on:

'On a fine evening in February, I was standing alone in one of the deserted rooms of the western turret at the Abbey looking at the sunset. Just before the sun went down, I felt a sensation stealing over me which it is impossible to explain. I saw nothing, heard nothing, knew nothing. This utter self-oblivion came suddenly; it was not fainting, for I did not fall to the ground, did not move an inch from my place. If such a thing could be, I should say it was the temporary separation of soul and body, without death: but all description of my situation at that time is impossible. Call my state what you will, trance or catalepsy, I know that I remained standing by the window utterly unconscious – dead, mind and body – until the sun had set. Then I came to my senses again; and then, when I opened my eyes, there was the apparition of Stephen Monkton standing opposite to me, faintly luminous, just as it stands opposite me at this very moment by your side.'

'Was this before the news of the duel reached England?' I asked.

'*Two weeks before* the news of it reached us at Wincot. And even when we heard of the duel, we did not hear of the day on which it was fought. I only found that out when the document which you have read was published in the French newspaper. The date of that document, you will remember, is February 22nd, and it is stated that the duel was fought two days afterwards. I wrote down in my pocket-book, on the evening when I saw the phantom, the day of the month on which it first appeared to me. That day was the 24th of February.'

He paused again, as if expecting me to say something. After the words he had just spoken, what could I say? what could I think?

'Even in the first horror of first seeing the apparition,' he went on, 'the prophecy against our house came to my mind, and with it the conviction that I beheld before me, in that spectral presence, the warning of my own doom. As soon as I recovered a little, I determined, nevertheless, to test the reality of what I saw – to find out whether I was the dupe of my own diseased fancy, or not. I left the turret; the phantom left it with me. I made an excuse to have the drawing-room at the Abbey brilliantly lighted up – the figure was still opposite me. I walked out into the park – it was there in the clear starlight. I went away from home, and travelled many miles to the seaside; still the tall dark man in his death agony was with me. After this, I strove against the fatality no more. I returned to the Abbey, and tried to resign myself to my misery. But this was not to be. I had a hope that was dearer to me than my own life; I had one treasure belonging to me that I shuddered at the prospect of losing, and when the phantom presence stood a warning obstacle between me and this one treasure, this dearest hope – then my misery grew heavier than I could bear. You know what I am alluding to; you must have heard often that I was engaged to be married?'

'Yes, often. I have some acquaintance myself with Miss Elmslie.'

'You never can know all she has sacrificed for me – never can imagine what I have felt for years and years past' – his voice trembled, and the tears came into his eyes – 'but I dare not trust myself to speak of that: the thought of the old happy days in the Abbey almost breaks my heart now. Let me get back to the other subject. I must tell you that I kept the frightful vision which pursued me, at all times, and in all places, a secret from everybody; knowing the vile reports about my having inherited madness from my family, and fearing that an unfair advantage would be taken of any confession that I might make. Though the phantom always stood opposite to me, and therefore always appeared either before or by the side of any person to whom I spoke, I soon schooled myself to hide from others that I was looking at it, except on rare occasions – when I have perhaps betrayed myself to you. But my self-possession availed me nothing with Ada. The day of our marriage was approaching.'

He stopped and shuddered. I waited in silence till he had controlled himself.

'Think,' he went on, 'think of what I must have suffered at looking always on that hideous vision, whenever I looked on my betrothed wife! Think of my taking her hand, and seeming to take it through the figure of the apparition! Think of the calm angel-face and the tortured spectre-face being always together, whenever my eyes met hers! Think of this, and you will not wonder that I betrayed my secret to her. She eagerly entreated to know the worst – nay more, she insisted on knowing it. At her bidding I told all; and then left her free to break our engagement. The thought of death was in my heart as I spoke the parting words – death by my own act, if life still held out after our separation. She suspected that thought; she knew it, and never left me till her good influence had destroyed it for ever. But for her, I should not have been alive now – but for her, I should never have attempted the project which has brought me here.'

'Do you mean that it was Miss Elmslie's suggestion that you came to Naples?' I asked in amazement.

'I mean that what she said, suggested the design which has brought me to Naples,' he answered. 'While I believed that the phantom had appeared to me as the fatal messenger of death, there was no comfort, there was misery rather in hearing her say that no power on earth should make her desert me, and that she would live for me, and for me only, through every trial. But it was far different when we afterwards reasoned together about the purpose which the apparition had come to fulfil – far different when she showed me that its mission might be for good, instead of for evil; and that the warning it was sent to give, might be to my profit instead of to my loss. At those words, the new idea which gave the new hope of life came to me in an instant. I believed then, what I believe now, that I have a supernatural warrant for my errand here. In that faith I live; without it I should die. *She* never ridiculed it, never scorned it as insanity. Mark what I say! The spirit that appeared to me in the Abbey, that has never left me since, that stands there now by your side, warns me to escape from the fatality which hangs over our race, and commands me, if I would avoid it, to bury the unburied dead. Mortal loves and mortal interests must bow to that awful bidding. The spectre-presence will never leave me till I have sheltered the corpse that cries to the earth to cover it! I dare not return – I dare not marry till I have filled the place that is empty in Wincot vault.'

His eyes flashed and dilated; his voice deepened; a fanatic ecstacy shone in his expression as he uttered these words. Shocked and grieved as I was, I made no attempt to remonstrate or to reason with him. It would have been useless to have referred to any of the usual common-places about optical delusions, or diseased imaginations – worse than useless to have attempted to account by natural causes for any of the extraordinary coincidences and events of which he had spoken. Briefly as he had referred to Miss Elmslie, he had said enough to show that the only hope of the poor girl who loved him best and had known him longest of any one, was in humouring his delusions to the last. How faithfully she still clung to the belief that she could restore him! How resolutely was she sacrificing herself to his morbid fancies, in the hope of a happy future that might never come! Little as I knew of Miss Elmslie, the mere thought of her situation, as I now reflected on it, made me feel sick at heart.

'They call me "Mad Monkton!"' he exclaimed, suddenly breaking the silence between us during the last few minutes.

'Here and in England everybody believes I am out of my senses, except Ada and you. She has been my salvation; and you will be my salvation too. Something told me that, when I first met you walking in the Villa Reale. I struggled against the strong desire that was in me to trust my secret to you; but I could resist it no longer when I saw you tonight at the ball – the phantom seemed to draw me on to you, as you stood alone in the quiet room. Tell me more of that idea of yours about finding the place where the duel was fought. If I set out tomorrow to seek for it myself, where must I go first? – where?' He stopped; his strength was evidently becoming exhausted, and his mind was growing confused. 'What am I to do! I can't remember. You know everything – will you not help me? My misery had made me unable to help myself!'

He stopped, murmured something about failing if he went to the frontier alone, and spoke confusedly of delays that might be fatal; then tried to utter the name of 'Ada'; but in pronouncing the first letter his voice faltered, and turning abruptly from me he burst into tears.

My pity for him got the better of my prudence at that moment, and without thinking of responsibilities, I promised at once to do for him whatever he asked. The wild triumph in his expression, as he started up and seized my hand, showed me that I had better have been more cautious; but it was too late now to retract what I had said. The next best thing to do was to try if I could not induce him to compose himself a little, and then to go away and think coolly over the whole affair by myself.

'Yes, yes,' he rejoined, in answer to the few words I now spoke to try and calm him, 'don't be afraid about me. After what you have said, I'll answer for my own coolness and composure under all emergencies. I have been so long used to the apparition that I hardly feel its presence at all except on rare occasions. Besides, I have here, in this little packet of letters, the medicine for every malady of the sick heart. They are Ada's letters; I read them to calm me whenever my misfortune seems to get the better of my endurance. I wanted that half hour to read them in tonight, before you came, to make myself fit to see you; and I shall go through them again after you are gone. So, once more don't be afraid about me. I know I shall succeed with your help; and Ada shall thank you as you deserve to be thanked when we get back to England. If you hear the fools at Naples talk about my being mad, don't trouble yourself to contradict them: the scandal is so contemptible that it must end by contradicting itself.'

I left him, promising to return early the next day.

When I got back to my hotel, I felt that any idea of sleeping, after all that I had seen and heard, was out of the question. So I lit my pipe, and sitting by the window – how it refreshed my mind just then to look at the calm moonlight! – tried to think what it would be best to do. In the first place, any appeal to doctors or to Alfred's friends in England was out of the question. I could not persuade myself that his intellect was sufficiently disordered to justify me, under existing circumstances, in disclosing the secret which he had entrusted to my keeping. In the second place, all attempts on my part to induce him to abandon the idea of searching out his uncle's remains would be utterly useless after what I had incautiously said to him. Having settled these two conclusions, the only really great difficulty which remained to perplex me was whether I was justified in aiding him to execute his extraordinary purpose.

Supposing that with my help he found Mr. Monkton's body, and took it back with him to England, was it right in me thus to lend myself to promoting the marriage which would most likely follow these events – a marriage which it might be the duty of every one to prevent at all hazards? This set me thinking about the extent of his madness, or, to speak more mildly and more correctly, of his delusion. Sane he certainly was on ordinary subjects; nay, in all the narrative parts of what he had said to me on this very evening he had spoken clearly and connectedly. As for the story of the apparition, other men, with intellects as clear as the intellects of their neighbours, had fancied themselves pursued by a phantom, and had even written about it in a high strain of philosophical speculation. It was plain that the real hallucination in the case now before me, lay in Monkton's conviction of the truth of the old prophesy, and in his idea that the fancied apparition was a supernatural warning to him to evade its denunciations. And it was equally clear that both delusions had been produced, in the first instance, by the lonely life he had led, acting on a naturally excitable temperament, which was rendered further liable to moral disease by an hereditary taint of insanity.

Was this curable? Miss Elmslie, who knew him far better than I did, seemed by her conduct to think so. Had I any reason or right to determine offhand that she was mistaken? Supposing I refused to go to the frontier with him, he would then most certainly depart by himself, to commit all sorts of errors, and perhaps to meet with all sorts of accidents; while I, an idle man, with my time entirely at my own disposal, was stopping at Naples, and leaving him to his fate after I had suggested the plan of his expedition, and had encouraged him to confide in me. In this way I kept turning the subject over and over again in my mind – being quite free, let me add, from looking at it in any other than a practical point of view. I firmly believed, as a derider of all ghost stories, that Alfred was deceiving himself in fancying that he had seen the apparition of his uncle, before the news of Mr. Monkton's death reached England; and I was on this account therefore uninfluenced by the slightest infection of my unhappy friend's delusions, when I at last fairly decided to accompany him in his extraordinary search. Possibly my harum-scarum fondness for excitement at that time, biassed me a little in forming my resolution; but I must add, in common justice to myself, that I also acted from motives of real sympathy for Monkton, and from a sincere wish to allay, if I could, the anxiety of the poor girl who was still so faithfully waiting and hoping for him far away in England.

Certain arrangements preliminary to our departure, which I found myself obliged to make after a second interview with Alfred, betrayed the object of our journey to most of our Neapolitan friends. The astonishment of everybody was of course unbounded, and the nearly universal suspicion that I must be as mad in my way as Monkton himself, showed itself pretty plainly in my presence. Some people actually tried to combat my resolution by telling me what a shameless profligate Stephen Monkton had been – as if I had a strong personal interest in hunting out his remains! Ridicule moved me as little as any arguments of this sort; my mind was made up, and I was as obstinate then as I am now.

In two days' time I had got everything ready, and had ordered the travelling carriage to the door some hours earlier than we had originally settled. We were jovially threatened with 'a parting cheer' by all our English acquaintances, and I thought it desirable to avoid this on my friend's account; for he had been more excited, as it was, by the preparations for the journey than I at all liked. Accordingly, soon after sunrise, without a soul in the street to stare at us, we privately left Naples.

Nobody will wonder, I think, that I experienced some difficulty in realising my own position, and shrank instinctively from looking forward a single day into the future, when I now found myself starting, in company with 'Mad Monkton', to hunt for the body of a dead duellist all along the frontier line of the Roman states!

CHAPTER V

I had settled it in my own mind that we had better make the town of Fondi, close on the frontier, our headquarters, to begin with; and I had arranged, with the assistance of the Embassy, that the leaden coffin should follow us so far, securely nailed up in its packing case. Besides our passports, we were well furnished with letters of introduction to the local authorities at most of the important frontier towns, and to crown all, we had money enough at our command (thanks to Monkton's vast fortune) to make sure of the services of anyone whom we wanted to assist us, all along our line of search. These various resources ensured us every facility for action – provided always that we succeeded in discovering the body of the dead duellist. But, in the very probable event of our failing to do this, our future prospects – more especially after the responsibility I had undertaken – were of anything but an agreeable nature to contemplate. I confess I felt uneasy, almost hopeless, as we posted, in the dazzling Italian sunshine, along the road to Fondi.

We made an easy two days' journey of it; for I had insisted, on Monkton's account, that we should travel slowly.

On the first day the excessive agitation of my companion a little alarmed me; he showed, in many ways, more symptoms of a disordered mind that I had yet observed in him. On the second day, however, he seemed to get accustomed to contemplate calmly the new idea of the search on which we were bent, and, except on one point, he was cheerful and composed enough. Whenever his dead uncle formed the subject of conversation, he still persisted – on the strength of the old prophecy, and under the influence of the apparition which he saw, or thought he saw, always – in asserting that the corpse of Stephen Monkton, wherever it was, lay yet unburied. On every other topic he deferred to me with the utmost readiness and docility; on this, he maintained his strange opinion with an obstinacy which set reason and persuasion alike at defiance.

On the third day we rested at Fondi. The packing-case with the coffin in it, reached us, and was deposited in a safe place under lock and key. We engaged some mules, and found a man to act as guide who knew the country thoroughly. It occurred to me that we had better begin by confiding the real object of our journey only to the most trustworthy people we could find among the better-educated classes. For this reason we followed, in one respect, the example of the duelling-party, by starting, early on the morning of the fourth day, with sketch-books and colour-boxes, as if we were only artists in search of the picturesque.

After travelling some hours in a northerly direction within the Roman frontier, we halted to rest ourselves and our mules at a wild little village, far out of the track of tourists in general.

The only person of the smallest importance in the place was the priest, and to him I addressed my first inquiries, leaving Monkton to await my return with the guide. I spoke Italian quite fluently and correctly enough for my purpose, and was extremely polite and cautious in introducing my business; but, in spite of all the pains I took, I only succeeded in frightening and bewildering the poor priest more and more with every fresh word I said to him. The idea of a duelling-party and a dead man seemed to scare him out of his senses. He bowed, fidgeted, cast his eyes up to heaven, and piteously shrugging his shoulders, told me, with rapid Italian circumlocution, that he had not the faintest idea of what I was talking about. This was my first failure. I confess I was weak enough to feel a little dispirited when I joined Monkton and the guide.

After the heat of the day was over, we resumed our journey.

About three miles from the village, the road, or rather cart-track, branched off in two directions. The path to the right, our guide informed us, led up among the mountains to a convent about six miles off. If we penetrated beyond the convent, we should soon reach the Neapolitan frontier. The path to the left led far inwards on the Roman territory, and would conduct us to a small town where we could sleep for the night. Now the Roman territory presented the first and fittest field for our search, and the convent was always within reach, supposing we returned to Fondi unsuccessful. Besides, the path to the left led over the widest part of the country we were starting to explore; and I was always for vanquishing the greatest difficulty first – so we decided manfully on turning left. The expedition in which this resolution involved us lasted a whole week, and produced no results. We discovered absolutely nothing, and returned to our headquarters at Fondi so completely baffled that we did not know whither to turn our steps next.

I was made much more uneasy by the effect of our failure on Monkton than by the failure itself. His resolution appeared to break down altogether as soon as we began to retrace our steps. He became first fretful and capricious, then silent and desponding. Finally, he sank into a lethargy of body and mind that seriously alarmed me. On the morning after our return to Fondi, he showed a strange tendency to sleep incessantly, which made me suspect the existence of some physical malady in his brain. The whole day he hardly exchanged a word with me, and seemed to be never fairly awake. Early the next morning I went into his room, and found him as silent and lethargic as ever. His servant, who was with us, informed me that Alfred had once or twice before exhibited such physical symptoms of mental exhaustion as we were now observing during his father's lifetime at Wincot Abbey. This piece of information made me feel easier, and left my mind free to return to the consideration of the errand which had brought us to Fondi.

I resolved to occupy the time until my companion got better in prosecuting our search by myself. That path to the right hand which led to the convent, had not yet been explored. If I set off to trace it, I need not be away from Monkton more than one night; and I should at least be able on my return to give him the satisfaction of knowing that one more uncertainty regarding the place of the duel had been cleared up. These considerations decided me. I left a message for my friend, in case he asked where I had gone, and set out once more for the village at which we had halted when starting on our first expedition.

Intending to walk to the convent, I parted company with the guide and the mules where the track branched off, leaving them to go back to the village and await my return.

For the first four miles the path gently ascended through an open country, then became abruptly much steeper, and led me deeper and deeper among the thickets and endless woods. By the time my watch informed me that I must have nearly walked my appointed distance, the view was bounded on all sides, and the sky was shut out overhead, by an impervious screen of leaves and branches. I still followed my only guide, the steep path; and in ten minutes, emerging suddenly on a plot of tolerably clear and level ground, I saw the convent before me.

It was a dark, low, sinister-looking place. Not a sign of life or movement was visible anywhere about it. Green stains streaked the once white facade of the chapel in all directions. Moss clustered thick in every crevice of the heavy scowling wall that surrounded the convent. Long lank weeds grew out of the fissures of roof and parapet, and drooping far downward, waved wearily in and out of the barred dormitory windows. The very cross opposite the entrance-gate, with a shocking life-sized figure in wood nailed to it, was so beset at the base with crawling creatures, and looked so slimy green, and rotten all the way up, that I absolutely shrank from it.

A bell rope with a broken handle hung by the gate. I approached it – hesitated, I hardly knew why – looked up at the convent again, and then walked round to the back of the building, partly to gain time to consider what I had better do next; partly from an unaccountable curiosity that urged me, strangely to myself, to see all I could of the outside of the place before I attempted to gain admission at the gate.

At the back of the convent I found an outhouse, built on to the wall – a clumsy, decayed building, with the greater part of the roof fallen in, and with a jagged hole in one of its sides, where in all probability a window had once been. Behind the outhouse the trees grew thicker than ever. As I looked towards them, I could not determine whether the ground beyond me rose or fell – whether it was grassy, or earthy, or rocky. I could see nothing but the all-pervading leaves, brambles, ferns, and long grass.

Not a sound broke the oppressive stillness. No bird's note rose from the leafy wilderness around me; no voices spoke in the convent garden behind the scowling wall; no clock struck in the chapel-tower; no dog barked in the ruined outhouse. The dead silence deepened the solitude of the place inexpressibly. I began to feel it weighing on my spirits – the more because woods were never favourite places with me to walk in. The sort of pastoral happiness which poets often represent, when they sing of life in the woods, never, to my mind, has half the charm of life on the mountain or in the plain. When I am in a wood, I miss the boundless loveliness of the sky, and the delicious softness that distance gives to the earthly view beneath. I feel oppressively the change which the free air suffers when it gets imprisoned among leaves; and I am always awed, rather than pleased, by that mysterious still light which shines with such a strange dim lustre in deep places among trees. It may convict me of want of taste and absence of due feeling for the marvellous beauties of vegetation, but I must frankly own that I never penetrate far into wood without finding that the getting out of it again is the pleasantest part of my walk – the getting out on to the barest down, the wildest hillside, the bleakest mountain-top – the getting out anywhere so that I can see the sky over me and the view before me as far as my eye can reach.

After such a confession as I have now made, it will appear surprising to no one that I should have felt the strongest possible inclination, while I stood by the ruined outhouse, to retrace my steps at once, and make the best of my way out of the wood. I had indeed actually turned to depart, when the remembrance of the errand which had brought me to the convent suddenly stayed my feet. It seemed doubtful whether I should be admitted into the building if I rang the bell; and more than doubtful if I were let in, whether the inhabitants would be able to afford me any clue to the information of which I was in search. However, it was my duty to Monkton to leave no means of helping him in his desperate object untried; so I resolved to go round to the front of the convent again, and ring the gate-bell at all hazards.

By the merest chance I looked up as I passed the side of the outhouse where the jagged hole was, and noticed that it was pierced rather high in the wall.

As I stopped to observe this, the closeness of the atmosphere in the wood seemed to be affecting me more unpleasantly than ever.

I waited a minute and untied my cravat.

Closeness? – surely it was something more than that. The air was even more distasteful to my nostrils than to my lungs. There was some faint, indescribable smell loading it – some smell of which I thought (now that my attention was directed to it) grew more and more certainly traceable to its source the nearer I advanced to the outhouse.

By the time I had tried the experiment two or three times, and had made myself sure of this fact, my curiosity became excited. There was plenty of fragments of stone and brick lying about me. I gathered some of them together, and piled them up below the hole, then mounted to the top, and feeling rather ashamed of what I was doing, peeped into the outhouse.

The sight of horror that met my eyes the instant I looked through the hole, is as present to my memory now as if I had beheld it yesterday. I can hardly write of it at this distance of time without a thrill of the old terror running through me again to the heart.

The first impression conveyed to me, as I looked in, was of a long recumbent object, extended on trestles, and bearing a

certain hideous, half-formed resemblance to the human face
and figure. I looked again, and felt certain of it. There were
the prominences of the forehead, nose and chin, dimly
shown as under a veil – there, the round outline of the chest,
and the hollow below it – there, the points of the knees, and
the stiff, ghastly upturned feet. I looked again, yet more
attentively. My eyes got accustomed to the dim light stream-
ing in through the broken roof; and I satisfied myself,
judging by the great length of the body from head to foot,
that I was looking at the corpse of a man – a corpse that had
apparently once had a sheet spread over it – and that had lain
rotting on the trestles under the open sky long enough for
the linen to take the livid, light-blue tinge of mildew and
decay which now covered it.

How long I remained with my eyes fixed on that dread
sight of death, on that tombless, terrible wreck of humanity,
poisoning the still air, and seeming even to stain the faint
descending light that disclosed it, I know not. I remember a
dull, distant sound among the trees, as if the breeze were
rising – the slow creeping on of the sound near the place
where I stood – the noiseless, whirling fall of a dead leaf on
the corpse below me, through the gap in the outhouse roof –
and the effect of awakening my energies, of relaxing the
heavy strain on my mind, which even the slight change
wrought in the scene I beheld by the falling leaf, produced in
me immediately. I descended to the ground, and, sitting
down on the heap of stones, wiped away the thick perspiration which covered my face, and which I now became aware
of for the first time. It was something more than the hideous
spectacle unexpectedly offered to my eyes which had shaken
my nerves, as I felt that they were shaken now. Monkton's
prediction that, if we succeeded in discovering his uncle's
body, we should find it unburied, recurred to me the instant
I saw the trestles and their ghastly burden. I felt assured on
the instant that I had found the dead man – the old prophecy
recurred to my memory – a strange yearning sorrow, a
vague foreboding of ill, an inexplicable terror, as I thought of
the poor lad who was awaiting my return in the distant
town, struck through me with a chill of superstitious dread,
robbed me of my judgement and resolution, and left me,

when I had at last recovered myself, weak and dizzy as if I had just suffered under some pang of overpowering physical pain.

I hastened round to the convent gate, and rang immediately at the bell – waited a little while, and rang again – then heard footsteps.

In the middle of the gate, just opposite my face, there was a small sliding panel, not more than a few inches long; this was presently pushed aside from within. I saw, through a bit of iron grating, two dull, light grey eyes staring vacantly at me, and heard a feeble, husky voice saying:–

'What do you please to want?'

'I am a traveller – ' I began.

'We live in a miserable place. We have nothing to show travellers here.'

'I don't come to see anything. I have an important question to ask, which I believe someone in this convent will be able to answer. If you are not willing to let me in, at least come out and speak to me here.'

'Are you alone?'

'Quite alone.'

'Are there no women with you?'

'None.'

The gate was slowly unbarred; and an old Capuchin, very infirm, very suspicious, and very dirty, stood before me. I was far too excited and impatient to waste any time in prefatory phrases; so telling the monk at once how I had looked through the hole in the outhouse, and what I had seen inside, I asked him in plain terms who the man had been whose corpse I had beheld, and why the body was left unburied?

The old Capuchin listened to me with watery eyes that twinkled suspiciously. He had a battered tin snuff-box in his hand; and his finger and thumb slowly chased a few scattered grains of snuff round and round the inside of the box all the time I was speaking. When I had done, he shook his head, and said, 'that was certainly an ugly sight in their outhouse; one of the ugliest sights, he felt sure, that ever I had seen in all my life!'

'I don't want to talk of the sight,' I rejoined impatiently; 'I want to know who the man was, how he died, and why he is not decently buried. Can you tell me?'

The monk's finger and thumb having captured three or four grains of snuff at last, he slowly drew them into his nostrils, holding the box open under his nose the while, to prevent the possibility of wasting even one grain, sniffed once or twice, luxuriously – closed the box – then looked at me again, with his eyes watering and twinkling more suspiciously than before.

'Yes,' said the monk, 'that's an ugly sight in our outhouse – a very ugly sight, certainly!'

I never had more difficulty in keeping my temper in my life, than at that moment. I succeeded, however, in repressing a very disrespectful expression on the subject of monks in general, which was on the tip of my tongue, and made another attempt to conquer the old man's exasperating reserve. Fortunately for my chances of succeeding with him, I was a snuff-taker myself; and I had a box full of excellent English snuff in my pocket, which I now produced as a bribe. It was my last resource.

'I thought your box seemed empty just now,' said I; 'will you try a pinch out of mine?'

The offer was accepted with an almost youthful alacrity of gesture. The Capuchin took the largest pinch I ever saw held between any man's finger and thumb, inhaled it slowly, without spilling a single grain – half closed his eyes – and, wagging his head gently, patted me paternally on the back.

'Oh! my son!' said the monk, 'what delectable snuff! Oh, my son and amiable traveller, give the spiritual father who loves you, yet another tiny, tiny pinch!'

'Let me fill your box for you. I shall have plenty left for myself.'

The battered tin snuff-box was given to me before I had done speaking – the paternal hand patted my back more approvingly than ever – the feeble, husky voice grew glib and eloquent in my praise. I had evidently found out the weak side of the old Capuchin; and, on returning him his box, I took instant advantage of the discovery.

'Excuse my troubling you on the subject again,' I said, 'but I have particular reasons for wanting to hear all that you can tell me in explanation of that horrible sight in the outhouse.'

'Come in,' answered the monk.

He drew me inside the gate, closed it, and then leading the way across a grass-grown courtyard, looking out on a weedy kitchen garden, showed me into a long room with a low ceiling, a dirty dresser, a few rudely-carved stall seats, and one or two grim mildewed pictures for ornaments. This was the sacristy.

'There's nobody here, and it's nice and cool,' said the old Capuchin. It was so damp that I actually shivered. 'Would you like to see the church?' said the monk; 'a jewel of a church, if we could only keep it in repair; but we can't. Ah! malediction and misery, we are too poor to keep our church in repair!'

Here he shook his head, and began fumbling with a large bunch of keys.

'Never mind the church now!' said I 'Can you, or can you not, tell me what I want to know?'

'Everything, from beginning to end – absolutely every-thing! Why, I answered the gate-bell – I always answer the gate-bell here,' said the Capuchin.

'What, in heaven's name, has the gate bell to do with the unburied corpse in your outhouse?'

'Listen, son of mine, and you shall know. Some time ago – some months – ah, me, I'm old; I've lost my memory; I don't know how many months – ah! miserable me, what a very old, old monk I am!' Here he comforted himself with another pinch of my snuff.

'Never mind the exact time,' said I. 'I don't care about that.'

'Good,' said the Capuchin. 'Now I can go on. Well, let us say, it is some months ago – we in this convent are all at breakfast – wretched, wretched breakfast, son of mine in this convent! – we are at breakfast, and we hear *bang! bang!* twice over. "Guns," says I. "What are they shooting for?" says brother Jeremy. "Game," says brother Vincent. "Aha! game," says brother Jeremy. "If I hear more, I shall send out and discover what it means," says the father superior. We hear no more, and we go on with our wretched breakfasts.'

'Where did the report of firearms come from?' I inquired.

'From down below, beyond the big trees at the back of the convent, where there's some clear ground – nice ground, if it wasn't for the pools and puddles. But, ah, misery! how damp we are in these parts! how very, very damp!'

'Well, what happened after the report of firearms?'

'You shall hear. We are still at breakfast, all silent – for what have we to talk about here? What have we but our devotions, our kitchen garden, and our wretched, wretched bits of breakfasts and dinners? I say we are all silent, when there comes suddenly such a ring at the bell as never was heard before – a very devil of a ring – a ring that caught us all with our bits – our wretched, wretched bits! – in our mouths, and stopped us before we could swallow them. "Go, brother of mine!" says the father superior to me – "go, it is your duty – go to the gate." I am brave – a very lion of a Capuchin. I slip out on tiptoe – I wait – I listen – I pull back our little shutter in the gate – I wait, I listen again – I peep through the hole – nothing, absolutely nothing, that I can see. I am brave – I am not to be daunted. What do I do next! I open the gate. Ah! Sacred Mother of Heaven, what do I behold lying all along our threshold? A man – dead! – a big man; bigger than you, bigger than me, bigger than anybody in this convent – buttoned up tight in a fine coat, with black eyes, staring, staring up at the sky; and blood soaking through and through the front of his shirt. What do I do? I scream once – I scream twice – and run back to the father superior!'

All the particulars of the fatal duel which I had gleaned from the French newspaper in Monkton's room at Naples, recurred vividly to my memory. The suspicion that I had felt when I looked into the outhouse, became a certainty as I listened to the old monk's last words.

'So far I understand,' said I. 'The corpse I have just seen in the outhouse, is the corpse of the man whom you found dead outside your gate. Now tell me why you have not given the remains decent burial?'

'Wait – wait – wait,' answered the Capuchin. 'The father superior hears me scream, and comes out; we all run together to the gate; we lift up the big man, and look at him close. Dead! dead as this' (smacking the dresser with his hand). 'We look again, and see a bit of paper pinned to the collar of his coat. Aha! son of mine, you start at that. I thought I should make you start at last.'

I have started indeed. That paper was doubtless the leaf mentioned in the second's unfinished narrative as having been torn out of his pocket-book, and inscribed with the statement of how the dead man had lost his life. If proof positive were wanted to identify the dead body, here was such proof found.

'What do you think was written on the bit of paper?' continued the Capuchin. 'We read, and shudder. This dead man has been killed in a duel – he, the desperate, the miserable, has died in the commission of mortal sin; and the men who saw the killing of him, ask us Capuchins, holy men, servants of Heaven, children of our lord the pope – they ask *us* to give him burial! Oh! but we are outraged when we read that; we groan, we wring our hands, we turn away, we tear our beards, we—'

'Wait one moment,' said I, seeing that the old man was heating himself with his narrative, and was likely, until I stopped him, to talk more and more fluently to less and less purpose – 'wait a moment. Have you preserved the paper that was pinned to the dead man's coat; and can I look at it?'

The Capuchin seemed on the point of giving me an answer, when he suddenly checked himself. I saw his eyes wander away from my face, and at the same moment heard a door softly opened and closed behind me.

Looking round immediately, I observed another monk in the sacristy – a tall, lean, black-bearded man, in whose presence my old friend with the snuff-box suddenly became quite decorous and devotional to look at. I suspected I was in the presence of the father superior; and I found that I was right the moment he addressed me.

'I am the father superior of this convent,' he said in quiet, clear tones, and looking me straight in the face while he spoke, with coldly attentive eyes. 'I have heard the latter part of your conversation, and I wish to know why you are so particularly anxious to see the piece of paper that was pinned to the dead man's coat?'

The coolness with which he avowed that he had been listening, and the quietly imperative manner in which he put his concluding questions, perplexed and startled me. I hardly knew at first what tone I ought to take in answering him. He observed my hesitation, and attributing it to the wrong cause, signed to the old Capuchin to retire. Humbly stroking his long grey beard, and furtively consoling himself with a private pinch of the 'delectable snuff,' my venerable friend shuffled out of the room, making a profound obeisance at the door just before he disappeared.

'Now,' said the father superior, as coldly as ever; 'I am waiting sir, for your reply.'

'You shall have it in the fewest possible words,' said I, answering him in his own tone. 'I find, to my disgust and horror, there is an unburied corpse in an outhouse attached to this convent. I believe that corpse to be the body of an English Gentleman of rank and fortune, who was killed in a duel. I have come into this neighbourhood, with the nephew and only relation of the slain man, for the express purpose of recovering his remains; and I wish to see the paper found on the body, because I believe that paper will identify it to the satisfaction of the relative to whom I have referred. Do you find my reply sufficiently straightforward? And do you mean to give me permission to look at the paper?'

'I am satisfied with your reply, and see no reason for refusing you a sight of the paper,' said the father superior; 'but I have something to say first. In speaking of the impression produced on you by beholding the corpse, you used the words "disgust" and "horror". This licence of expression in relation to what you have seen in the precincts of a convent, proves to me that you are out of the pale of the Holy Catholic Church. You have no right, therefore, to expect any explanation; but I will give you one, nevertheless, as a favour. The slain man died, unabsolved, in the commission of mortal sin. We infer so much from the paper which we found on his body; and we know, by the evidence of our own eyes and ears, that he was killed on the territories of the church, and in the act of committing direct violation of those special laws against the crime of duelling, the strict enforcement of which the holy father himself has urged on the faithful throughout his dominions, by letters signed with his own hand. Inside this convent the ground is consecrated; and we Catholics are not accustomed to bury the outlaws of our religion, the enemies of our Holy Father, and the violators of our most sacred laws, in consecrated ground. Outside this convent, we have no rights and no powers; and, if we had both, we should remember that we are monks, not grave-diggers, and that the only burial with which *we* can have any concern, is burial with prayers of the church. That is all the explanation I think it necessary to give. Wait for me here, and you shall see the paper.' With those words the father superior left the room as quietly as he had entered it.

I had hardly time to think over this bitter and ungracious explanation, and to feel a little piqued by the language and manner of the person who had given it to me, before the father superior returned with the paper in his hand. He placed it before me on the dresser; and I read hurriedly traced in pencil, the following lines:–

'*This paper is attached to the body of the late Mr. Stephen Monkton, an Englishman of distinction. He has been shot in a duel, conducted with perfect gallantry and honour on both sides. His body is placed at the door of this convent, to receive burial at the hands of its inmates, the survivors of the encounter being obliged to separate and secure their safety by immediate flight. I, the second of the slain man, and the writer of this explanation, certify, on my word of honour as a gentleman that the shot which killed my principal on the instant, was fired fairly, in the strictest accordance with the rules laid down beforehand for the conduct of the duel.*
(signed) '*F*'

'F.' I recognised easily enough as the initial letter of Monsieur Foulon's name, the second of Mr. Monkton, who had died of consumption at Paris.

The discovery and the identification were now complete. Nothing remained but to break the news to Alfred, and to get permission to remove the remains in the outhouse. I began almost to doubt the evidence of my own senses, when I reflected that the apparent impracticable object with which we had left Naples was already, by the merest chance, virtually accomplished.

'The evidence of the paper is decisive,' I said, handing it back. 'There can be no doubt that the remains in the outhouse are the remains of which we have been in search. May I inquire if any obstacles will be thrown in our way, should the late Mr. Monkton's nephew wish to remove his uncle's body to the family burial-place in England?'

'Where is this nephew?' asked the father superior.

'He is now waiting my return at the town of Fondi.'

'Is he in a position to prove his relationship?'

'Certainly; he has papers with him which will place it beyond a doubt.'

'Let him satisfy the civil authorities of his claim, and he need expect no obstacle to his wishes from anyone here.'

I was in no humour for talking a moment longer with my sour-tempered companion than I could help. The day was wearing on fast; and, whether night overtook me or not, I was resolved never to stop on my return till I got back to Fondi. Accordingly, after telling the father superior that he might expect to hear from me again immediately, I made my bow, and hastened out of the sacristy.

At the convent gate stood my old friend with the tin snuff-box, waiting to let me out.

'Bless you, my son,' said the venerable recluse, giving me a farewell pat on the shoulder; 'come back soon to your spiritual father who loves you; and amiably favour him with another tiny, tiny pinch of the delectable snuff.'

CHAPTER VI

I returned at the top of my speed to the village where I had left the mules, had the animals saddled immediately, and succeeded in getting back to Fondi a little before sunset.

While ascending the stairs of our hotel, I suffered under the most painful uncertainty as to how I should best communicate the news of my discovery to Alfred. If I could not succeed in preparing him properly for my tidings, the result – with such an organisation as his – might be fatal. On opening the door of his room, I felt by no means sure of myself; and when I confronted him, his manner of receiving me took me so much by surprise that, for a moment or two, I lost my self-possession altogether.

Every trace of the lethargy in which he was sunk when I had last seen him, had disappeared. His eyes were bright, his cheeks deeply flushed. As I entered, he started up, and refused my offered hand.

'You have not treated me like a friend,' he said passionately; 'you had no right to continue the search unless I searched with you – you had no right to leave me here alone. I was wrong to trust you: you are no better than all the rest of them.'

I had by this time recovered a little from my first astonishment, and was able to reply before he could say anything more. It was quite useless, in his present state, to reason with him, or to defend myself. I determined to risk everything, and break my news to him at once.

'You will treat me more justly, Monkton, when you know that I have been doing you good service during my absence,' I said. 'Unless I am greatly mistaken, the object for which we have left Naples may be nearer attainment by both of us than—'

The flush left his cheeks almost in an instant. Some expression in my face, or some tone in my voice, of which I was not conscious, had revealed to his nervously-quickened perception more than I had intended that he should know at first. His eyes fixed themselves intently on mine; his hand grasped my arm; and he said to me in an eager whisper:

'Tell me the truth at once. Have you found him?'

It was too late to hesitate. I answered in the affirmative.

'Buried or unburied?'

His voice rose abruptly as he put the question, and his unoccupied hand fastened on my other arm.

'Unburied.'

I had hardly uttered the word before the blood flew back into his cheeks; his eyes flashed again as they looked into mine, and he burst into a fit of triumphant laughter, which shocked and startled me inexpressibly.

'What did I tell you? What do you say to the old prophecy now?' he cried, dropping his hold on my arms, and pacing backwards and forwards in the room. 'Own you were wrong. Own it, as all Naples shall own it, when once I have got him safe in his coffin!'

His laughter grew more and more violent. I tried to quiet him in vain. His servant and the landlord of the inn entered the room; but they only added fuel to the fire, and I made them go out again. As I shut the door on them, I observed lying on a table near at hand, the packet of letters from Miss Elmslie, which my unhappy friend preserved with such care, and read and re-read with such unfailing devotion. Looking towards me just when I passed by the table, the letters caught his eyes. The new hope for the future, in connection with the writer of them, which my news was already awakening in his heart, seemed to overwhelm him in an instant at sight of the treasured memorials that reminded him of his betrothed wife. His laughter ceased, his face changed, he ran to the table, caught the letters up in his hand, looked from them to me for one moment with an altered expression which went to my heart, then sank down on his knees at the table, laid his face on the letters, and burst into tears. I let the new emotion have its way uninterruptedly, and quitted the room, without saying a word. When I returned, after a lapse of some little time, I found him sitting quietly in his chair, reading one of the letters from the packet which rested on his knee.

His look was kindness itself; his gesture almost womanly in its gentleness as he rose to meet me, and anxiously held out his hand.

He was quite calm enough now to hear in detail all that I had to tell him. I suppressed nothing but the particulars of the state in which I had found the corpse. I assumed no right of direction as to the share he was to take in our future proceedings, with the exception of insisting beforehand that he should leave the absolute superintendence of the removal of the body to me, and that he should be satisfied with a sight of M. Foulon's paper, after receiving my assurance that the remains placed in the coffin were really and truly the remains of which we had been in search.

'Your nerves are not so strong as mine,' I said, by way of apology for my apparent dictation; 'and for that reason I must beg leave to assume the leadership in all that we have now to do, until I see the leaden coffin soldered down and safe in your possession. After that, I shall resign all my functions to you.'

'I want words to thank you for your kindness,' he answered. 'No brother could have borne with me more affectionately, or helped me more patiently, than you.'

He stopped, and grew thoughtful, then occupied himself in tying up slowly and carefully the packet of Miss Elmslie's letters, and then looked suddenly towards the vacant wall behind me, with that strange expression the meaning of which I knew so well. Since we had left Naples, I had purposely avoided exciting him by talking on the useless and shocking subject of the apparition by which he believed himself to be perpetually followed. Just now, however, he seemed so calm and collected – so little likely to be violently agitated by any allusion to the dangerous topic – that I ventured to speak out boldly.

'Does the phantom still appear to you,' I asked, 'as it appeared at Naples?'

He looked at me, and smiled.

'Did I not tell you that it followed me everywhere?' His eyes wandered back again to the vacant space, and he went on speaking in that direction, as if he had been continuing the conversation with some third person in the room. 'We shall part,' he said slowly and softly, 'when the empty place is filled in Wincot vault. Then I shall stand with Ada before the altar in the Abbey chapel; and when my eyes meet hers, they will see the tortured face no more.'

Saying this, he leaned his head on his hand, sighed, and began repeating softly to himself the lines of the old prophecy:

> When in Wincot vault a place
> Waits for one of Monkton's race:
> When that one forlorn shall lie
> Graveless under open sky,
> Beggared of six feet of earth,
> Though lord of acres from his birth—
> That shall be a certain sign
> Of the end of Monkton's line.
> Dwindling ever faster, faster,
> Dwindling to the last-left master;
> From mortal ken, from light of day,
> Monkton's race shall pass away.

Fancying that he pronounced the last lines a little incoherently, I tried to make him change the subject. He took no notice of what I said, and went on talking to himself.

'Monkton's race shall pass away!' he repeated; 'but not with *me*. The fatality hangs over my head no longer. I shall bury the unburied dead; I shall fill the vacant place in Wincot vault. And then – then the new life, the life with Ada!' – That name seemed to recall him to himself. He drew his travelling desk towards him, placed the packet of letters in it, and then took out a sheet of paper. 'I am going to write to Ada,' he said, turning to me, 'and tell her the good news. Her happiness, when she knows it, will be even greater than mine.'

Worn out by the events of the day, I left him writing, and went to bed. I was, however, either too anxious or too tired to sleep. In this waking condition, my mind naturally occupied itself with the discovery at the convent, and with the events to which that discovery would in all probability lead. As I thought on the future, a depression for which I could not account weighed on my spirits. There was not the slightest reason for the vague melancholy forebodings that oppressed me. The remains, to the finding of which my unhappy friend attached so much importance, had been traced; they would certainly be placed at his disposal in a few days; he might take them to England by the first merchant vessel that sailed from Naples; and, the gratification of his strange caprice thus accomplished, there was at least some reason to hope that his mind might recover its tone, and that the new life he would lead at Wincot might result in making him a happy man. Such considerations as these were, in themselves, certainly not calculated to exert any melancholy influence over me; and yet, all through the night, the same inconceivable, unaccountable depression weighed heavily on my spirits – heavily through the hours of darkness – heavily even when I walked out to breathe the first freshness of the early morning air.

With the day came the all-engrossing business of opening negotiations with the authorities.

Only those who have had to deal with Italian officials can imagine how our patience was tried by everyone with whom we came in contact. We were bandied about from one authority to the other, were stared at, cross-questioned, mystified – not in the least because the case presented any special difficulties or intricacies, but because it was absolutely necessary that every civil dignitary to whom we applied, should assert his own importance by leading us to our object in the most roundabout manner possible. After our first day's experience of official life in Italy, I left the absurd formalities, which we had no choice but to perform, to be accomplished by Alfred alone, and applied myself to considering the really serious question of how the remains in the convent outhouse were to be safely removed.

The best plan that suggested itself to me was to write to a friend at Rome, where I knew that it was a custom to embalm the bodies of high dignitaries of the church, and where, I consequently inferred, such chemical assistance as was needed in our emergency might be obtained. I simply stated in my letter that the removal of the body was imperative, then described the condition in which I had found it, and engaged that no expense on our part should be spared if the right person or persons could be found to help us. Here again more difficulties interposed themselves, and more useless formalities were to be gone through; but, in the end, patience, perseverance, and money triumphed, and two men came expressly from Rome to undertake the duties we required of them.

It is unnecessary that I should shock the reader by entering into any detail in this part of my narrative. When I have said that the progress of decay was so far suspended by chemical means as to allow the remains being placed in the coffin, and to ensure their being transported to England with perfect safety and convenience, I have said enough. After ten days had been wasted in useless delays and difficulties, I had the satisfaction of seeing the convent outhouse empty at last; passed through a final ceremony of snuff-taking, or rather, of snuff-giving, with the old Capuchin; and ordered the travelling carriage to be ready at the inn door. Hardly a month had elapsed since our departure, when we entered Naples successful in the achievement of a design, which had been ridiculed as wildly impracticable by every friend of ours who had heard of it.

The first object to be accomplished on our return was to obtain the means of carrying the coffin to England – by sea, as a matter of course. All inquiries after a merchant vessel on the point of sailing for any British port, led to the most unsatisfactory results. There was only one way of ensuring the immediate transportation of the remains to England, and that was to hire a vessel. Impatient to return, and resolved not to lose sight of the coffin till he had seen it placed in Wincot vault, Monkton decided immediately on hiring the first ship that could be obtained. The vessel in port which we were informed could soonest be got ready for sea, was a Sicilian brig; and this vessel my friend accordingly engaged. The best dockyard artisans that could be got were set to work, and the smartest captain and crew to be picked up on an emergency in Naples, were chosen to navigate the brig.

Monkton, after again expressing in the warmest terms his gratitude for the services I had rendered him, disclaimed any intention of asking me to accompany him on the voyage to England. Greatly to his surprise and delight, however, I offered of my own accord to take passage in the brig. The strange coincidences I had witnessed, the extraordinary discovery I had hit on, since our first meeting in Naples, had made his one great interest in life my one great interest for the time being, as well. I shared none of his delusions, poor fellow; but it is hardly an exaggeration to say that my eagerness to follow our remarkable adventure to its end, was as great as his anxiety to see the coffin laid in Wincot vault. Curiosity influenced me, I am afraid, almost as strongly as friendship, when I offered myself as the companion of his voyage home.

We set sail for England on a calm and lovely afternoon.

For the first time since I had known him, Monkton seemed to be in high spirits. He talked and jested on all sorts of subjects, and laughed at me for allowing my cheerfulness to be affected by the dread of sea-sickness. I had really no such fear; it was my excuse to my friend for a return of that unaccountable depression under which I had suffered at Fondi. Everything was in our favour; everybody on board the brig was in good spirits. The captain was delighted with the vessel; the crew, Italians and Maltese, were in high glee at the prospect of making a short voyage on high wages in a well-provisioned ship. I alone felt heavy at heart. There was no valid reason that I could assign to myself for the melancholy that oppressed me, and yet I struggled against it in vain.

Late on our first night at sea, I made a discovery which was by no means calculated to restore my spirits to their usual equilibrium. Monkton was in the cabin, on the floor of which had been placed the packing-case containing the coffin; and I was on deck. The wind had fallen almost to a calm, and I was lazily watching the sails of the brig as they flapped from time to time against the masts, when the captain approached, and, drawing me out of hearing of the man at the helm, whispered in my ear:

'There's something wrong among the men forward. Did you observe how suddenly they all became silent just before sunset?'

I had observed it, and told him so.

'There's a Maltese boy on board,' pursued the captain, 'who is a smart lad enough, but a bad one to deal with. I have found out that he has been telling the men there is a dead body inside that packing-case of your friend's in the cabin.'

My heart sank as he spoke. Knowing the superstitious irrationality of sailors – of foreign sailors especially – I had taken care to spread a report on board the brig, before the coffin was shipped, that the packing case contained a valuable marble statue which Mr. Monkton prized highly, and was unwilling to trust out of his own sight. How could this Maltese boy have discovered that the pretended statue was a human corpse? As I pondered over the question, my suspicions fixed themselves on Monkton's servant, who spoke Italian fluently, and whom I knew to be an incorrigible gossip. The man denied it when I charged him with betraying us, but I have never believed his denial to this day.

'The little imp won't say where he picked up this notion of his about the dead body,' continued the captain. 'It's not my place to pry into secrets; but I advise you to call the crew aft and contradict the boy, whether he speaks the truth or not. The men are a parcel of fools, who believe in ghosts, and all the rest of it. Some of them say they would never have signed our articles if they had known they were going to sail with a dead man; others only grumble; but I'm afraid we shall have some trouble with them all, in case of rough weather, unless the boy is contradicted by you or the other gentleman. The men say that if either you or your friend tell them on your words of honour that the Maltese is a liar, they will hand him up to be rope's ended accordingly; but that if you won't, they have made up their minds to believe the boy.'

Here the captain paused, and awaited my answer. I could give him none. I felt hopeless under our desperate emergency. To get the boy punished by giving my word of honour to support a direct falsehood, was not to be thought of even for a moment. What other means of extrication from this miserable dilemma remained? None that I could think of. I thanked the captain for his attention to our interests, told him I would take time to consider what course I should pursue, and begged that he would say nothing to my friend about the discovery he had made. He promised to be silent, sulkily enough, and walked away from me.

We had expected the breeze to spring up with the morning, but no breeze came. As it wore on towards noon, the atmosphere became insufferably sultry, and the sea looked as smooth as glass. I saw the captain's eye turn often and anxiously to windward. Far away in that direction, and alone in the blue heaven, I observed a little black cloud, and asked if it would bring us any wind.

'More than we want,' the captain replied shortly; and then, to my astonishment, ordered the crew aloft to take in sail. The execution of this manœuvre showed but too plainly the temper of the men; they did their work sulkily and slowly, grumbling and murmuring among themselves. The captain's manner, as he urged them on with oaths and threats, convinced me we were in danger. I looked again to windward. The one little cloud had enlarged to a great bank of murky vapour, and the sea at the horizon had changed in colour.

'The squall will be on us before we know where we are,' said the captain. 'Go below; you will be only in the way here.'

I descended to the cabin, and prepared Monkton for what was coming. He was still questioning me about what I had observed on deck, when the storm burst on us. We felt the little brig strain for an instant as if she would part in two, then she seemed to be swinging round with us, then to be quite still for a moment, trembling in every timber. Last, came a shock which hurled us from our seats, a deafening crash, and a flood of water pouring into the cabin. We clambered, half drowned, to the deck. The brig had, in the nautical phrase, 'Broached to,' and she now lay on her beam ends.

Before I could make out anything distinctly in the horrible confusion, except the one tremendous certainty that we were entirely at the mercy of the sea, I heard a voice from the fore part of the ship which stilled the clamouring and shouting of the rest of the crew in an instant. The words were Italian, but I understood their fatal meaning only too easily. We had sprung a leak, and the sea was pouring into the ship's hold like the race of a mill-stream. The captain did not lose his presence of mind in this fresh emergency. He called for his axe to cut away the foremast, and ordering some of the crew to help him, directed the others to rig out the pumps.

The words had hardly passed his lips, before the men broke into open mutiny. With a savage look at me, their ringleader declared that the passengers might do as they pleased, but that he and his messmates were determined to take the boat, and leave the accursed ship, and *the dead man in her,* to go to the bottom together. As he spoke there was a shout among the sailors, and I observed some of them pointing derisively behind me. Looking round, I saw Monkton, who had hitherto kept close at my side, making his way back to the cabin. I followed him directly, but the water and confusion on deck, and the impossibility, from the position of the brig, of moving the feet without the slow assistance of the hands, so impeded my progress that it was impossible for me to overtake him. When I had got below, he was crouched upon the coffin, with the water on the cabin floor whirling and splashing about him, as the ship heaved and plunged. I saw a warning brightness in his eyes, a warning flush on his cheeks, as I approached and said to him:

'There is nothing left for it, Alfred, but to bow to our misfortune, and do the best we can to save our lives.'

'Save yours,' he cried, waving his hand to me, 'for *you* have a future before you. Mine is gone when this coffin goes to the bottom. If the ship sinks, I shall know that the fatality is accomplished, and shall sink with her.'

I saw that he was in no state to be reasoned with or persuaded, and raised myself again to the deck. The men were cutting away all obstacles, so as to launch the long boat, placed amidships, over the depressed bulwark of the brig, as she lay on her side; and the captain, after having made a last vain exertion to restore his authority, was looking on at them in silence. The violence of the squall seemed already to be spending itself, and I asked whether there was really no chance for us if we remained by the ship. The captain answered that there might have been the best chance if the men had obeyed his orders, but that now there was none. Knowing that I could place no dependence on the presence of mind of Monkton's servant, I confided to the captain, in the fewest and plainest words, the condition of my unhappy friend, and asked if I might depend on his help. He nodded his head, and we descended together to the cabin. Even at this day, it costs me pain to write of the terrible necessity to which the strength and obstinacy of Monkton's delusion reduced us, in the last resort. We were compelled to secure his hands, and drag him by main force to the deck. The men were on the point of launching the boat, and refused at first to receive us into it.

'You cowards!' cried the captain, 'have we got the dead man with us this time? Isn't he going to the bottom along with the brig? Who are you afraid of when we get into the boat?'

This sort of appeal produced the desired effect; the men became ashamed of themselves, and retraced their refusal.

Just as we pushed off from the sinking ship, Alfred made an effort to break from me, but I held him firm, and he never repeated the attempt. He sat by me, with drooping head, still and silent, while the sailors rowed away from the vessel: still and silent, when with one accord they paused at a little distance off, and we all waited and watched to see the brig sink: still and silent, even when that sinking happened, when the labouring hull plunged slowly into a hollow of the sea – hesitated, as it seemed, for one moment – rose a little again – then sank to rise no more.

Sank with her dead freight: sank, and snatched for ever from our power the corpse which we had discovered almost by a miracle – those jealously-preserved remains on the safe keeping of which rested so strangely the hopes and the love-destinies of two living beings! As the last signs of the ship disappeared in the depths of the waters, I felt Monkton trembling all over as he sat close at my side, and heard him repeating to himself, sadly, and many times over, the name of 'Ada.'

I tried to turn his thoughts to another subject, but it was useless. He pointed over the sea to where the brig had once been, and where nothing was left to look at but the rolling waves.

'The empty place will now remain empty for ever in Wincot vault.'

As he said those words, he fixed his eyes for a moment sadly and earnestly on my face, then looked away, leant his cheek upon his hand, and spoke no more.

We were sighted long before nightfall by a trading vessel, were taken on board, and landed at Cartagena in Spain. Alfred never held up his head, and never once spoke to me of his own accord, the whole time we were at sea in the merchantman. I observed, however, with alarm, that he talked often and incoherently to himself – constantly muttering the lines of the old prophecy – constantly referring to the fatal place that was empty in Wincot vault – constantly repeating in broken accents which it affected me inexpressibly to hear, the name of the poor girl who was awaiting his return to England. Nor were these the only causes for the apprehension that I now felt on his account. Towards the end of our voyage he began to suffer from alternation of fever fits and shivering fits, which I ignorantly imagined to be attacks of ague. I was soon unde-cieved. We had hardly been a day on shore before he became so much worse that I secured the best medical assistance Cartagena could afford. For a day or two the doctors differed, as usual, about the nature of his complaint, but ere long alarming symptoms displayed themselves. The medical men declared that his life was in danger, and told me that his disease was brain fever.

Shocked and grieved as I was, I hardly knew how to act at first under the fresh responsibility now laid upon me. Ulti-mately, I decided on writing to the old priest who had been Alfred's tutor, and who, as I knew, still resided at Wincot Abbey. I told this gentleman all that had happened, begged him to break my melancholy news as gently as possible to Miss Elmslie, and assured him of my resolution to remain with Monkton to the last.

After I had despatched my letter, and had sent to Gibralter to secure the best English medical advice that could be obtained, I felt that I had done my best, and that nothing remained but to wait and hope.

Many a sad and anxious hour did I pass by my poor friend's bedside. Many a time did I doubt whether I had done right in giving any encouragement to his delusion. The reasons for doing so which had suggested themselves to me, after my first interview with him, seemed, however, on reflection, to be valid reasons still. The only way of hastening his return to England and to Miss Elmslie, who was pining for that return, was the way I had taken. It was not my fault that a disaster which no man could foresee, had overthrown all his projects and all mine. But now that the calamity had happened, and was irretrievable, how, in the event of his physical recovery, was his moral malady to be combatted?

When I reflected on the hereditary taint in his mental organisation, on that childish fright of Stephen Monkton from which he had never recovered, on the perilously secluded life that he had led at the Abbey, and on his firm persuasion of the reality of the apparition by which he believed himself to be constantly followed, I confess I despaired of shaking his superstitious faith in every word and line of the old family prophecy. If the series of striking coincidences which appeared to attest its truth had made a strong and lasting impression on *me* (and this was assuredly the case), how could I wonder that they had produced the effect of absolute conviction on *his* mind, constituted as it was? If I argued with him, and he answered me, how could I rejoin? If he said, 'The prophecy points at the last of the family: *I* am the last of the family. The prophecy mentions an empty place in Wincot vault: there is such an empty place there at the moment. On the faith of the prophecy I told you that Stephen Monkton's body was unburied, and you found that it was unburied' – if he said this, of what use would it be for me to reply, 'These are only strange coincidences, after all'?

The more I thought of the task that lay before me, if he recovered, the more I felt inclined to despond. The oftener the English physician who attended on him said to me, 'He may get the better of the fever, but he has a fixed idea, which never leaves him night or day, which has unsettled his reason, and which will end in killing him, unless you or some of his friends can remove it' – the oftener I heard this, the more acutely I felt my own powerlessness, the more I shrank from every idea that was connected with the hopeless future.

I had only expected to receive my answer from Wincot in the shape of a letter. It was consequently a great surprise, as well as a great relief, to be informed one day that two gentlemen wished to speak with me, and to find that of these two gentlemen the first was the old priest, and the second a male relative of Mrs. Elmslie.

Just before their arrival the fever symptoms had disappeared, and Alfred had been pronounced out of danger. Both the priest and his companion were eager to know when the sufferer would be strong enough to travel. They had come to Cartagena expressly to take him home with them, and felt far more hopeful than I did of the restorative effects of his native air. After all the questions connected with the first important point of the journey to England had been asked and answered, I ventured to make some inquiries after Miss Elmslie. Her relative informed me that she was suffering both in body and in mind from excess of anxiety on Alfred's account. They had been obliged to deceive her as to the dangerous nature of his illness, in order to deter her from accompanying the priest and her relation on their mission to Spain.

Slowly and imperfectly, as the weeks wore on, Alfred regained something of his former physical strength, but no alteration appeared in his illness as it affected his mind.

From the very first day of his advance towards recovery, it had been discovered that the brain fever had exercised the strangest influence over his faculties of memory. All recollection of recent events was gone from him. Everything connected with Naples, with me, with his journey to Italy, had dropped in some mysterious manner entirely out of his remembrance. So completely had all late circumstances passed from his memory, that, though he recognised the old priest and his own servant easily on the first days of his convalescence, he never recognised me, but regarded me with such a wistful, doubting expression, that I felt inexpressibly pained when I approached his bedside. All his questions were about Miss Elmslie and Wincot Abbey; and all talk referred to the period when his father was yet alive.

The doctors augured good rather than ill from this loss of memory of recent incidents saying that it would turn out to be temporary, and that it answered the first great healing purpose of keeping his mind at ease. I tried to believe them – tried to feel as sanguine, when the day came for his departure, as the old friends felt who were taking him home. But the effort was too much for me. A foreboding that I should never see him again, oppressed my heart, and the tears came into my eyes as I saw the worn figure of my poor friend half helped, half lifted into the travelling carriage, and borne away gently on the road towards home.

He had never recognised me, and the doctors had begged that I would give him, for some time to come, as few opportunities as possible of doing so. But for this request I should have accompanied him to England. As it was, nothing better remained for me to do than to change the scene, and recruit as I best could my energies of body and mind, depressed of late by much watching and anxiety. The famous cities of Spain were not new to me, but I visited them again, and revived old impressions of the Alhambra and Madrid. Once or twice I thought of making a pilgrimage to the East, but late events had sobered and altered me. That yearning unsatisfied feeling which we call 'homesickness,' began to prey upon my heart, and I resolved to return to England.

I went back by way of Paris, having settled with the priest that he should write to me at my banker's there, as soon as he could after Alfred had returned to Wincot. If I had gone to the East, the letter would have been forwarded to me. I wrote to prevent this; and, on my arrival at Paris, stopped at the banker's before I went to my hotel.

The moment the letter was put into my hands, the black border on the envelope told me the worst. He was dead.

There was but one consolation – he had died calmly, almost happily, without once referring to those fatal chances which had wrought the fulfilment of the ancient prophecy. 'My beloved pupil,' the old priest wrote, 'seemed to rally a little the first few days after his return, but he gained no real strength, and soon suffered a slight relapse of fever. After this he sank gradually and gently day by day, and so departed from us on the last dread journey. Miss Elmslie (who knows that I am writing this) desires me to express her deep and lasting gratitude for all your kindness to Alfred. She told me when we brought him back, that she had waited for him as his promised wife, and that she would nurse him now as a wife should; and she never left him. His face was turned towards her, his hand was clasped in hers, when he died. It will console you to know that he never mentioned events at Naples, or the shipwreck that followed them from the day of his return to the day of his death.'

Three days after reading the letter I was at Wincot, and heard all the details of Alfred's last moments from the priest. I felt a shock which it would not be very easy for me to analyse or explain, when I heard that he had been buried, at his own desire, in the fatal Abbey vault.

The priest took me down to see the place – a grim, cold, subterranean building, with a low roof, supported on heavy Saxon arches. Narrow niches, with the ends only of coffins visible within them, ran down each side of the vault. The nails and silver ornaments flashed here and there as my companion moved past them with a lamp in his hand. At the lower end of the place he stopped, pointed to a niche, and said: 'He lies there, between his father and mother.' I looked a little further on and saw what appeared at first like a long dark tunnel. 'That is only an empty niche,' said the priest, following me. 'If the body of Mr. Stephen Monkton had been brought to Wincot, his coffin would have been placed there.'

A chill came over me, and a sense of dread which I am ashamed of having felt now, but which I could not combat then. The blessed light of day was pouring down gaily at the other end of the vault through the open door. I turned my back on the empty niche, and hurried into the sunlight and the fresh air.

As I walked across the grass glade leading down to the vault, I heard the rustle of a woman's dress behind me, and, turning round, saw a young lady advancing, clad in deep mourning. Her sweet, sad face, her manner as she held out her hand, told me who it was in an instant.

'I heard that you were here,' she said, 'and I wished' – her voice faltered a little. My heart ached as I saw how her lip trembled, but before I could say anything, she recovered herself and went on – 'I wished to take your hand, and thank you for your brotherly kindness to Alfred; and I wanted to tell you that I am sure, in all you did, you acted tenderly and considerately for the best. Perhaps you may be soon going away from home again, and we may not meet any more. I shall never, never forget that you were kind to him when he wanted a friend, and that you have the greatest claim of anyone on earth to be gratefully remembered in my thoughts as long as I live.'

The inexpressible tenderness of her voice, trembling a little all the while she spoke, the pale beauty of her face, the artless candour in her sad, quiet eyes, so affected me that I could not trust myself to answer her at first, except by gesture. Before I recovered my voice, she had given me her hand once more and had left me.

I never saw her again. The chances and changes of life kept us apart. When I last heard of her, years and years ago, she was faithful to the memory of the dead, and was Ada Elmslie still, for Alfred Monkton's sake.

A TERRIBLY STRANGE BED

A TERRIBLY STRANGE BED

Shortly after my education at college was finished I happened to be staying at Paris with an English friend. We were both young men then, and lived, I am afraid, rather a wild life, in the delightful city of our sojourn. One night we were idling about the neighbourhood of the Palais Royal, doubtful to what amusement we should next betake ourselves. My friend proposed a visit to Frascati's; but his suggestion was not to my taste. I knew Frascati's, as the French saying is, by heart; had lost and won plenty of five-franc pieces there, merely for amusement's sake, until it was amusement no longer, and was thoroughly tired, in fact, of all the ghastly respectabilities of such a social anomaly as a respectable gambling-house. 'For Heaven's sake,' said I to my friend, 'let us go somewhere where we can see a little genuine, blackguard, poverty-stricken gaming, with no false gingerbread glitter thrown over it at all. Let us get away from fashionable Frascati's, to a house where they don't mind letting in a man with a ragged coat, or a man with no coat, ragged or otherwise.' – 'Very well,' said my friend, 'we needn't go out of the Palais Royal to find the sort of company you want. Here's the place just before us; as blackguard a place, by all report, as you could possibly wish to see.' In another minute we arrived at the door, and entered the house.

When we got up stairs, and had left our hats and sticks with the doorkeeper, we were admitted into the chief gambling-room. We did not find many people assembled there. But, few as the men were who looked up at us on our entrance, they were all types – lamentably true types – of their respective classes.

We had come to see blackguards; but these men were something worse. There is a comic side, more or less appreci-able, in all blackguardism – here there was nothing but tragedy – mute, weird tragedy. The quiet in the room was horrible. The thin, haggard, long-haired young man, whose sunken eyes fiercely watched the turning up of the cards, never spoke; the flabby, fat-faced, pimply player, who pricked his piece of pasteboard perseveringly, to register how often black won, and how often red – never spoke; the dirty, wrinkled old man, with the vulture eyes and the darned greatcoat, who had lost his last *sou*, and still looked on desperately, after he could play no longer – never spoke. Even the voice of the croupier sounded as if it were strangely dulled and thickened in the atmosphere of the room. I had entered the place to laugh; but the spectacle before me was something to weep over. I soon found it necessary to take refuge in excitement from the depression of spirits which was fast stealing on me. Unfortunately I sought the nearest excite-ment, by going to the table, and beginning to play. Still more unfortunately, as the event will show, I won – won prodi-giously; won incredibly; won at such a rate, that the regular players at the table crowded round me; and staring at my stakes with hungry, superstitious eyes, whispered to one another, that the English stranger was going to break the bank.

The game was *Rouge et Noir*. I had played at it in every city in Europe, without, however, the care or the wish to study the Theory of Chances – that philosopher's stone of all gamblers! And a gambler, in the strict sense of the word, I had never been. I was heart-whole from the corroding passion for play. My gaming was a mere idle amusement. I never resorted to it by necessity, because I never knew what it was to want money. I never practised it so incessantly as to lose more than I could afford, or to gain more than I could coolly pocket without being thrown off my balance by my good luck. In short, I had hitherto frequented gambling-tables – just as I frequented ballrooms and opera-houses – because they amused me, and because I had nothing better to do with my leisure hours.

But on this occasion it was very different – now, for the first time in my life, I felt what the passion for play really was. My success first bewildered, and then, in the most literal meaning of the word, intoxicated me. Incredible as it may appear, it is nevertheless true, that I only lost when I attempted to estimate chances, and played according to previous calculation. If I left everything to luck, and staked without any care or considera-tion, I was sure to win – to win in the face of every recognised probability in favour of the bank. At first, some of the men present ventured their money safely enough on my colour; but I speedily increased my stakes to sums which they dared not risk. One after another they left off playing, and breathlessly looked on at my game.

Still, time after time, I staked higher and higher, and still won. The excitement in the room rose to fever pitch. The silence was interrupted by a deep, muttered chorus of oaths and exclamations in different languages, every time the gold was shovelled across to my side of the table – even the imperturbable croupier dashed his rake on the floor in a (French) fury of astonishment at my success. But one man present preserved his self-possession; and that man was my friend. He came to my side, and whispering in English, begged me to leave the place satisfied with what I had already gained. I must do him the justice to say, that he repeated his warnings and entreaties several times; and only left me and went away, after I had rejected his advice (I was to all intents and purposes gambling-drunk) in terms which rendered it impossible for him to address me again that night.

Shortly after he had gone, a hoarse voice behind me cried: – 'Permit me, my dear sir! – permit me to restore to their proper place two Napoleons which you have dropped. Wonderful luck, sir! I pledge you my word of honour as an old soldier, in the course of my long experience in this sort of thing, I never saw such luck as yours! – never! Go on, sir – *Sacré mille bombes!* Go on boldly, and break the bank!'

I turned round and saw, nodding and smiling at me with inveterate civility, a tall man, dressed in a frogged and braided surtout.

If I had been in my senses, I should have considered him, personally, as being rather a suspicious specimen of an old soldier. He had goggling bloodshot eyes, mangy mustachios, and a broken nose. His voice betrayed a barrack-room intona-tion of the worst order, and he had the dirtiest pair of hands I ever saw – even in France. These little personal peculiarities exercised, however, no repelling influence on me. In the mad excitement, the reckless triumph of that moment, I was ready to 'fraternize' with anybody who encouraged me in my game. I accepted the old soldier's offered pinch of snuff; clapped him on the back, and swore he was the honestest fellow in the world – the most glorious relic of the Grand Army that I had ever met with. 'Go on!' cried my military friend, snapping his fingers in ecstasy, – 'Go on, and win! Break the bank – *Mille tonnerres!* my gallant English comrade, break the bank!'

And I *did* go on – went on at such a rate, that in another quarter of an hour the croupier called out: 'Gentlemen! the bank has discontinued for tonight.' All the notes, and all the gold in that 'bank,' now lay in a heap under my hands; the whole floating capital of the gambling-house was waiting to pour into my pockets!

'Tie up the money in your pocket-handkerchief, my worthy sir,' said the old soldier, as I wildly plunged my hands into my heap of gold. 'Tie it up, as we used to tie up a bit of dinner in the Grand Army; your winnings are too heavy for any breeches pockets that ever were sewed. There! that's it! – shovel them in, notes and all! *Credié!* what luck! – Stop! another Napoleon on the floor! *Ah! sacré petit polisson de Napoleon!* have I found thee at last? Now then, sir – two tight double knots each way with your honourable permission, the money's safe. Feel it! feel it, fortunate sir! hard and round as a cannon ball – *Ah, bah!* if they had only fired such cannon balls at us at Austerlitz – *nom d'une pipe!* if they only had! And now, as an ancient grenadier, as an ex-brave of the French army, what remains for me to do? I ask what? Simply this: to entreat my valued English friend to drink a bottle of champagne with me, and toast the goddess Fortune in foaming goblets before we part!'

Excellent ex-brave! Convivial ancient grenadier! Champagne by all means! An English cheer for an old soldier! Hurrah! hurrah! Another English cheer for the goddess Fortune! Hurrah! hurrah! hurrah!

'Bravo! the Englishman; the amiable, gracious Englishman, in whose veins circulates the vivacious blood of France! Another glass? *Ah, bah!* – the bottle is empty! Never mind! *Vive le vin!* I, the old soldier, order another bottle, and half-a-pound of *bon-bons* with it!'

'No, no, ex-brave; never – ancient grenadier! *Your* bottle last time; *my* bottle this. Behold it! Toast away! The French Army! – the great Napoleon! – the present company! the croupier! the honest croupier's wife and daughters – if he has any! the Ladies generally! Everybody in the world!'

By the time the second bottle of champagne was emptied, I felt as if I had been drinking liquid fire – my brain seemed all a-flame. No excess in wine had ever had this effect on me before in my life. Was it the result of a stimulant acting upon my system when I was in a highly excited state? Was my stomach in particularly disordered condition? Or was the champagne amazingly strong?

'Ex-brave of the French Army!' cried I, in a mad state of exhilaration, '*I* am on fire! how are *you?* You have set me on fire! Do you hear; my hero of Austerlitz? Let us have a third bottle of champagne to put the flame out!'

The old soldier wagged his head, rolled his goggle eyes, until I expected to see them slip out of their sockets; placed his dirty forefinger by the side of his broken nose; solemnly ejaculated 'Coffee!' and immediately ran off into an inner room.

The word pronounced by the eccentric veteran seemed to have a magical effect on the rest of the company present. With one accord they all rose to depart. Probably they had expected to profit by my intoxication; but finding that my new friend was benevolently bent on preventing me from getting dead drunk, had now abandoned all hope of thriving pleasantly on my winnings. Whatever their motive might be, at any rate they went away in a body. When the old soldier returned, and sat down again opposite to me at the table, we had the room to ourselves. I could see the croupier, in a sort of vestibule which opened out of it, eating his supper in solitude. The silence was now deeper than ever.

A sudden change, too, had come over the 'ex-brave.' He assumed a portentously solemn look; and when he spoke to me again, his speech was ornamented by no oaths, enforced by no finger-snapping, enlivened by no apostrophes or exclamations.

'Listen, my dear sir,' said he, in mysteriously confidential tones – 'listen to an old soldier's advice. I have been to the mistress of the house (a very charming woman, with a genius for cookery!) to impress on her the necessity of making us some particularly strong and good coffee. You must drink this coffee in order to get rid of your little amiable exaltation of spirits before you think of going home – you *must*, my good and gracious friend! With all that money to take home tonight, it is a sacred duty to yourself to have your wits about you. You are known to be a winner to an enormous extent by several gentlemen present tonight, who, in a certain point of view, are very worthy and excellent fellows; but they are mortal men, my dear sir, and they have their amiable weaknesses! Need I say more? Ah, no, no! you understand me! Now, this is what you must do – send for a cabriolet when you feel quite well again – draw up all the windows when you get into it – and tell the driver to take you home only through the large and well-lighted thorough-fares. Do this; and you and your money will be safe. Do this; and tomorrow you will thank an old soldier for giving you a word of honest advice.'

Just as the ex-brave ended his oration in very lachrymose tones, the coffee came in, ready poured out in two cups. My attentive friend handed me one of the cups with a bow. I was parched with thirst, and drank it off at a draught. Almost instantly afterwards, I was seized with a fit of giddiness, and felt more completely intoxicated than ever. The room whirled round and round furiously; the old soldier seemed to be regularly bobbing up and down before me like the piston of a steam-engine. I was half deafened by a violent singing in my ears; a feeling of utter bewilderment, helplessness, idiocy, overcame me. I rose from my chair, holding on by the table to keep my balance; and stammered out, that I felt dreadfully unwell – so unwell that I did not know how I was to get home.

'My dear friend,' answered the old soldier, and even his voice seemed to be bobbing up and down as he spoke – 'my dear friend, it would be madness to go home in *your* state; you would be sure to lose your money; you might be robbed and murdered with the greatest ease. *I* am going to sleep here: do *you* sleep here, too – they make up capital beds in this house – take one; sleep off the effects of the wine, and go home safely with your winnings tomorrow – tomorrow, in broad daylight.'

I had but two ideas left: – one, that I must never let go hold of my handkerchief full of money; the other, that I must lie down somewhere immediately, and fall off into a comfortable sleep. So I agreed to the proposal about the bed, and took the offered arm of the old soldier, carrying my money with my disengaged hand. Preceded by the croupier, we passed along some passages and up a flight of stairs into the bedroom which I was to occupy. The ex-brave shook me warmly by the hand; proposed that we should breakfast together, and then, followed by the croupier, left me for the night.

I ran to the wash-hand stand; drank some of the water in my jug; poured the rest out, and plunged my face into it – then sat down in a chair and tried to compose myself. I soon felt better. The change for my lungs, from the fetid atmosphere of the gambling-room to the cool air of the apartment I now occupied; the almost equally refreshing change for my eyes, from the glaring gas-lights of the 'Salon' to the dim, quiet flicker of one bedroom candle; aided wonderfully the restorative effects of cold water. The giddiness left me, and I began to feel a little like a reasonable being again. My first thought was of the risk of sleeping all night in a gambling-house; my second, of the still greater risk of trying to get out after the house was closed, and of going home alone at night, through the streets of Paris with a large sum of money about me. I had slept in worse places than this on my travels, so I determined to lock, bolt, and barricade my door, and take my chance till the next morning.

Accordingly, I secured myself against all intrusion; looked under the bed, and into the cupboard; tried the fastening of the window; and then, satisfied that I had taken every proper precaution, pulled off my upper clothing, put my light, which was a dim one, on the hearth among a feathery litter of wood ashes, and got into bed, with the handkerchief full of money under my pillow.

I soon felt not only that I could not go to sleep, but that I could not even close my eyes. I was wide awake, and in a high fever. Every nerve in my body trembled – every one of my senses seemed to be preternaturally sharpened. I tossed and rolled, and tried every kind of position, and perseveringly sought out the cold corners of the bed, and all to no purpose. Now, I thrust my arms over the clothes; now, I poked them under the clothes; now, I violently shot my legs straight out down to the bottom of the bed; now, I convulsively coiled them up as near my chin as they would go; now, I shook out my crumpled pillow, changed it to the cool side, patted it flat, and lay down quietly on my back; now, I fiercely doubled it in two, set it up on end, thrust it against the board of the bed, and tried a sitting-posture. Every effort was in vain; I groaned with vexation, as I felt that I was in for a sleepless night.

What could I do? I had no book to read. And yet, unless I found out some method of diverting my mind, I felt certain that I was in the condition to imagine all sorts of horrors; to rack my brain with forebodings of every possible and impossible danger; in short, to pass the night in suffering all conceivable varieties of nervous terror.

I raised myself on my elbow, and looked about the room – which was brightened by a lovely moonlight pouring straight through the window – to see if it contained any pictures or ornaments that I could at all clearly distinguish. While my eyes wandered from wall to wall, a remembrance of Le Maistre's delightful little book, 'Voyage autour de ma Chambre,' occurred to me. I resolved to imitate the French author, and find occupation and amusement enough to relieve the tedium of my wakefulness, by making a mental inventory of every article of furniture I could see, and by following up to their sources the multitude of associations which even a chair, a table, or a wash-hand stand may be made to call forth.

In the nervous unsettled state of my mind at that moment, I found it much easier to make my inventory than to make my reflections, and thereupon soon gave up all hope of thinking in Le Maistre's fanciful track – or, indeed, of thinking at all. I looked about the room at the different articles of furniture, and did nothing more.

There was, first, the bed I was lying in; a four-post bed, of all things in the world to meet with in Paris! – yes, a thorough clumsy British four-poster, with the regular top lined with chintz – the regular fringed valance all round – the regular stifling unwholesome curtains, which I remembered having

mechanically drawn back against the posts without particularly noticing the bed when I first got into the room. Then
there was the marble-topped wash-hand stand, from which
the water I had spilt, in my hurry to pour it out, was still
dripping, slowly and more slowly, on to the brick-floor. Then
two small chairs, with my coat, waistcoat, and trousers flung
on them. Then a large elbow-chair covered with dirty-white
dimity, with my cravat and shirt-collar thrown over the back.
Then a chest of drawers with two of the brass handles off, and
a tawdry, broken china inkstand placed on it by way of
ornament for the top. Then the dressing-table, adorned by a
very small looking-glass, and a very large pin-cushion. Then
the window – an unusually large window. Then a dark old
picture, which the feeble candle dimly showed me. It was the
picture of a fellow in a high Spanish hat, crowned with a
plume of towering feathers. A swarthy sinister ruffian, looking upward, shading his eyes with his hand, and looking
intently upward – it might be at some tall gallows at which he
was going to be hanged. At any rate, he had the appearance of
thoroughly deserving it.

This picture put a kind of constraint upon me to look
upward too – at the top of the bed. It was a gloomy and not an
interesting object, and I looked back at the picture. I counted
the feathers in the man's hat – they stood out in relief – three
white, two green. I observed the crown of his hat, which was
of a conical shape, according to the fashion supposed to have
been favoured by Guido Fawkes. I wondered what he was
looking up at. It couldn't be at the stars; such a desperado was
neither astrologer nor astronomer. It must be at the high
gallows, and he was going to be hanged presently. Would the
executioner come into possession of his conical crowned hat
and plume of feathers? I counted the feathers again – three
white, two green.

While I still lingered over this very improving and intellectual employment, my thoughts insensibly began to wander.
The moonlight shining into the room reminded me of a
certain moonlight night in England – the night after a picnic
party in a Welsh valley. Every incident of the drive homeward, through lovely scenery, which the moonlight made
lovelier than ever, came back to my remembrance, though I

had never given the picnic a thought for years; though, if I had *tried* to recollect it, I could certainly have recalled little or nothing of that scene long past. Of all the wonderful faculties that help to tell us we are immortal, which speaks the sublime truth more eloquently than memory? Here was I, in a strange house of the most suspicious character, in a situation of uncertainty, and even of peril, which might seem to make the cool exercise of my recollection almost out of the question; nevertheless, remembering, quite involuntarily, places, people, conversations, minute circumstances of every kind, which I had thought forgotten for ever, which I could not possibly have recalled at will even under the most favourable auspices. And what cause had produced in a moment the whole of this strange, complicated, mysterious effect? Nothing but some rays of moonlight shining in at my bedroom window.

I was still thinking of the picnic – of our merriment on the drive home – of the sentimental young lady who *would* quote Childe Harold because it was moonlight. I was absorbed by these past scenes and past amusements, when, in an instant, the thread on which my memories hung snapped asunder: my attention immediately came back to present things more vividly than ever, and I found myself, I neither knew why nor wherefore, looking hard at the picture again.

Looking for what?

Good God, the man had pulled his hat down on his brows! – No! the hat itself was gone! Where was the conical crown? Where the feathers – three white, two green? Not there! In place of the hat and feathers, what dusky object was it that now hid his forehead, his eyes, his shading hand?

Was the bed moving?

I turned on my back and looked up. Was I mad? drunk? dreaming? giddy again? or was the top of the bed really moving down – sinking slowly, regularly, silently, horribly, right down throughout the whole of its length and breadth – right down upon Me, as I lay underneath?

My blood seemed to stand still. A deadly paralyzing coldness stole all over me, as I turned my head round on the pillow, and determined to test whether the bed-top was really moving or not, by keeping my eye on the man in the picture.

The next look in that direction was enough. The dull, black, frowsy outline of the valance above me was within an inch of being parallel with his waist. I still looked breathlessly. And steadily, and slowly – very slowly – I saw the figure, and the line of frame below the figure, vanish, as the valance moved down before it.

I am, constitutionally, anything but timid. I have been on more than one occasion in peril of my life, and have not lost my self-possession for an instant; but when the conviction first settled on my mind that the bed-top was really moving, was steadily and continuously sinking down upon me, I looked up shuddering, helpless, panic-stricken, beneath the hideous machinery for murder, which was advancing closer and closer to suffocate me where I lay.

I looked up, motionless, speechless, breathless. The candle, fully spent, went out; but the moonlight still brightened the room. Down and down, without pausing and without sound-ing, came the bed-top, and still my panic-terror seemed to bind me faster and faster to the mattress on which I lay – down and down it sank, till the dusty odour from the lining of the canopy came stealing into my nostrils.

At that final moment the instinct of self-preservation star-tled me out of my trance, and I moved at last. There was just room for me to roll myself sideways off the bed. As I dropped noiselessly to the floor, the edge of the murderous canopy touched me on the shoulder.

Without stopping to draw my breath, without wiping the cold sweat from my face, I rose instantly on my knees to watch the bed-top. I was literally spell-bound by it. If I had heard footsteps behind me, I could not have turned round; if a means of escape had been miraculously provided for me, I could not have moved to take advantage of it. The whole life in me was, at that moment, concentrated in my eyes.

It descended – the whole canopy, with the fringe round it, came down – down – close down; so close that there was not room now to squeeze my finger between the bed-top and the bed. I felt at the sides, and discovered that what had appeared to me from beneath to be the ordinary light canopy of a four-post bed, was in reality a thick, broad mattress, the substance of which was concealed by the valance and its fringe. I looked up and saw the four posts rising hideously bare. In the middle of the bed-top was a huge wooden screw that had evidently worked it down through a hole in the ceiling, just as ordinary presses are worked down on the substance selected for compression. The frightful apparatus moved without making the faintest noise. There had been no creaking as it came down; there was now not the faintest sound from the room above. Amid a dead and awful silence I beheld before me – in the nineteenth century, and in the civilized capital of France – such a machine for secret murder by suffocation as might have existed in the worst days of the Inquisition, in the lonely inns among the Hartz Mountains, in the mysterious tribunals of Westphalia! Still, as I looked on it, I began to recover the power of thinking, and in a moment I discovered the murderous conspiracy framed against me in all its horror.

My cup of coffee had been drugged, and drugged too strongly. I had been saved from being smothered by having taken an overdose of some narcotic. How I had chafed and fretted at the fever-fit which had preserved my life by keeping me awake! How recklessly I had confided myself to the two wretches who had led me into this room, determined, for the sake of my winnings, to kill me in my sleep by the surest and most horrible contrivance for secretly accomplishing my destruction! How many men, winners like me, had slept, as I had proposed to sleep, in that bed, and had never been seen or heard of more! I shuddered at the bare idea of it.

But, erelong, all thought was again suspended by the sight of the murderous canopy moving once more. After it had remained on the bed – as nearly as I could guess – about ten minutes, it began to move up again. The villains who worked it from above evidently believed that their purpose was now accomplished. Slowly and silently, as it had descended, that horrible bed-top rose towards its former place. When it reached the upper extremities of the four posts, it reached the ceiling too. Neither hole nor screw could be seen; the bed became in appearance an ordinary bed again – the canopy an ordinary canopy, even to the most suspicious eyes.

Now, for the first time, I was able to move – to rise from my knees – to dress myself in my upper clothing – and to consider of how I should escape. If I betrayed, by the smallest noise, that the attempt to suffocate me had failed, I was certain to be murdered. Had I made any noise already? I listened intently, looking towards the door.

No! no footsteps in the passage outside – no sound of a tread, light or heavy, in the room above – absolute silence everywhere. Besides locking and bolting my door, I had moved an old wooden chest against it, which I had found under the bed. To remove this chest (my blood ran cold as I thought what its content *might* be!) without making some disturbance was impossible; and, moreover, to think of escaping through the house, now barred up for the night, was sheer insanity. Only one chance was left me – the window. I stole to it on tiptoe.

My bedroom was on the first floor, above an *entresol*, and looked into the back street. I raised my hand to open the window, knowing that on that action hung, by the merest hair's-breadth, my chance of safety. They keep vigilant watch in a House of Murder. If any part of the frame cracked, if the hinge creaked, I was a lost man! It must have occupied me at least five minutes, reckoning by the time – five *hours*, reckoning my suspense – to open that window. I succeeded in doing it silently – in doing it with all the dexterity of a housebreaker – and then looked down into the street. To leap the distance beneath me would be almost certain destruction! Next, I looked round at the sides of the house. Down the left side ran a thick water-pipe – it passed close by the outer edge of the window. The moment I saw the pipe, I knew I was saved. My breath came and went freely for the first time since I had seen the canopy of the bed moving down upon me!

To some men the means of escape which I had discovered might have seemed difficult and dangerous enough – to *me* the prospect of slipping down the pipe into the street did not suggest even a thought of peril. I had always been accustomed, by the practice of gymnastics, to keep up my school-boy powers as a daring and expert climber; and knew that my head, hands, and feet would serve me faithfully in any hazards of ascent or descent. I had already got one leg over the window-sill, when I remembered the handkerchief filled with money under my pillow. I could well have afforded to leave it

behind me, but I was revengefully determined that the mis-
creants of the gambling-house should miss their plunder as
well as their victim. So I went back to the bed and tied the
heavy handkerchief at my back by my cravat.

Just as I had made it tight and fixed it in a comfortable place,
I thought I heard a sound of breathing outside the door. The
chill feeling of horror ran through me again as I listened. No!
dead silence still in the passage – I had only heard the night-air
blowing softly into the room. The next moment I was on the
window-sill – and the next I had a firm grip on the water-pipe
with my hands and knees.

I slid down into the street easily and quietly, and I thought I
should, and immediately set off at the top of my speed to a
branch 'Prefecture' of Police, which I knew was situated in the
immediate neighbourhood. A 'Sub-prefect,' and several
picked men among his subordinates, happened to be up,
maturing, I believe, some scheme for discovering the perpetrator of a mysterious murder which all Paris was talking of
just then. When I began my story, in a breathless hurry and in
very bad French, I could see that the Sub-prefect suspected me
of being a drunken Englishman who had robbed somebody;
but he soon altered his opinion as I went on, and before I had
anything like concluded, he shoved all the papers before him
into a drawer, put on his hat, supplied me with another (for I
was bare-headed), ordered a file of soldiers, desired his expert
followers to get ready all sorts of tools for breaking open
doors and ripping up brick-flooring, and took my arm, in the
most friendly and familiar manner possible, to lead me with
him out of the house. I will venture to say, that when the
Sub-prefect was a little boy, and was taken for the first time to
the Play, he was not half as much pleased as he was now at the
job in prospect for him at the gambling-house!

Away we went through the streets, the Sub-prefect cross-
examining and congratulating me in the same breath as we
marched at the head of our formidable *posse comitatus*. Sen-
tinels were placed at the back and front of the house the
moment we got to it; a tremendous battery of knocks was
directed against the door; a light appeared at a window; I was
told to conceal myself behind the police – then came more
knocks, and a cry of 'Open in the name of the law!' At that

terrible summons bolts and locks gave way before an invisible hand, and the moment after the Sub-prefect was in the passage, confronting a waiter half-dressed and ghastly pale. This was the short dialogue which immediately took place:–

'We want to see the Englishman who is sleeping in this house?'

'He went away hours ago.'

'He did no such thing. His friend went away; *he* remained. Show us to his bedroom!'

'I swear to you, Monsieur le Sous-prefet, he is not here! He–'

'I swear to you, Monsieur le Garçon, he is. He slept here – he didn't find your bed comfortable – he came to us to complain of it – here he is among my men – and here am I ready to look for a flea or two in his bedstead. Renaudin! (calling to one of the subordinates, and pointing to the waiter) collar that man, and tie his hands behind him. Now, then, gentlemen, let us walk up stairs!'

Every man and woman in the house was secured – the 'Old Soldier' the first. Then I identified the bed in which I had slept, and then we went into the room above.

No object that was at all extraordinary appeared in any part of it. The Sub-prefect looked round the place, commanded everybody to be silent, stamped twice on the floor, called for a candle, looked attentively at the spot he had stamped on, and ordered the flooring there to be carefully taken up. This was done in no time. Lights were produced, and we saw a deep raftered cavity between the floor of this room and the ceiling of the room beneath. Through this cavity there ran perpendicularly a sort of case of iron thickly greased; and inside the case appeared the screw, which communicated with the bed-top below. Extra lengths of screw, freshly oiled; levers covered with felt; all the complete upper works of a heavy press – constructed with infernal ingenuity so as to join the fixtures below, and when taken to pieces again to go into the smallest possible compass – were next discovered and pulled out on the floor. After some little difficulty the Sub-prefect succeeded in putting the machinery together, and, leaving his men to work it, descended with me to the bedroom. The smothering canopy was then lowered, but not so noiselessly as I had seen it lowered. When I mentioned this to the Sub-prefect, his answer, simple as it was, had a terrible significance. 'My men,' said he, 'are working down the bed-top for the first time – the men whose money you won were in better practice.'

We left the house in the sole possession of two police agents – every one of the inmates being removed to prison on the spot. The Sub-prefect, after taking down my '*procès-verbal*' in his office, returned with me to my hotel to get my passport. 'Do you think,' I asked, as I gave it to him, 'that any men have really been smothered in that bed, as they tried to smother *me?*'

'I have seen dozens of drowned men laid out at the Morgue,' answered the Sub-prefect, 'in whose pocket-books were found letters, stating that they had committed suicide in the Seine, because they had lost everything at the gaming-table. Do I know how many of those men entered the same gambling-house that *you* entered? won as *you* won? took that bed as *you* took it? slept in it? were smothered in it? and were privately thrown into the river, with a letter of explanation written by the murderers and placed in their pocket-books? No man can say how many or how few have suffered the fate from which you have escaped. The people of the gambling-house kept their bedstead machinery a secret from *us* – even from the police! The dead kept the rest of the secret for them. Good night, or rather good morning, Monsieur Faulkner! Be at my office again at nine o'clock – in the meantime, *au revoir!*'

The rest of my story is soon told. I was examined and re-examined; the gambling-house was strictly searched all through from top to bottom; the prisoners were separately interrogated; and two of the less guilty among them made a confession. *I* discovered that the Old Soldier was the master of the gambling-house – *justice* discovered that he had been drummed out of the army as a vagabond years ago; that he had been guilty of all sorts of villanies since; that he was in possession of stolen property, which the owners identified; and that he, the croupier, another accomplice, and the woman who had made my cup of coffee, were all in the secret of the bed-stead. There appeared some reason to doubt whether the inferior persons attached to the house knew anything of the suffocating machinery; and they received the benefit of that doubt, by being treated simply as thieves and vagabonds. As for the Old Soldier and his two head-myrmidons, they went to the galleys; the woman who had drugged my coffee was imprisoned for I forget how many years; the regular attendants at the gambling-house were considered 'suspicious,' and placed under 'surveillance;' and I became, for one whole week (which is a long time), the head 'lion' in Parisian society. My adventure was dramatised by three illustrious playmakers, but never saw theatrical daylight; for the censorship forbade the introduction on the stage of a correct copy of the gambling-house bedstead.

One good result was produced by my adventure which any censorship must have approved:– it cured me of ever again trying 'Rouge et Noir' as an amusement. The sight of a green cloth, with packs of cards and heaps of money on it, will henceforth be for ever associated in my mind with the sight of a bed-canopy descending to suffocate me in the silence and darkness of the night.

SHERIDAN LE FANU

IN A GLASS DARKLY

With Dr Martin Hesselius, five of whose 'cases' are brought together in this superb collection, Sheridan Le Fanu contributed a major figure to the ranks of those occult doctors, forensic experts, and special investigators who enthralled the Victorian reading public.

Each case presents its own peculiar revelation. In 'Green Tea' a quiet English clergyman is haunted by a spectral monkey. Captain Barton of Dublin is scared literally to death by the appearance *in miniature* of a man whom he knows to have died in Naples; this is his 'Familiar'. The young narrator of 'The Room in the Dragon Volant' is more or less buried alive in a French roadside inn. The hanging judge, Mr Justice Harbottle, in the story of that name, is condemned to hang himself. 'Carmilla' links sexual perversion and vampirism in the woods of lower Austria.

THOMAS HARDY

A GROUP OF NOBLE DAMES

The ten stories contained in *A Group of Noble Dames* are ranged around a '. . . store of ladies, whose bright eyes rain influence'.

Hardy plumbs the hidden depths of county families to reveal what went on behind the scenes, transforming half-remembered incidents into palpitating drama. Barbara of the House of Grebe, Lady Mottisfont, Anna, Lady Baxby, The Lady Penelope and The Honourable Laura, together with the other Noble Dames, will live long in the mind of the reader.

THOMAS HARDY

LIFE'S LITTLE IRONIES

Hardy considered 'The Son's Veto' to be his best short story, while 'On The Western Circuit' was Florence Hardy's favourite. It is difficult to argue with either judgement, for each of the tales in *Life's Little Ironies* will be championed by different readers. Suffice it to say that they show Hardy at his characteristic best in the Wessex countryside he made his own.

As a pendant to the tales, Hardy added a series of stories linked under the heading 'A Few Crusted Characters', harking back to an earlier age. The characters are here in good measure – Tony Kytes, Andrey Satchel and the rest – their stories told to a returning native by Burthen, the Longpuddle Carrier, during a golden afternoon in autumn.

W.M. THACKERAY

THE IRISH SKETCHBOOK

Here is Thackeray's marvellously detailed account of a four-month tour of Ireland he made during the summer and winter of 1842. The whole of contemporary Irish life is here: horse-racing, agricultural fairs, fishing, sight-seeing, the great cities and cathedrals, country inns, universities, schools and convents, grand balls and beggars.

The book's interest is two-fold today, providing as much of an insight into Thackeray's own character as into that of the Irish. Clearly an Englishman abroad, he nevertheless paints a vivid portrait of Ireland and the harsh realities of Irish life, tempering his humour and satire with descriptions of the country's great natural beauty and the warmth of the people.

The Irish Sketchbook was one of Thackeray's early successes and is a fascinating and colourful kaleidoscope of Irish life on the eve of the Great Famine.

ANTHONY TROLLOPE

THE VICAR OF BULLHAMPTON

Here is another of Trollope's splendid galleries of characters. Harry Gilmore, the Squire, Captain Walter Marrable, the Reverend Frank Fenwick and Mrs Fenwick, who is as good a specimen of an English country parson's wife as you will meet in any county: good-looking, fond of the society around her, with a little dash of fun, knowing in blankets and corduroys and coals and tea – and also in beer and gin and tobacco.

Between them, the Vicar of Bullhampton and his wife are acquainted with every man and woman in the parish, including the Balfours, Mary Lowther and the Brattles – the Brattles who live across the meadows at the old mill and who are to figure so prominently in this story, set in a quiet Wiltshire backwater.